Daisy Canfield

BEN HAAS

SIMON AND SCHUSTER • NEW YORK

C,1

Published by Simon and Schuster
Rockefeller Center, 630 Fifth Avenue
New York, New York 10020

First printing

SBN 671-21484-5
Library of Congress Catalog Card Number: 72-90795
Manufactured in the United States of America

*For Dot and Ott and Steve and Bobbie
and all the nephews and nieces,
with love.*

Author's Note

The Outer Banks of the Carolinas and Virginia do not include Harriot and Shoal Islands, which are fictitious, as are the municipalities, governmental units, and characters thereon. Only the islands of Ocracoke, Hatteras, and Portsmouth really exist; otherwise, the locale and characters of this novel are fictitious and no resemblance is intended between characters in the book and actual persons, living or dead.

Southern policeman reopens murder
case in an attempt to find purpose in
his own life.

Chapter 1

There had been a fair blow that morning, with some rain; now it had swept out northwestward, leaving only freshness. Even indoors, Chief of Police Daniel Wahab Rush, who was as sensitive to the weather as a bird or cat, felt the change with an instinct bred into him, passed down to him, by generations of ancestors whose lives had been bounded by water, who, islanders, had made the sea their pasture and their mine.

Leaning back in the chair behind the desk in his tiny office, Chief Rush stared at the poster on the opposite wall. THIS IS BLACKBEARD COUNTRY! A florid lithographed pirate, jackbooted, head bound in red bandanna, cutlass brandished, bared white teeth in a mass of curling purple whiskers. SEE! THE THRILLING OUTDOOR DRAMA "BLACKBEARD!" NIGHTLY EXCEPT MONDAYS! JUNE 10–AUGUST 25, BUCCANEER THEATER, HARRIOT ISLAND!

Chief Rush sighed. Tonight, down on Hatteras, the fish

would be running in the surf, excited by the foul weather's aftermath. He wished that he were there, thigh deep in water under a moon just again becoming visible, with the fine raw wind blowing on him, instead of in this little air-conditioned concrete-block cubicle in the Municipal Building of the Town of Harriot. He wished that, like Felix, he were free of responsibility, of duty, and of worry. Instead— His mouth twisted and he looked down at the pocket checkbook before him, in which most of the stubs were blank.

Danny Rush had managed to evade all but the most basic arithmetic in his eleven years of schooling and, at thirty-three, still found simple addition and subtraction taxing. Nevertheless, he had to admit that there was no one to blame but himself for his predicament; as Marshall at the bank had told him in blunt exasperation last month, any man fit to head a police force should be able to balance a checkbook. But somehow he never seemed able to do that; something in him balked at that much system and order. Supervising his three men and keeping the necessary records of the Force exhausted all the precision in him.

Standing, Rush would have been about six feet, his body, undistinguished by any massive width of chest or shoulder, fully male and utilitarian, ropy muscles well constructed by nearly a full lifetime on the Outer Banks, that long, thin, curving linkage of offshore islands forming a barrier between the Atlantic and the Virginia-Carolina coast. When Danny Rush had been growing up on Hatteras fifteen or twenty years before, there had been no living to be made but from the sea; and he had been toughened by pulling oars, handling nets, gathering salvage and flotsam, fishing, swimming, contending against not only water but deep and omnipresent sand. He was lean and hard everywhere except his belly, which was beginning to bulge roundly from too much drinking. His face was long, his skin seamed and grainy from exposure to sun and sand and salt, the frontal line of his black hair rapidly retreating, gray beginning to show above his ears. There were dark halfmoons of fatigue and dissipation beneath his deep-set black eyes, and his teeth needed dental work which he could not afford.

In fact, at this moment, he could afford nothing at all. He had been sweating over the checkbook for a half hour, but he could not tell whether he had ten dollars left in the account or was ten dollars overdrawn. And one thing was certain; he could not go to the bank to find out, because if he were overdrawn it would be four days until he could cover the deficit.

He'd have been all right, he thought, except for Ruth. He'd had fifteen dollars cash, which would have seen him through, but when he'd come to work this morning, Mayor Jordan had sent for him.

The Mayor owned Jordan's Insurance and Realty. A small brisk man, never without coat and tie even in the hottest weather, he was a native Banker who had grown up on Harriot Island and, like everyone else, been poor until the land boom started. Now he owned three dozen beach houses, a restaurant, and, jointly with Sheriff Claude Bristow, two motels. It was likely that he was a millionaire; yet he had never lost the common touch, and Danny could not help liking him and wanting his respect, which had made things even more embarrassing.

There had been some preliminaries, in which Jordan had carefully established his friendship for and faith in Danny. Then: "Chief, if there's one thing I hate, it's getting mixed up in somebody else's personal affairs. But your wife, your ex-wife, I mean, called me at home last night, and she was mighty upset. It seems she's been phoning you for two days now and leaving word for you to call back, and you won't return her call, and it's some sort of emergency. Don't you think you'd better take an hour off and go out and see what she wants?"

The bitch, thought Danny savagely. His thoughts raced, but his answer was lame. "I meant to call her back, but it slipped my mind."

"Yeah, we're all too busy sometimes these days. All the same— Danny, I'll be frank. She said it was about money, she had to have some money. Now I don't know what the problem is and I don't want to know. But I *don't* want her calling me at home any more." He paused. "Danny, can I give you some advice, friend to friend?"

"Yes, sir."

"All of us have complications in our personal affairs, and money troubles too. And, Danny, we can't neglect those things, not if we're going to do our jobs properly and be of service to our fellow man. Now . . . I know we don't pay you what you're worth. I've tried to get more for you from the town council, but there's only so much to go around and— Well, we all have to manage with what we've got, and if we don't, we're in trouble, and a man in trouble can't think clearly and do his job right. So all of us have to put first things first and cut our coats, as the saying goes, to fit our cloth. Do you read me? I mean, Danny, you can't fully be of service to your fellow man if your private life is disorganized. Now, I think the world of you, but— Well, a word to the wise is sufficient. I just hope you'll go out and see her right away and get all your problems cleared up so it won't be necessary for her to bother me again."

"Yes, sir," Danny said. "I'll do that."

"Take all the time you need," Jordan said.

● ●

Twenty minutes later, driving east along the highway to the trailer park where she lived, he felt as if something inside him were wound so tight that one notch more and it would break and fly apart, and he would fly apart with it. He had already made up his mind; in his own trailer there was a tag end of whiskey in a bottle, and once he was through here he'd swing by there and finish it to calm his nerves.

Ruth. What he could not understand was why she had changed so after the wedding. When he had met her down in Fayetteville when he was in the MPs and she was tending bar, she had been a good old girl, had liked the things he liked, getting high, hitting the honky-tonks, making love wherever there was a place and time enough, a real party girl. He had looked forward to marrying her, to being a good husband during the week and the two of them partying every weekend, sobering up in bed on Sundays, watching television and having sex . . .

But after marriage she had changed as quickly as a window coming down. Suddenly she wanted only to stay in the trailer all weekend and keep him with her; and that would not have been too bad, except that she had turned against drinking and loving, both. All she could think about was how much the whiskey cost; and when it came to sex, she had become a supply sergeant, grudging everything doled out and making sure that she gave nothing without getting due return. She repudiated all his friends with whom she had been so happy to carouse before, and all she seemed to care about was owning him completely, bending him to her will. The only place she ever wanted to go was to her mother's, where the two women could sit talking endlessly about sick and dying people or running down Danny and all of Danny's friends.

Well, he had tried it her way for a while, though it nearly drove him crazy. It had been better after the children came,

Junior one year after marriage and Linda ten months after him. Being home suited him more, because he loved the kids, loved playing with them. But they had increased his financial burden so much that Ruth's hold on him had tightened to the breaking point. Before, he had been able to slip out for a binge with a clear conscience, now he knew as well as she that there was no money for his carousing. Presently it had seemed that the less there was to spend the more necessary it was for him to spend it, if only to assert that he really existed and had a will of his own.

Anyhow, it had all gone sour; but it was she who had divorced him, not the other way around. He would have stuck it out for the children's sake. He had been raised to believe a bargain was a bargain, something, apparently, that women were never taught. To them a bargain meant getting something valuable for less than you should have paid. But in the long run maybe she had been right; maybe it was better for the kids not to have to listen to their constant fighting, and maybe he just didn't have in him what it took to be a decent husband. . . .

When he had pulled up beside the gleaming Monel mobile home in the sandy trailer park surrounded by dark pines, the blue water of the Sound gleaming just beyond the point, Junior, riding his tricycle hell-for-leather among all the other trailers, had jumped off the wheel so quickly it fell over. "Daddy, Daddy, Daddy!" he cried, running to his father, ribby body tanned, black hair long and matted. Danny scooped him up, grinning, plastered him with kisses, and held him close. "Hey, boy." Then as the four-year-old leaned backward on his crooked arm, he saw the gnats crawling in a black line around and over the child's eyes. "Don't move," he said and purged them with his thumb.

"Daddy, what you bring me?"

Danny frowned. He hadn't thought about a present. "Fifteen cents for you to buy a funny book with," he said, recovering quickly.

"Funny books cost a quarter," Junior whined.

"Goddlemighty, they done gone up again?" Four years old, he thought, and already he knows what things cost. "A quarter, then—"

The screen door of the trailer burst open and Linda tumbled down the steps, blond hair in straggling spirals, round face smudged with snot and dust. "Daddy!"

He picked her up too, wet training pants and all. "Gimme some sugar." Burying his face in the child-smelling sweaty softness of her neck, he kissed her hungrily. "What oo bing me, Daddy?" she asked.

Suddenly he felt tired and she was very heavy. "A quarter for you and Junior to get a funny book," he said and put her down. They followed him to the door, and Ruth was there, holding open the screen.

Her hair, neither brown nor blond, was rolled up on huge curlers, which seemed to pull her skin up and taut, giving her the look of a hungry chicken. She wore a blouse left over from her last pregnancy to conceal the belly that had never gone down, and baggy shorts, and her dusty feet were unshod. "Well, you finally come," she said.

"I come." The trailer was neither clean nor very dirty. The children scrambled in behind him. He took a quarter from his pocket. "I promised 'em a funny book."

She took the coin and slid it in the pocket of the shorts. "We'll git it tomorrow, maybe." Then, to the children: "Y'all go outside and play. Daddy and I got business to talk."

Danny waited until the protesting died and the kids were finally shoved outside. Then he released his anger. "God damn it, don't you have any better sense than to call Jordan, and especially at home? You tryin to make me lose my job?"

"All you had to do was call me back." But there was a light in her eyes that he knew, remembered. Once, when they'd had a fight, she'd seized the possession she loved best, a thin blue glass vase a girl friend married to a soldier had brought her from Germany, and brandished it. But instead of throwing it at him, she'd smashed it to the floor at her own feet, then just stood looking at the fragments and smiling triumphantly, as if by punishing herself she had taken terrible revenge on him. Which she had, because he knew how much she admired that vase, and he had felt guilty for inciting anger enough in her to smash it. "Anyhow," she said, "I got to have some money."

Danny's stomach clenched. "How much?"

"At least thirteen dollars and fifty cents. Darrel Fox is fixin to cut the water off. We're three months behind and this is the last day."

"Three months?" he yelled incredulously.

"What you expect," she shouted back, "when you sixty dollars behind in your child support?"

It was true, and it disarmed him. He sucked in a breath. "Okay, I'll write you a check."

Ruth snorted. "Darrel won't take no more of your checks. It was ten days before you picked up the last one." She looped her hands across her pot belly, and he wondered fleetingly if she were pregnant by somebody else, but he knew she was not. By now she hated the very thought of sex. "I got to have some cash," she said. "You got plenty of money for beer and funny books, but I got to call the Mayor to keep the water on."

After laying out the quarter, Danny had fourteen dollars and forty cents in his pocket. He brought it out slowly, but in the knowledge that the children came first; so did the bargain.

He counted out exactly thirteen dollars and fifty cents, leaving him ninety cents. "All right. That do?"

"I oughta have some more for groceries."

Danny exploded. "God damn it, woman, I ain't got no more! That's the last cash I got."

He was surprised when she did not flare back. "All right," she said, sounding as weary as he felt. "I reckon I can make out on what I got here until you git paid, only except for milk and Sugar Pops. You know Junior won't eat nothin for breakfast but Sugar Pops."

Danny's head twisted toward the screen, then he delved in his pocket and brought out the last of his change. "There. That's all I got. You oughta be able to buy Sugar Pops for that. Besides, you got the quarter for the funny book."

"I know," she said and took the money. Her eyes scanned his face. "This leave you anything?" she asked in a softer voice.

"I'll make out."

"Yeah." She turned away. Her shoulder blades, bony and prominent, showed where the blouse was cut low in back. "You'll find somebody to give you credit so you can keep on drinkin. You coulda bought a head boat long ago with what you spend on whiskey."

"I don't want no head boat."

"You could make a lotta money with a head boat."

"I ain't no fuckin fisherman!" he almost yelled. "I'm a police officer!"

"Don't you use that language around me!" She whirled. "You use it with your friends, but not in my house, you hear?"

"I'm sorry. Look, when I git paid, I'll come straight out here and try to catch up—"

"Yeah," she said. "Yeah, sure."

"I mean it."

"Sure, you always mean it. Well, just let me see some money on the table there, you let me see sixty dollars cash and I'll believe it. You think I want to have to keep on callin and callin you, a dime every time, and havin people tell me you ain't in? When we divorced, you promised to see to me and the kids. You run behind ever' month since then. I don't put dependence in nothin more you say."

"Well, you can now. I'll git straightened out, I promise you."

"You better. There's doctor's bills too. You know that fungus in Linda's belly button—"

"If you'd spray some bug stuff on 'em to keep those damn gnats off—"

"They wear it off quick as I can put it on, and it costs two dollars a can. Now you listen. I can make out till payday. But that very day you better be out here with some money, or I'll call the Mayor again."

"You do that, I'll lose my job. And I can't git no job nowhere else without him to recommend me. You want to cut off your nose to spite your face?"

"You jest be here payday," she said, moved past him, and changed the channel on the television set, which had been muttering all this time. Somebody roared, *"The Dating Game!"* and there was wild applause. "My program's on," Ruth said and sat down at the table, eyes fixed on the screen. Light raying through the Venetian blinds struck her face, and Danny wondered at how old she looked. She had gone from thirty to fifty in two years. "This is my program," she repeated.

"Yeah," Danny said. "Yeah, well, I'll see you payday."

She did not answer. He left the trailer, the children ran to him, and he scooped them up once more. "Daddy," Junior begged, "we wanta sleep with you. When can we come sleep with you again?"

"Soon. Y'all be good, you can come to sleep with Daddy soon."

"Now."

"No, not now. Later on, when I can buy some candy bars and Sugar Pops. Sat'dy a week from now, maybe. We'll sit up and watch *Gunsmoke*, okay?"

They shrilled something, and he had held them tightly, his eyes closed; and in that interval he was refreshed, seeing himself with their vision, tall, magnificent, worthy of their love. For a moment he felt cleansed. Gently he kissed and put them down and warned them to stand well clear as he got in the cruiser and drove away.

Now he folded the checkbook and put it in his pocket. Well, face it, he was broke. There was only one way to get through until payday—find somebody to cash a check. That would not be so easy. He had bounced checks at so many places on Harriot and Shoal Islands, although always he had made them good. Still, someone who had two or three already might complain to the Mayor about another one. Well, he would think of some place tomorrow and—

By his elbow the phone buzzed. He picked it up, grateful for the breaking of his thoughts. "Police. Chief Rush."

"Chief." The voice was deep, rich, black, and relieved. "Glad I caught you in. I got another one for you. This Grover. Reckon you could come down here and git her before she causes trouble?"

"Ain't there no boy with her?"

"She all alone. She and another white girl come here two hours ago, no way I could make 'em stay out, and the other one done left, but this un wouldn't go. She drunk as seven hundred dollars, makin a play for ever' man in the place, and either she gonna cause a cuttin or she gonna go off with somebody that might hurt her. I'd appreciate it if you'd come and git her."

Chief Rush sighed. "Okay, Grover. I'll be right there." His voice was thick with the accent of the Outer Banks, converting *I* to *Oi*.

"Much obliged. I watch her till you git here."

Danny hung up, rose, plucked at the sweaty seat of blue uniform trousers, and strapped on his service belt with all its accouterments: night stick, flashlight, handcuffs, and the Colt .357 Magnum revolver, the latter his personal property. He went through the empty offices of the town government to the garage of the volunteer fire department. There he checked out with the man on duty, who sprawled on a cot reading a paperback called *Incest Contest*. "You need me, call me on the CB." Then he went out and got into the police car parked before the building.

Chapter 2

As he had expected, the wind was moderate, clean, and cool. He rolled down the car windows to let it in, then groped beneath the seat. He brought out a pint bottle with an inch of whiskey left in it and uncapped it with the luxurious realization that he knew now where he could get a fifth to last him through tonight and tomorrow morning. He drained the flask, popped a lighted cigarette in his mouth, backed up the car, and threw the bottle into a dark vacant lot. Then he drove away.

Harriot Island was a zigzag nine miles long of black muck overlaid with deep sand, shagged with tall pines and thick scrub. It was not one of the Outer Banks proper, for it lay in the Sound, but it adjoined Shoal Island, which was; and it was close enough to Hatteras, where Daniel Rush had been born and raised, so he could be back on his own home grounds within an hour. Still, as a Hatterasman, he felt a certain contempt for this protected island, secure from the worst, primary fury of the ocean, a frontiersman's derision of tame civilization behind wild outlying barriers.

But, he thought, driving through darkness, all the islands had changed so much in the past twenty years that sometimes he felt as if he were a stranger on them. In his childhood they had been isolated and almost totally captive to the sea. The paved roads had stopped at Nags Head and Roanoke Island; only ferries and mail boats linked the lower Banks with the mainland at all, and they were infrequent and slow. From Shoal to Ocracoke there were only sand roads overlaid with the kind of metal grillwork used on assault beaches in the war—those and the lighthouses warning coastal shipping of the terrible reefs of Cape Hatteras, of Diamond Shoals, of the cruel area they called the Graveyard of the Atlantic.

It had been better then, he thought, when people had lived as they had always lived: fishing, salving, beachcombing, serving in the Coast Guard. Rough, yes, but it had been simple. Now everything was so complicated . . .

He drove through the outskirts of the town, old houses dreaming under live oaks that had sprouted when George Washington was still in swaddling clothes, then paused at the town's only stoplight. Turning right, he thought, Man, in only twenty years. . . . Ahead a solid bank of neon glittered down the highway: motels, restaurants, and shops.

For centuries the only inhabitants of the islands had been descendants of early seamen, wandering here from other colonies or stranded on the more than hundred miles of shore by the wrecking of their wooden ships. Hatteras, Ocracoke, Portsmouth—they had all been islands lost in time, drowsing in another century, families inbreeding, wary of anyone who did not know the sea.

Then, twenty years before, a great hunger for sand and

ocean had exploded in the souls of mainlanders, pushing them across the Sound to the Outer Banks. First came a vanguard seeking solitude and freedom: as they multiplied developers followed, like gulls and sharks behind a ship. They exerted leverage; bridges replaced the ferries, highways the sandy roads; and tourists seeking sun, salt water, and space poured in. As their numbers threatened to destroy the islands, the Federal government intervened, and the Outer Banks had become the country's first National Seashore. That had only brought in more outsiders, and Danny Rush, returning to Hatteras after four years in the Army, found it a place he had never seen before. Bronzed young men and almost naked girls swarmed over it like ants atop a sugar cube; cars backed up for miles, waiting for the ferries; fishing piers multiplied; campgrounds were jammed with tents and trailers; beach houses, both cheap and expensive, pimpled the seaside dunes; and money, which once had been as scarce as fresh water, coursed in gushing streams.

Harriot had undergone the same transformation. Although in winter the town still counted less than eight hundred people, in summer the island was packed. There were at least four thousand on it, another fifteen thousand on Shoal Island, and thousands more in transit. And, of course, there was the Theater.

On Roanoke Island, farther north, an outdoor drama called *The Lost Colony* had been a smashing tourist attraction for more than three decades. In unashamed imitation, an amphitheater had been constructed here on Harriot at the Sound's edge. The Island's only claim to historical significance was the legend that Edward Teach, Blackbeard, and his pirates had occasionally used it as a hiding place. But that was enough. The resulting play combined buccaneering, blood, and sex and had filled every seat for half a dozen summers. Annually a cast and crew of more than a hundred people were mustered here to present it, and, thought Danny, turning from the highway on to a sandclay road, they were more trouble than any other element in his jurisdiction. The girl in Grover's, there was no doubt that she was from the Theater. Like Daisy Canfield . . .

Along here houses were small, unpainted, their yards crammed with junk; and in between them dead and wheelless cars, hoods sprung open and gaping skyward, were overgrown with vines and scrub. This was Oystertown, the Negro section, and it was not unusual for Chief Rush to have to extricate a white girl from it. He could not understand why so many of them, especially from the North, had such a thing about black men. Grover did his best to keep them out of his Pleasure Palace, but they kept forcing themselves in, looking for a pickup. Imagining a white girl kissing a black man, rubbing up against him, Danny Rush felt a sick disgust. At the same time, involuntarily, he had an erection. He did his best to ignore it, but finally he touched it with one hand. "Well, by damn," he said aloud, "I'll put this up against anything she can find at Grover's."

Rounding a curve, he slowed, then turned the cruiser into a rutted ungraded drive. Ahead, in a grove of pines on a low hillock, lights were yellow in blue darkness. Cars were parked among the trees, and the long single-story never-painted building bore a big sign: GROVER'S PLEASURE PALACE —DRINK COCA-COLA.

Danny drew up by the front door, turned on the flashing light, stopped the engine, and got out. Driving funky music spilled from the open door. He hitched at his belt and loosened the strap behind the revolver's hammer; it always seemed to him that, despite his uniform and Grover's invitation, he was on strange and dangerous ground when entering this place.

Rickety steps trembled under his weight as he climbed the porch and went inside. There he moved immediately to place his back against the wall and scan the room, thumbs hooked in belt. For a moment he had the exhilarating sensation of being someone else—John Wayne or James Arness—as conversation slowly died, awareness of his presence spreading like an infection.

In here there was a bar, booths, bright light. Beyond, there was a door with a crudely lettered sign—*Couples onley*—and past that the darkness of a cave. From this annex Grover came, squat and black in pearl-gray suit, dark cheek puckered with old bullet scar. "She in yonder," he said, face close to Rush's.

"Still not with nobody?"

"No. 'Lone and skunk-drunk, dodgin in and outa booths. Ever'body afraid to touch her this far, but with all them young studs and hot bitches in there, hell due to pop."

"Okay, I'll see to her." He unsnapped his flashlight. "Grover."

"Yayh," he said warily.

"While I'm back yonder, suppose you slide a fifth under the front seat."

"Sho. Be glad to." But Grover's voice was grudging.

Danny nodded, passed through the door into the other room. This was a dance hall, with a single red bulb dangling from a pigtail socket in the middle of the floor, a jukebox gleaming at the far end, booths all around the walls. Danny raked his light from right to left, then he saw the girl.

She leaned over a table in a booth, standing on one foot, the other leg pointed out behind, sandal dangling. Her miniskirt had ridden up, and Danny's light came to rest on the

27

diaphragm of nylon across the lower slopes of rounded buttocks. The girl did not even notice. Hands braced on the table, she went on talking earnestly to a young Negro man sitting with a black girl. The man was trying hard not to look at her, and the black girl's lip was poked far out as, savagely, she turned her glass around and around. The eyes of both gleamed in the flashlight beam.

Softly Danny walked up behind the plump outstretched leg. The girl remained oblivious. "Tell you," she was insisting, "my brother, you understand? Personal *friend* of James Chaney." The extended leg waved excitedly. "He and Mike Schwerner were in school together and then they both joined COFO—"

"Don't know nothin about no Chaney, no COFO," the black man said. "But, chick, you better look out . . . because they is a great big policeman standin right behind you."

"Police—" The girl's leg was motionless, then it came down. "All right, miss, " Danny said, tapping her on the shoulder.

She turned, slowly coming upright, pushing back a thick strand of brown hair from one eye. When she let it go, it fell right back, obscuring half her face, which was pale and puffy, cheeks round and doughy, mouth small and red. Danny moved the beam over her body. Her breasts were large beneath a white blouse with dark spots of sweat beneath the arms, her waist was thick, her hips wide. He raised the light again and she blinked. "Well," she said hoarsely, "if it isn't Chuck." She jerked her head toward the black man. "Hey, drill the Chuck pig just walked in."

The young man said nothing. Danny said, "Miss, it's time to go."

She tossed her head, but the hair flopped back in the same

place. Not over twenty, Danny thought. "Go where, you fucking pig?" she asked, and from the thickness of her voice he knew to be careful of all the beer she had in her. He stifled the disgust and, yes, excitement he always felt when he heard a girl use that word. "Home," he answered.

"You can't make me go anywhere, you motherf—"

"Watch it girl!" the black man in the booth snapped angrily.

"The management don't want you here," said Danny with careful patience. "This is a place for colored. They've asked me to get you to leave. Now, which is it? Either I take you home or take you into town and book you and call your parents. I'd rather take you home."

"Up yours, pig," she said, glaring at him, swaying slightly. "*Listen* to him." Her voice rose, indignant, shrill. "You gonna stand by and let this Goddamn *racist* dictate to everybody?" Even slurred and drunken, her Northern accent grated harshly on Danny's ears.

The room was wholly silent.

"This fucking white racist?" she screamed. "This totalitarian bastard?"

Nobody spoke or moved.

"What the hell's the matter with everybody?" the girl shrieked. Grover materialized by Danny's elbow. "It in the car."

The girl whirled on Grover. "Listen, you ass-kissing Tom—"

"That'll be enough." Danny seized her upper arm, fingers digging into soft, watery flesh. "Come on."

She tried to jerk away. "Lemme go, you Nazi! Big man with a gun! That gun, you'd like to ram it up my snatch, huh? Big man wears his prick in a holster—"

"I'll swear, Chief," Grover muttered, "*I* don't know how they git this way."

"Come on, lady," Danny said and pulled again.

"Lemme go, you fucking—" In midsentence, clear green vomit gushed from her mouth in a thick stream, and Danny and Grover jumped back just in time. Her eyes widened in astonishment as the liquid poured out in amazing quantity.

Danny remembered a bird he had found under a yaupon bush when he was small. Whatever it was, it had eaten so many berries it could not fly; it only lay on its back with legs kicking feebly, berries trickling from its mouth. When he had picked it up, held it head down, they had poured from it as beer came now from the girl.

"Jesus," Grover said disgustedly. "Well, I go send a mop and bucket." He turned away, and Danny went behind the vomiting girl and cradled her forehead in his hand, standing well back out of the splash, as he had used to do with Junior. She leaned hard into it, and finally she was retching without yielding anything. A shapeless Negro woman came with bucket and mop and looked and sighed. The black man in the booth said, "Here some napkins," and passed Danny a wad of paper.

He wiped her mouth. "All right. There." He felt not so much disapproval as sympathy; he had been this drunk himself more than once.

"Jesus," the girl said, and she sagged against him, shuddering, soft buttocks pressing, her hair in his face.

"You want to come with me now?"

"I don't care." She shook her head, gasped. "Anywhere."

"Grover," Danny said. "Her pocketbook. Check it."

"Here it is," the girl in the booth said. Grover looked inside. "Five dollars, some change."

"Right." Danny took the handbag. "I got twelve-fifteen. That right with you?"

"On the dot."

"Okay, here we go. Miss, what's your name, where you live?"

"Stern," she wheezed. "Deborah Stern . . . Canfield Complex . . . Number Four."

She went docilely as he led her from the room; she smelled of perspiration, vomit, perfume worn too long. Grover followed them to the front door, watched as Danny helped her down the steps. At the bottom she stumbled, and, steadying her, his hand closed on one big spongy breast. He held her that way until they reached the cruiser. There he opened the door to the back seat. "Now, you got to throw up again, you go ahead and do it. But not in the vehicle."

"No," she wheezed. "No, nothing left inside." She slid in, skirt riding up around her loins. Danny saw darkness behind the thin panties where her legs veed together. He shut the door, which locked automatically, and went around and got behind the wheel. He started the engine and drove away from Grover's Pleasure Palace.

At the sandclay road he turned right. In the rearview mirror he saw Deborah Stern sprawled on the seat, separated from him by a barrier of bulletproof glass. Her mouth was opening and closing like a landed fish's.

Danny drove through lonesome country—pine woods, thickets, old fields—eyes flicking from headlight glare to mirror and back again. Once he switched on the rear domelight; she blinked in its glare; again he saw her pubic region. He cut the light off, sucked in a long breath, feeling his pants bulge with his extending flesh. It had been almost ten days since he had had a woman . . .

"Hey, cop," she said from in back.

"Chief," he said. "I'm the Police Chief."

"Yeah, big deal, cop. Cop? Look." Her voice was thick, slurred. "Hey, stop the car. I wanta tell you somethin."

"Tell me while we're riding."

"No, *stop*."

Fearing she'd be sick again, he put on brakes. Deborah laughed. "Better," she said. "You know what? Let's fuck."

Danny stiffened. "Miss—"

"Come on, damn it, less me'n you fuck." Her voice rose. "I wanta fuck, you understand? I really wanta fuck!"

Danny's hands clamped on the wheel. He sat there staring straight ahead for a moment, then he switched on the dome-light once more. She lay half sprawled on the seat, and she had pulled her skirt off and she was peeling down her underpants and he saw the thick brown shag between her thighs. "Fuck," she said. "All right? Come on, honey—"

Danny cut off the light. He looked at the roadside on right and left; ahead there was a narrow trail just wide enough to accommodate a car. He could pull in there and . . . It would all be over in five minutes and likely she would not even remember it in the morning, or if she did, probably she would come back for more. . . . He reached for the handle of the door.

Then he said harshly, "No!" He threw the car in gear, gunned the engine. The girl rolled off the seat, bumped on the floor, let out a squawk. "Put your skirt back on," Danny snarled. "You hear? Get your fool self dressed!"

"Honey," she whined.

The car roared along the road, reached the highway. In its headlight beams Danny saw the sign, its reflectors like the eyes of a pack of great animals shining in the darkness. An arrow pointed left: BUCCANEER THEATER. CANFIELD COMPLEX. 1 MILE. She was lucky, he thought savagely as the cruiser shot into the highway, that Grover's was inside the town limits. If it had been in the county, some deputy would have been humping her right now and then swearing out a warrant for public drunkenness.

"Honey," she wailed, but the car sped along the road, and when it branched, roared down the left fork through a stand of ancient pines. It forked again, the left branch leading to the Theater on the edge of the waters of the Sound; he took the right one. This led uphill and ended in a paved parking lot. Beyond, a compound of modern single-story duplexes was brightly lit by floodlights. In that glare Danny saw, turning, that the girl had fumbled her skirt back on. Fuming, he jerked open his door and then the one in back.

"All right, Miss Stern."

She still could hardly stand; she leaned against him. "Cop," she muttered, "please, don't wanta go home, wanta fuck."

Almost in vengeance, Danny squeezed one big breast, slid his hand down her hip, under her skirt, felt her ass, then around to her crotch, then drew back. He said, "Come on." He led her into the compound and up the steps of a redwood duplex with picture windows and lights over the doors. He rang the bell.

"I got a key," Deborah Stern said, fumbling in her handbag, then dropping it.

Danny picked it up and stood wide away from her and rang the bell again. Presently a tall blond young woman in a short blue nylon robe opened the door, blinking groggily. "Debbie, what in the world?" Her voice trailed off as she saw Danny's blue hat and uniform, the badge glittering on his chest in the moonlight.

Behind her he could see the living room, with sofa and chairs and record player and wall-to-wall carpeting, a kitchen dinette behind it and to the side, a hallway that led to two bedrooms, each shared by two girls. They paid, these Theater people, ten dollars weekly each for such a place, and he felt a pang of envy. This was the kind of place he and Ruth had

33

wanted before things had got so messed up. . . . "Miss, is this your roommate?"

"Yes." She rubbed her face. Then she took Debbie by the arm, led her inside, and dropped her in a chair. The girl leaned sideways and began to snore.

Danny whipped notebook and pen from his shirt pocket. "Miss, what's your name?"

"I'm Frances Goodson, but—"

"I found this young lady in Grover's Pleasure Palace. Grover made a complaint—"

"I know. I was there with her, and then when I left she wouldn't come. Is she . . . under arrest?"

"No," said Danny. "But she will be if she ever goes back there again. Now, will you please check the money in her handbag?"

The girl opened it. "Five dollars and sixty-seven cents."

"All right. What time is it?"

She looked at a tiny wristwatch. "Twelve twenty-eight."

"Remember that," Danny said. The snoring broke off. Deborah had roused and was looking at him through tangled hair; and seeing her in good light, he no longer wanted her at all. "Now," he said fiercely, "let me tell you something, both of you. The next time Grover complains about one of you kids, you're goin straight to jail." He whirled on Deborah. "You. What would you have done if I hadn't come and got you? Walked home by yourself in the dark? You want to wind up like Daisy Canfield?"

"Who?" Frances Goodson asked.

Danny spun back to her. "The young lady they named these apartments for. That's why they built this place, so you young ladies wouldn't have to go back and forth between here and town at night. *She* did exactly what Miss Stern let herself in for. Stayed out late and tried to walk home early in the

morning, three years ago, and got herself picked up by somebody on a road near Oystertown and raped and strangled and
her body throwed off the draw of the mainland bridge. It was
two weeks before they found her in the Sound, and the man
that done it ain't never been brought to justice. He mighta
been in that place you was in tonight. Now, you been warned.
Both of you, you stay outa Grover's and watch your step, you
hear?"

From down the corridor another girl's voice, thick with
sleep, called, "What the hell's going on out there?"

"Nothing, Gerry," Frances Goodson snapped. "Go back to
sleep." Her resentment at being lectured crackled in her
voice. "Thank you," she said thinly, "for bringing my
roommate home. Good night."

Danny opened his mouth, then closed it. "Good night," he
said shortly. Feeling the press of anger and frustration within
his skull, he whirled, went out the door, and closed it solidly.
He was panting when he reached the car, although his way
had been all downhill. Getting in, he fumbled beneath the
seat. "Bitches," he said aloud. "Christ, what the young kids
comin to?" In the complex the lights went out in Apartment
Four. Danny shone his flash on the bottle of whisky, snorting
when he read the label. "Damn cheapskate." It was rotten
stuff; even Grover was showing contempt for him and his
office.

But he needed it, and he broke the seal, eased far down on
the seat, and drank. Then he drove away from the complex,
angry, excited, disturbed. At the fork he turned toward the
Theater.

A quarter of a mile brought him to a log palisade decorated
with wooden cutouts of sailing ships flying the Jolly Roger.
The enormous stockade enclosed a three-thousand-seat amphitheater, a stage built so that the water of the Sound

formed a backdrop for scenes on-ship and ashore, and a large complex of costume, dressing, and rehearsal rooms. Danny parked the cruiser, looked around carefully, took the bottle, got out, and walked down a path that led him to the Sound.

Here he was backstage. Water rippled on the shore, a halfmoon's reflection shattered and washing in it, fragments of silver paving a jagged path to nowhere across an infinity of darkness. Paralleling that, a dock stretched its long finger outward. To Danny's right, heavy wooden rails supported a mock-up of a barkentine's superstructure, masts and plywood sails on a truck with railroad wheels. Beyond, the backstage housing, also rustic like the palisade, was a dark blob.

He walked out on the dock, sat on its end, made sure no one lurked in the dark places behind the dressing rooms, and took another drink. Inside he still seethed, not only with desire but with frustration and shame.

Water sucked at pilings; he caught the familiar loin smell of marshes. He was, he thought, a Goddamned fool. Five minutes would have done it, five minutes in the brush along the road. There had been a dozen places he could have pulled over. . . .

But he had been on duty, and that was what had made the difference.

Danny pondered that. He was a man who lived in constant fear of himself and his inability to master his own desires; always it seemed to him that he walked a tightrope over a chasm of disaster, knowing that no one else would unbalance him, but that he himself might, carelessly or deliberately, send himself hurtling to his doom. He thoroughly expected to be the instrument of his own destruction and was always startled and pleased when he passed up an opportunity. That was what he had done tonight, simply because it had not been his business to lay that little girl but to see her safely home.

He had taken an oath to protect people like her. If she had been thirty, that would have been a different case.

And yet it would have been so good. To have done something with somebody, anybody. He was so Goddamned lonely. Oh, there was Felix and Larry, but this was a different kind of loneliness, a vacancy in a different quarter of his soul. He wanted a woman, but what he wanted of her was something he had not got from Ruth. It was not just sex, he thought, although that was a big part of it. But it was what came afterwards, the quiet place to rest, the cradle in the darkness. What he wanted was a woman who would treat him all the time as if he had just satisfied her, who would love him all the time as much as all women loved you for the moment just afterwards. The life he led was too much for him, too complicated for one man alone; he needed someone to carry part of the weight and untangle the things his fingers were too clumsy for. He wanted someone to reassure him that he was strong enough to keep on going, and to make it worthwhile to be strong.

All this he sensed more than thought, for he was tired and felt the whiskey and was never too good with words anyhow. He regretted the missed chance with Deborah Stern as all his life, while he was potent, he would regret a missed chance with any woman. But she wasn't worth it. Not that he was afraid she would cry rape. Not that he was saving himself for someone else. But only because he was on duty, and the trust that implied was the tightrope he walked. The badge he wore was more his protection than hers; it marked the limit beyond which he must not let himself go if he were not to fall off that tightrope. That was all he had, the badge, the fact that he was Chief, all he had salvaged.

He drank once more, capped the bottle, rose, and climbed the hill to the cruiser. After he got in, he looked around the empty parking area and the silent woods. He thought about Daisy Canfield. She had lived here; it was possible that she had died here. Once he had thought her death would be his salvation, but he knew better now. He had been crazy, under Felix's spell, even to take the confession in the first place, much less carry it to Jordan and Bristow. Oh, it would make him famous; he would be the man who had solved Daisy Canfield's murder.

He laughed harshly, bitterly, started the car, drove up through the woods, and when he reached the highway, halted and checked in with the volunteer fire department on the CB radio. There had been no calls for him, so he went directly to shut down the town. As he drove back to Harriot, he lapsed into sexual fantasies, imagining what he would have done with two girls at once, or they with him.

Even though Harriot was the largest municipality in Midyette County, which encompassed this island, Shoal Island, and a great sprawling wilderness of mainland swamps and forests, there were only about six blocks of it to cruise, not counting Oystertown. Most of the recent expansion and new population lay outside the city limits on the highway. Rush checked the downtown business district—the single tavern, the pool hall, the one movie theater, a handful of stores—and found them all closed and secure. The sidewalks were deserted now at one, although there would be seething activity on the beaches all around the clock.

Danny made a circuit of the town square, dominated by the high ancient white-painted courthouse, with its clock tower like a belfry. In the shadow of its great granite steps he saw something move, halted the cruiser, switched on the spotlight. He swore softly. "All right, Bubba. Go on home. You're out too late."

The figure in the spotlight beam was nearly seven feet tall, so scrawny that the work shirt hung around it like a tent and the faded blue jeans were like bags. Nearly vacant eyes shone in the yellow gleam, and large front teeth like a muskrat's glinted too. "Ch-Chief Rush." The stuttering voice was falsetto, effeminate. "Jus— Jus checkin on things f-for S-Sheriff B-Bristow. L-Like I a-always d-do."

"Yeah, like you always do," Danny said. "Checking on things for Cousin Claude. God damn it, you go on home, Bubba. Your momma'll be waitin up."

"Yuy-yeah, you r-right. G-G'night, Ch-Chief."

"Good night," Danny snapped and watched the gangling figure shuffle off. You simple-minded lying son of a bitch, he thought, as Bubba Dixon was swallowed up by darkness. All the shit you put me through. The cruiser's engine roared as he gunned it and raced to the City Hall. There, in the parking lot, he checked with the volunteer fireman again, cleaned the bottle and all scraps of broken seal from the patrol car, left it locked and parked, and got in his own ancient Ford. When he started it, the car roared like thunder, its muffler bad and tailpipe bracket broken. Danny hated the sound it made as he drove home.

Chapter 3

Home. That was another trailer park, one so new, bulldozer tracks were still engraved in its dust. No lights burned here at this time of morning, and Danny hoped the car's gutted roar would not awaken any sleeping babies. He quickly cut it off before one of the smaller, badly dented mobile homes.

He unlocked the door and entered, flicked on the light and looked around disgustedly. The bed was as he had left it when he had crawled out this morning; the tiny kitchen overflowed with dirty dishes and accumulated garbage; the stove was piled with greasy frying pans. "Jesus, you're a lousy housekeeper," Danny said aloud.

But it was so hard to get organized, he thought, setting down the bottle. On duty, he was all right; off, he simply could not force himself into any kind of discipline. "I got to clean this place up tomorrow," he said determinedly, and that released him from any obligation tonight. Feeling better, he got ice from the little refrigerator, dumped it in a cloudy jelly glass, made a strong highball. He carried it to the foldout table, sat down on the leatherette bench there, drank deeply, and sighed. Presently he slipped off his shoes without untying them, aware that he was scuffing leather and not caring. He peeled off cheap dark socks plastered to his feet like decals and absently rubbed the fingers of his left hand between his gummy toes as he drank. He could smell the odor, knew a bath was needed, but that could wait until tomorrow too. He had tomorrow and the next day off, so everything could wait until tomorrow. Right now he would drink some whiskey. He would drink just enough to make himself believe that after a good rest tonight everything would be all right tomorrow. He would be clearheaded, orderly, and he would clean up the trailer; he would know where to cash a check; he would have fresh willpower to cut out the cigarettes and booze. He knew it was a lie, but he could drink enough tonight to make it seem the truth, and that was almost as good. It should take about half the bottle; it took a little more every time.

He hitched around, unstrapped his service belt, laid it coiled on the table with the gun on top, butt toward his hand. He drank half the glass, and idly he wondered what it would feel like to be somebody else, somebody born in New York or Hollywood and grown up there, rich and smart and never worried, able to spend twenty or thirty dollars any time you took a notion. It was so strange and random, he thought, how and where people were born and what they got. He deserved so much more than he had got, and yet he had so much more than others; he was Wahab Rush's son.

"And you had better fuckin well not forget it," he said aloud. "That is one thing you had better fuckin well not forget." He thought about getting up to turn on the television, but it would only have an old movie about to end. He sat there quietly, thinking about the girls, building more fantasies and exciting himself. Presently he got up and made another drink and sat down again, one hand rubbing his crotch beneath the table.

Then his eyes came to rest on the holstered gun. *Prick in a holster . . . ram it up my snatch . . .* By damn, she had imagination, anyway. That was something out of a dirty paperback. He unsnapped the strap, pulled the gun from its scabbard. Everything else on the belt was property of the town, but this revolver belonged to him. He laid his hand over it, and the solid cold metal seemed to transmit reassurance to him. By God, he owned three good things, anyhow: his son, his daughter, and this gun.

Besides his children, it was the only thing he had ever possessed that somebody had not used before, including Ruth. Up in Manteo with a full paycheck in his pocket and a sixpack in his belly, he had seen it in a hardware store and fallen helplessly in love with it. On impulse, he had bought it for a quarter of his monthly salary. Later, home and with the alcohol wearing off, he was almost afraid to face Ruth and try to explain why he had ruined their budget. But after a lifetime of buying the cheapest and using the shoddy, he had simply not been able to walk away from that fine gun.

But there was no way he could justify it to her, for it was a man's thing beyond her understanding. Even when he pointed out that it might save his life, that the .38s the town provided were inadequate, but a Magnum could drop a man in his tracks through sheer shock, she had reminded him that he had never had to use a pistol anyhow. But there was always a first time, he'd tried to make her see, and when it came, you had to have enough gun for the job. She did not know about the fights, the narrow escapes, and daring showdown battles he had fought in his imagination until they were real.

Anyhow, he was glad he'd bought it. By now the financial scar had healed, and there was not a day he did not take satisfaction in it. Somehow its existence attested to him that he existed too and that, no matter what else happened, he was Chief of Police of the Town of Harriot, and that was something beyond the ordinary. "So, what the hell," he said aloud and spun the cylinder lovingly. When he went to bed an hour later, after drinking half the bottle, the Colt hung beside him within easy reach.

It was well past noon when he awakened the next day, stomach upset, head aching, mouth burnt and bitter. The thought of food made his entrails roil; in his jockey shorts he lurched across the trailer, poured an ounce of whiskey, dashed in a little water, and drank it quickly. He waited a moment, then had another drink, and presently the turmoil was damped down a little by the alcohol. The hangover, though, was not the worst of it. He was gripped by a heavy depression stemming from the knowledge of what he must do today: cash a check that he could not be sure was good, indeed was certain to bounce unless by some miracle it did not reach the bank till payday. Oh, no one would lose a cent by it except himself—the bank would charge him three dollars—but it was a kind of lying, and if not stealing, at least it was close to begging. He hated it, hated the damage it would do his reputation and his pride. And he hated Ruth for making it necessary. But most of all he hated himself, for in the end the responsibility was his.

He had another drink and hated that too, for once he'd had an inflexible rule never to drink in the morning, much less before he'd eaten. He knew all too well what that could lead to; it seemed a pit yawned before him. But he was helpless to keep from marching toward it; there was too much chaos in him.

Sitting there in his shorts, grimy from the day before, looking around the littered trailer in the bleak morning light, he was suddenly panic-stricken. He did not want to be alone in such a mood, here with the gun. He was afraid of himself and of the gun, because now it seemed to him that it was his last friend, his last defense against all he had endured. All at once, with determination, he sprang up, stripped off the shorts, and grimaced as he stepped into the dirty shower stall with its mildewed curtain. Under the penance of cold water, he revived. Later, still naked, he shaved. Having no clean civilian clothes, he put on his spare uniform, then heated water, drank a cup of instant coffee, and went outside.

At this season the climate of the Outer Banks was superb. The air was crystalline, the sunlight undulled by haze or smoke, the wind from the sea strong and fresh. Danny drew in deep breaths, stretched, flexed his arms. He looked around the trailer camp, feeling hopeful again. Children shouted as they ran and played; women at their brightly flapping clothes-lines talked to one another; the surrounding pines coughed and whispered. He lit a cigarette and pondered the matter of the check. Presently he had an inspiration, and he got in the old car and drove eastward on the highway to where it forked.

The right turn took him through marshes like endless prairies, choked with grass and staked with occasional gaunt half-drowned trees. After a mile of this he reached the fishing village of Finley Harbor, the only other settlement on the island. It was a place of small houses and neat front yards, in some of which little wiry ponies of the kind that had once run wild up and down the Banks cropped grass. In the past decade the wild ones had been rounded up once and for all to prevent overgrazing of the precious grass that held the dunes together; only a token herd of a dozen remained on pasture on the southern island of Ocracoke as a tourist attraction. With all the people on the Banks now, there was less room for wild things; since the government had come in, everything was regulated.

Finley Harbor had no business district; Harriot served it in that regard. Its heart was the wharves. Rickety and surrounded by a cluster of big ramshackle wooden buildings, they were, save for one small marina, wholly utilitarian. Half a dozen scabby little wooden trawlers rode at anchorage, nets furled and booms locked; abandoned car and truck bodies, tangled nets and cordage, rusting winches, piles of oyster shells, and general rubbish hillocked the terrain for hundreds of yards around. On a wooden crate an old man sat carefully painting plastic bleach bottles orange to be used as buoys for his crab pots. The dirt parking lot was packed with cars, and two big refrigerated trailers were backed up to the loading dock of Dooly Gray's fish house and supply store.

Danny parked the car and got out, sucking in deeply the familiar intermingled tangs of dirty brackish water, fish, sea-breeze, and motor oil. To him it was a good smell, conjuring memories. He had served his time on fishing boats such as these four days or a week at a time on the Gulf Stream. He knew what a hard, brutal, chancy life it could be, but for a moment he felt a deep yearning for its simplicity, strenuous-ness, and masculine companionship. He walked out on docks littered with trash fish and tiny dried stars and crabs and all manner of little dead sea organisms for which there was no market, sizing up each tied boat professionally.

In the open shed of the fish house, men in rubber aprons and boots sorted, weighed, boxed, and iced mackerel, bluefish, even a few red snapper brought to them gleaming and wide-eyed on a conveyor. They knew Danny, and he chatted with them a moment, then went through a door into

45

the general store and marine supply house area of Gray's complex. Dooly Gray was behind the counter, wiry, white-haired, face and body like something made of driftwood, and Danny carefully put on a casual manner.

Gray's greeting held genuine cordiality and Danny relaxed. "Where you been so long?"

"Well, a man stays busy."

"Yeah, I reckon police work keeps you hoppin." Gray's voice was rich with the Banker brogue. "Well, good to see you."

Having checked the boats, Danny knew the next question was wholly safe. "Jeff Furman in?"

"Nope, he's still out, won't put in until tomorrow. You know him, he fishes till he's full. Any message I can give him? I can raise him on the radio. He ain't in trouble with the law, is he?"

"Naw, I'm off today, just thought I'd have a beer with him if he was around. Well—" Danny half turned to go, then paused. "While I'm here, Dooly, gimme a pack of Winstons."

"Sure." Gray took one from behind the counter. Danny dug in his pocket, then snapped his fingers. "Son of a gun, I give the last cash I had to my wife yesterday evenin. You mind cashin a check?"

"No trouble. How much you want?"

"Well, I hate to ask you, for such a little bit of money, but—fifteen dollars okay?"

"Sure." Gray went to the cash register. Danny was careful to fill out the check stub, make a show of counting change with businesslike precision. "Much obliged."

"You welcome." Gray grinned. "When you gonna sell me that Colt, Danny?"

"That'll be the day." It was a standing joke between them; Gray coveted that Magnum. "Buy one of your own."

"Can't afford a new one."

Danny laughed. "Dooly, you could afford a closet full of 'em."

They joked a moment more, and Danny went out, depression lifting from him, the cash in his pocket like new blood in his veins. Now he had money, a day and a half of freedom, and Tuesday he would draw his check. The world, somewhat, fell back into focus. He started toward his car, but when he heard the grinding of an engine refusing to start, he looked around.

The blue Mustang was parked on the shoulder of the road, a woman bent over the wheel. Actuated by policeman's instinct, nothing else, he went to it and rapped on the window. "Excuse me, ma'am. Havin trouble?"

She looked up, and when she saw his uniform relief spread across her face. She was, he guessed, about his age, and he could not decide immediately whether she was pretty. Brown-blond hair cut short and curling in feathery tufts framed a triangle of a face devoid of makeup and slightly freckled. A short nose glowed with recent sunburn; eyes beneath pale brows were large, blue-gray; her upper lip was beaded with perspiration. Her sleeveless blue blouse was stained with sweat beneath the armpits. Automatically he inventoried her breasts, found them ample if not large, and the sun-reddened legs beneath white shorts were very good.

"I seem to be," she said, smiling ruefully. "It won't start and I get this red light." Her voice had a crisp, hard-edged Northern accent, but it was soft, pleasant. She gestured helplessly.

"Alternator. It's not working. Look, I got jumper cables in my car. Hold on a minute and I'll rig 'em up. Maybe you can start off my battery and then we'll see."

She wiped perspiration from her lip with a finger. "You're a lifesaver, Officer."

"Chief. I'm Police Chief of the town of Harriot."

She nodded, impressed. "Chief."

Danny parked his car nose to nose with hers, rigged the cables. With his engine idling, he went to the Mustang. "Now, move over."

She slid across the seat and he got behind the wheel. The car started at once, red light on the dash flickering on and off as he raced the engine. "Yep, alternator, it's cuttin out on you. Better have it fixed."

"Is there a garage here?"

"No, ma'am. Ford agency in Harriot, but I know a guy runs an Esso station on Shoal Island that's a good mechanic and a lot cheaper. Lemme unhook these cables and then I'll follow you. Go back up this road and when you cross the bridge to Shoal turn right again, go down one block, first Esso on your left. I'll be right behind you."

"Oh, thanks. I'd hate for this thing to die and leave me stranded in the swamps."

Danny grinned. "Won't let that happen." He disconnected and stowed the cables, got in his car, watched as she deftly swung around. As he moved out behind her, he noted that the Mustang bore a Pennsylvania license plate.

There had been no wedding ring on her left hand. As they drove in convoy toward Shoal Island, Danny built a fantasy, for this was different from the girl in Grover's; she was grown, and he was not on duty. He imagined taking her home, wherever that might be, she asking him in for a drink, and then— It was, as a matter of fact, not so wild a prospect. In the summer the islands swarmed with women of all ages on the loose, far from home and ready for a spree. Over the years, he'd encountered his share.

That had, of course, been one reason for the split between

himself and Ruth. He did like women; moreover, they liked him, and, exposed to constant temptation in his job, he was only human. But he had never been seriously mixed up with any other woman while he and Ruth were married; there had been only brief, almost anonymous, interludes with those who in a day or week would be moving on. He had seen nothing wrong with that, especially since she was not keeping him happy at home. He did not even think she knew about them, really, but only assumed he cheated on her, and she had closed up tighter, in revenge. That made him more wolfish away from home, and so they had been caught up in a kind of vicious circle.

Anyhow, he had time, money, and he was ready for a party if she was. It wouldn't hurt to try.

Her name was Paula Murphy, and while she paced the service bay of the station, smoking one cigarette after another like a father in a waiting room, Danny get a better look at her. She was neither tall nor short, a little broad in the hips, and she had a straightforward, almost sardonic manner and a wry sense of humor that he liked.

The alternator would have to be rebuilt. Doc Austin said he would try to have the car ready by tomorrow afternoon, and that likely it would cost at least forty dollars. "Oogh," she said, then shrugged. "Well, it's in your hands. Treat it tenderly." She turned to Danny. "Would it be possible for you to give me a lift? I've got a cottage just up the beach."

He was embarrassed for her to see how old and dirty his car was, upholstery torn, overhead sagging, leakstained. "I got to get a new one soon," he told her as he settled behind the wheel. "My kids have picked this one all to pieces."

"Oh, you're married?"

"Was. Divorced now, I got a boy and girl, they live with their mama." Leaving the station, he drove north along the narrow road that ran the length of the Shoal Island beach front, lined solidly on both sides with motels, restaurants, cottages, apartments, piers, gift shops, and other structures. Though the ocean was only three hundred yards distant on their right, it was impossible to see it. Danny wondered again how much money Mayor Jordan and Sheriff Bristow had made out of the explosive development of what, only ten years before, had been barren dunes.

"I'll bet from your accent you grew up down here."

"I did; I'm from Hatteras."

"I thought so." She was pleased. "That lovely accent. I've read about it, but I thought it would have died out by now. You know, television . . . Everybody talks the same way everywhere now."

"Most folks from Hatteras and Ocracoke and the eastern part of Midyette and Hyde County talk the way I do."

"Hoide County. I think that's delicious. Please, let me hear you say something else. Like, oh, 'I want to take a ride at high tide in Hyde County.'"

He said it and she laughed. "Oi want to tek a roide at hoigh toide— It's so *musical.*" Then, contritely, "I hope you don't think I'm making fun of you, as kind as you've been to me."

"Oh, we like to keep the tourists happy. We talk funny for 'em and start their cars even when we're off duty."

"You're not on duty?"

"No, ma'am. I'm off one weekend a month and this is it."

"I see." She pointed. "Over there, that's where I'm staying."

Danny turned into a court of wooden cottages around a badly paved drive. Wet bathing suits flapped from washlines and a fat woman and a skinny girl hung out more. "This one," she said, pointing to a small weatherbeaten house with a screen porch.

He stopped the car, got out, came around to open her door, but she had already done it for herself. Facing him, the top of her head barely came to his chin. "Well, Chief Rush, I thank you."

"Yes, ma'am, Miss Murphy. If I can be of help again, let us know."

There was a moment then when they looked at each other in silence, neither stirring. Then she said, as Danny was about to turn away, "I could offer you a drink, if you've got time. Since you're off duty, I suppose it's not against regulations."

Inwardly Danny grinned, but he kept his face expressionless. "Why, that would be real nice."

"I hope you like martinis, that's all I've got the makings for."

"That's fine. I'm very fond of martinis."

"Oim vurry fahnd of martinis." She smiled. "Then Oi would be vurry pleased to give you one, Chief Rush."

The beach house smelled of sun-dried wood, sand, salt. Its furniture was wicker, a sofa, two large chairs, a coffee table with a map spread over it. A cheap television set was on a stand, and nearby it a portable record player that must have been her own property. There was no air-conditioner, but a breeze blew in constant crossdraft through the room. She motioned Danny to the sofa. "Have a seat. I'll go wash my face and hands and make the drinks."

Sitting, he lit a cigarette, feeling a sense of luck and power; things were breaking right, absolutely right; he was pretty sure he knew how this weekend would work out now, and it would be a good one. He looked at the map, which was of the Coast and the Outer Banks, laid it aside, riffled through magazines beneath it: *Playboy, Cosmopolitan, Time*, and something called *Private Confessions*. He picked up the latter, which was the sort of thing Ruth had used to read. The cover showed a girl just beginning to peel off her sweater. I DANCED NAKED FOR THE HIGH SCHOOL FOOT-BALL TEAM, a legend said.

He was thumbing through that one when she came back with a tray, a pitcher, two glasses. Embarrassed, he quickly laid it aside. Paula Murphy grinned. "I see you've found my dirty little secret."

Danny looked at her blankly. "Huh?"

"The lead article. I wrote it. 'I Danced Naked . . .'"

He blinked at her. "You're a writer?"

"No, I teach fifth grade, in Washington, Pennsylvania. But I bat out those things in my spare time. They're not hard to do, and, for instance, I got four hundred dollars for that one."

Danny picked up the confession magazine again, opened it to the article. A girl in bra and skirt was surrounded, in its photographic illustration, by three young men in shoulder pads and jerseys. "I always thought these things was true. You didn't—"

Paula Murphy threw back her head and laughed. "No, unfortunately nobody ever asked me." Then, smiling, she went on. "But it *is* based on fact; I heard about an incident like it at a convention." She filled the glasses and handed one to him. He noticed that she had combed her hair and put on lipstick. Taking her own glass, she sat down in the chair opposite, the coffee table between them. "Well, Chief Rush, cheers."

The gin was cold and tasted clean. Danny said, "I got a friend you ought to meet. He teaches tenth grade in the high school, Larry Besser, and he wants to be a writer someday."

Paula grimaced. "Thanks, but I drove six hundred miles to get away from schoolteachers."

"I just thought if you were lonesome—"

"I'm not lonesome. I'm never lonesome when I'm in a place I've never been, meeting people I don't know. Like you. I've never had a drink with a police chief before."

"It's only me and three other officers."

"A chief's a chief in my book. Is it an exciting life?"

Danny laughed. "It's pretty quiet. My jurisdiction only goes to the town limits and Sheriff Bristow handles everything else. Once in a while we have a break-in or a wreck or maybe a fistfight outside of Carney's, that's the beer joint downtown. And then, of course, there's things like last night." He told her about the girl at Grover's, omitting the dirty words. "She was pretty wild. All the way back to the Canfield Complex she kept wantin me to get in the back seat with her."

Her brows went up. "Did you?"

"She was nothin but a kid, too drunk to know what she was doin. And I was on duty anyhow. What do you think I am?"

"I'm sorry," Paula said. "That was a nasty question. The Canfield Complex—what in the world is that?"

"It's where the girls in the Blackbeard play all live now. They built it after Daisy Canfield got murdered, so they wouldn't have to go about alone across the island at night."

"Daisy Canfield? Murdered?" Paula sat up straight. "What was that? Who was Daisy Canfield?"

"She was a girl had a part in *Blackbeard!* out at the Theater. Wasn't but nineteen, a real knockout, black hair, black eyes, a figure—" He described it with his hand. "Three years ago somebody raped and strangled her and throwed her off the bridge into the Sound."

"Who did it?"

"Nobody ever got convicted of it. It's still unsolved, officially anyhow. What happened was, she dated a young guy named Peter Hogan that played the organ they use for music in the show. He took her to his room early in the mornin and his story was that he was tired and full of beer and passed out on her and that she musta tried to walk home in the dark. If she did, somebody got her. Anyhow, it's not my jurisdiction, it's Bristow's and the State Bureau of Investigation. But it was a pretty famous thing for a while. You see, first she just vanished and ten days later some fishermen found her body in their nets, and in between time, we had the biggest manhunt down here you ever seen. Everybody was in on it, from the Boy Scouts to the Marines from up yonder at the base."

"You mean this what's-his-name said she was in his room and he just went to sleep and let her walk home?"

"That was his story. Anyhow, Bristow and them put him through the wringer and they never could shake it, so they couldn't hold him. But there was other suspects too. In fact, you could say there was thousands. I mean, in the summer all these young boys roamin around at night lookin for poonta— for girls. If she really was walkin home alone at two in the mornin, no tellin who grabbed her up." He drank deeply. "I guess Hogan's still the chief suspect. It's not none of my affair, and I don't know where things stand now. Except I know that the confession I took is still locked up in the Town Clerk's safe."

Paula Murphy stared at him. "You took a confession?"

"About a year ago. There's a kind of retarded kid named Bubba Dixon just hangs around town. In fact, he sweeps up the courthouse sometimes. Anyhow, he come to me and a friend of mine last year, said he had somethin important to tell us about Daisy Canfield. Pestered me so bad I finally took a statement from him. He said he saw it done, that he was hangin around town early that mornin and another boy from here come cruisin by lookin for girls and invited him to come along and they drove out a ways and saw Daisy Canfield and grabbed her up and tried to rape her. Only she fought, and so they took her out on the bridge and this other feller hit her and threw her over. I took it all down right, the way the Town Clerk said, and carried it to the Mayor, and he called a meetin of me and the Sheriff and the Director of the SBI from over in the capital, but the upshot of it was they didn't put no faith in it. You see, what they never released was that she'd been strangled with this rope, and the retarded guy didn't account for that in his story. So it come to nothin. So Hogan's still the target, but he's long gone from here, been gone three years." He smiled ruefully. "For a while, though, I sure thought I had something. I mean, the man that broke that case could write his own ticket. I'd already figured on runnin against Sheriff Bristow in the next election and likely winnin. When they sprung that part about the rope, it was like havin the chair pulled out from under me. And then they made it damned clear I was to stay out of what wasn't in my jurisdiction. So they've kept the confession locked up; you know, nuts are always confessin to murders they never did, but I'll swear, this boy sure fooled me."

"Well, I'm sorry you didn't get rich and famous."

He laughed without much mirth. "Tell the truth, I don't think they want it solved now. Not unless Bristow and the SBI can do it, and they've tried for three years and no luck so far. They gambled all their chips on Peter Hogan and couldn't crack him, never had enough to hold him. If it turned out it was somebody else, they'd sure look like fools. Besides, Bristow's been sheriff for eighteen years and he's not about to let anybody get in a position to hurt him in an election. And the SBI— Well, there's an awful lot of unsolved murder cases in this state that they've been in on. When the publicity dies down, they don't like it stirred up again, it embarrasses 'em. I guess nobody is really interested in who killed Daisy Canfield any more except her parents, and they live out in South Dakota."

"South Dakota? She came a long way to get murdered."

"Her father was a preacher on an Indian reservation out there. She was a quarter Indian herself. Anyhow, she got a scholarship to a college down here and she got interested in 'the stage,' as they call it out there at the Theater, and tried out for a part and got it. She'd have been a lot better off if she hadn't."

She rose and refilled his glass. "So you've given up on it?"

"I've learned my lesson. The Mayor and the Sheriff are good political buddies, and I got alimony to pay and child support. I need my job."

"And you'd lose it if you tried to find out who killed this girl?"

"Well, let's say that wouldn't help me any." He sipped his gin and maybe it was the alcohol but he felt an old anger rising in him. "I don't know. Sometimes I get kind of mad. Not because of that, but just because— I seen her when they brought her out of the water after nearly two weeks in the Sound and . . . I don't know. Right then and there, if I coulda got my hands on the man who done it, I think I mighta killed him myself." He gestured. "Well, let it ride. Anyhow, it's good for business for the island to have a mystery. Sort of matches the Lost Colony up on Roanoke that disappeared without a trace."

"Good for business," Paula said, voice sharp. "Well, that's comforting." She was looking at him speculatively across the glass. "And you felt . . . outrage, eh? Tell me, how did you get to be a policeman?"

"Well, I joined the Army and they put me in the MPs. Two years in California, two at Fort Bragg, and I was thinkin about bein a career soldier. Then I met Ruth and we got married and she didn't like that idea, so I didn't re-up. Instead we come to Harriot, and I got a job on the force. It paid more cash money than I was makin as a sergeant, but . . . no free doctors, no PX, I couldn't make her see how it wasn't as good a deal but . . . I wanted to make her happy. Only it didn't work out that way . . . And I just hung on here. I could make more somewhere else, I reckon, in a big city, but I wanta be near my kids. Anyhow, this is . . . home, sort of."

She asked a lot of questions, he thought, but it was somehow good to talk about himself to a woman who listened. He hadn't meant to brag, but then it broke from him. "My daddy was in the Coast Guard, you see, until he got drowned in a rescue. They give my mama a medal and named a cutter after him. The *Wahab Rush.*"

"Oh, really?" She looked impressed.

"Yeah, it was in the Second War. A Nazi U-boat hit a freighter out off Diamond Shoals and she run aground. But it was heavy weather and the way she laid, no way to git a breeches buoy to her, so they had to send out boats to take the crew off. The wind come up to gale and they was raisin twenty-foot seas and better, and there was still people on her after they'd made two trips, and come mornin she'd be broke in two and gone. My daddy, Coxswain Rush, he volunteered to take a surfboat out one more time, and his crew volunteered to go along if Wahab Rush was in charge. So they got the rest off, and they was comin back when they hit a suck and the boat got dragged broadside and she swamped and rolled and— They say it musta hit him when it went over. Anyhow, he was the only one didn't git to shore; they found him down on Ocracoke a month later."

"I understand now," she said softly. "So you joined the Army because you hated the sea."

He looked at her in surprise. "What for, hate it? I don't

hate the ocean, I put in my time on her when I was younger. You don't hate her and you don't love her, you just watch the bitch every minute. Hell, she's been eatin people off these islands long as there's been people here, and if you're afraid of her, you ain't a man."

Paula looked at her glass. "Driving up and down this beachfront, you get the idea that it's been tamed into a plaything. A provider of shore dinners, driftwood for your mantel, and conch shells painted with a sunset. Just a kind of natural Disneyland."

Danny laughed harshly. "The minute you think that way, you're dead. The Coast Guard asked me to sign up, but I turned 'em down, but it wasn't because I was scared."

"Then why?"

He groped for words. "I don't know," he said at last. "I guess it was my daddy. They still remember Wahab Rush and . . . and honor him. I guess I was afraid that if I went in the service I'd have been less a man and disgraced him, maybe, or . . . maybe I would have been a better man. And then maybe they would have forgot him and remembered me, and I didn't want that either."

He became aware that she was looking at him strangely, and suddenly he was self-conscious. He laughed again. "Boy, you're some teacher. You got me blatherin on like I was a kid recitin. Let's talk about you for a change."

Chapter 4

In the bathroom of the cottage Danny Rush zipped his fly and leaned against the wall, grinning broadly. He was high on gin, but more than that, he was having fun. She was the damnedest woman! He looked at his watch, swore in amazement. Three solid hours they had sat there talking and drinking and it had seemed only an instant. He closed his eyes, shook his head, tried to sort out everything she had said about herself.

She had never been married, seemed down on the whole idea. "I'm afraid my father wasn't as noble as yours. He was a middle-grade executive with a steel company and a son of a bitch. Strong as iron himself and cold, always using other people. He just ate up my mother, destroyed whatever personality she had, like a car being turned into scrap. No, thanks, I've seen one marriage."

"You're afraid of winding up like your mama?"

Paula Murphy had laughed. "You may be a good cop, but

you're a lousy psychologist. No, I'm too much like *him*, that's the trouble. In the long run I'd try to walk all over any man I married, and if he let me, I'd hate him and if he didn't I'd hate him too. So I teach my class—that's enough for anybody's maternal instincts—and write my lecherous little confessions for a few thousand extra every year and live the way I please. That way I don't hurt anybody and nobody hurts me."

Which was fair enough, Danny thought, emerging from the bathroom. If all women had that much sense and honesty— He liked her. By God, he liked her. He couldn't remember when he had really liked a woman, not just as something to get in bed but to actually sit and shoot the breeze with, the way he did with Felix, Larry. She was, he thought, swaying a little as he returned to the living room, a good old girl. And he'd see that she had a real good time tonight.

When he entered, she had the map spread out on the table, had hitched her chair up close, was bent over it, and now she had on glasses. On her they looked good, even sexy, Danny thought. He came up behind her, put his hand on her shoulder. "What you looking at?"

"Just planning my next move. I've given myself a whole month to soak up all the fresh air, sunshine, and salt water my system can take. In fact I tried to soak up too much yesterday. That's how I got this red nose and it's why I was just driving around today. Anyhow, after all those *National Geographic* articles and the piles of brochures, there's got to be something besides row after row of motels and beach houses. Where're all the shipwrecks and the endless beaches you can be alone on?"

"You'll play the devil being alone on a beach down here this time of year. Since they opened the campgrounds, there's people everywhere, from Duck to Ocracoke. I guess Portsmouth's the only place you could really be alone, and you can't get there."

"Where's Portsmouth?"

"Here." He touched a blob just south of Ocracoke. "There used to be a fishin village there, and a Coast Guard station. But the Coast Guard's pulled out and the last three people that lived in town, two old ladies and an old colored man, they finally got sick and died, I understand. And now there's nobody there."

Paula turned her head to look at him. "You mean it's a ghost town?"

"Sure is. Not a soul there, except duck hunters come there in the wintertime and a few visitors in the summer. There ain't no bridge and no ferry either, you got to hire somebody to take you over. Yeah, it's quite a trip, we'll go down there sometime."

"We?"

"Why not? I know these Banks like the back of my hand. You want to meet some real Bankers, I'll introduce you. Take you fishin if you want."

"No, thanks. I'm no fisherman. But the rest sounds pretty good."

His hand pressed down, stroked, caressed. "It will be. Maybe we'll camp down there and go out on the beach at night and see a ghost ship."

"What?"

"The old sailin ships. There's been a blue million of 'em wrecked down here, and the old folks used to say they had spirits just like people. Said if you set out long enough in full moon, you'd see a ghost come by, all sails set and a bone, like they say, in her teeth."

Paula cocked her head and eyes to see his face. "Did you ever see one?"

Danny massaged the nape of her neck. She straightened up, but he kept his hand there. "You'll laugh," he said.

"No, I won't. I promise."

"I watched all the time when I was a kid, but I never seen one. Then last September, me and Felix Britt and Larry Besser, my two drinkin buddies, we went down to Hatteras. It was one of them quiet times you git in hurricane season just before a blow, the ocean slick as glass. We stayed out all night, ate some fish, steamed some clams and—yeah, we saw one."

"Really?"

"I don't know what else it could have been. She was moving south against the moon and her hull was black and she had full sail set and, man, she was big, she was big and lovely, out there against the sky. We all three saw it, and we didn't say a word until she just disappeared, like she'd gone over the horizon, but she hadn't. Felix said she was a grain ship bound for the Roarin Forties, around the Horn and to Australia, but there's been no grain ship like that for forty years. And the only windjammers nowadays are cruise ships and maybe a foreign trainin ship. . . . Anyhow, she was a sight to see." He paused, then laughed. "Of course, we'd each of us done drunk a sixpack by then, and it's like Ruth, my ex-wife, said, what do you expect a bunch of drunks to see? I reckon she was right. Anyhow, I never told nobody else till now."

"I see," Paula Murphy said. Then she was silent and so was he. His hand tightened on her neck. She stiffened, and then she slipped from beneath it and stood up. She took off her glasses, laid them aside, looked up at him, gray eyes serious, small, rather thin lips pressed together. He saw her breasts rising and falling beneath the blouse; she was breathing hard. Then he pulled her to him and bent and kissed her.

She came easily enough and returned the kiss, but it was

not a commitment. After thirty seconds she shook free, stepped back, and she looked at him again, almost piercingly. Danny smiled gently at her.

"You and your Goddamned ghost ships," she said after a moment, and then she smiled faintly too. "All right," she said. "All right, come on."

Danny said nothing, did not move, and then she took his hand. Hers was small and soft against the great breadth of his hard palm. "Come on," she said, her voice half amused. And she led him a few steps along the hall into the bedroom. She shut the door. That made it quiet and warm in there, and the place smelled of woman's powder and perfumed soap. A brassiere hung over a chair's back. The bed was neatly made, the Venetian blinds closed so that the light was dim and golden.

Standing by the bed, Paula faced him, still with that faint smile, that amusement in her eyes. "The vacationing school-teacher and the cop," she said. "Well, I didn't come down here *entirely* for the sun. I guess you knew that all along." She pulled the blouse over her head. The brassiere was plain and white, her flesh above it very red. "You'll have to be easy, though. I almost broiled myself like a lobster yesterday, and I'm tender in the damnedest places."

Danny smiled. She made it all so good, so easy, and so nice. "That's all right," he said. "I'll be real careful."

She was naked before he was, standing unashamed before him. Her breasts fell down a little when she removed the bra, their nipples small, their points out. He liked the dimple of her navel, the way her belly rounded out beneath it, the thatch of brown hair, neither thick nor sparse, beneath it, the rather short, sturdy, yet cleanly modeled legs. She was all right; she was damned all right. When he was naked, she looked at him with a scrutiny just as appraising, and he thought she liked what she saw. He started toward her. "I don't have nothing with me," he said.

"It's all right. I take my pill every day, whether I need it or not."

"Then good," Danny said, and as she lay down on the bed, he stretched out beside her and they kissed.

It was two in the morning, the halfmoon balanced like a blob of silver on the edge of the pines around the trailer court. Whistling softly to himself, far from sleep, Danny Rush pushed the garbage deep into the overflowing can and silently, not to awake the neighbors, pressed the lid back on. Naked to the waist, he went back inside the trailer, paused to look around.

The soiled clothes that had been scattered everywhere were wrapped up in a shirt, stored in the closet. That was the last of the garbage; now the dishes and the pots and pans in the kitchen challenged him. Whistling louder, he unloaded the stacked-full sink, seized a cloth, found some cleanser, and began to scrub it, letting water run. When it was clean, he filled it, stacked the plates in the soapy hotness, and after letting them soak a moment poured the last of the bourbon from the bottle, added ice, and sipped it straight. He leaned against the little kitchen counter. "Son of a gun," he whispered jubilantly. "Son of a gun!"

There was no despair left in him, only a kind of wild joy; he felt masculine and confident and strong and eager for tomorrow. She had not let him spend the night, which was as well, since by eleven both had been exhausted. "But tomorrow," she said. "You will come back tomorrow?"

"You damn well told I will!"

"That's good. That's very good." She had lain there, drowsy, naked, watching him as he dressed. Then she had risen, slipped on a robe, and let him out.

"Ha!" Danny said now and lit a cigarette. He slapped his thigh. "Ha!" He took another drink, then turned and furiously began to scrub the encrusted dishes. While he worked, his mind leaped backward, forward, like a grasshopper.

She'd been ready all right. The first time, she'd exploded like a firecracker, crying out.

He thought of Ruth contemptuously. She didn't know what making love *was*. Compared to Paula Murphy, she was in kindergarten.

Then forward: What would it be like?

He knew a house for sale in Finley Harbor, nice, with a lawn and woods out back. She wouldn't even have to teach. She could stay home and write those stories. God, he could give her plenty stories: "I Danced Naked in Grover's Pleasure Palace." . . . If she sold one a month, that was near five thousand a year, and Jesus—

He broke a dish. "Watch it, Danny ole boy, ole boy," he said aloud. Suddenly he thought, But hell. A stupid son of a bitch like me—

She was the craziest woman. What had she said, lying on his arm? "Sometimes I'd like to write a book. A pornographic book."

"You mean a dirty book?"

"Why not?"

The thought aroused him. She went on: "After all, you've got a captive audience. You can say anything you want to say, no holds barred, no matter how wild or esoteric, as long as you put in enough sex to keep 'em reading. And you don't have to learn how to write to do it. I think it would be a lot of fun." Then she gave that deep soft chuckle that he liked so much. "Of course, there's the matter of the necessary research. But, then, I've got you."

She'd do it too, he thought. I'll be damned if she wouldn't. She's the wildest woman I ever met. And the smartest. Boy, when I think of all the stupid sluts I've— He threw the broken pieces of the dish away. "Now," he said aloud, "that pill, that's the thing. Ruth swore she could never take it, said it made her sick and made her bleed." He snorted. "Bullshit. She just wanted an excuse."

He drained the glass, felt a moment's regret at being out of whiskey, for tomorrow was Sunday and he could not buy any more. Then he said aloud, "What the hell. I can do without it." Anyhow, she had plenty of gin. Anyhow, he didn't really need the stuff. What he needed was to buckle down to work. Bristow wasn't any spring chicken. He couldn't stay up there in the courthouse forever, and when he retired, if Danny Rush was the most experienced lawman in Midyette County and the best liked . . . "So you wait five years," he said. "That gives you time to get things squared away. And her and you could live pretty good till then, you git your ducks in a row, and when you're Sheriff and makin twenty-five or thirty thou a year in fees and land deals and the like . . .

Sheriff Daniel Wahab Rush. And Mrs. Rush. And Linda Rush and Daniel Wahab Rush, Junior, because long before then he could take the children away from Ruth. She'd be glad to be rid of them. Maybe she could get that pot off of her and find some other poor sucker. Maybe—

Then he cursed.

The pickup truck needed a new muffler and its gears were shot, and the noise it made rolling across the trailer park was thunderous in the sleeping silence. Goddamn, thought Danny. Felix. I don't want to see him now.

What he had inside himself he wanted to cherish in solitude, savor without interruption or distraction. His mind raced, seeking a way that he could fob off Felix, and Larry if he was along, without hurting their feelings. He decided he would just tell them to go. It was late, he had to get the trailer clean, and he was in no mood for a party.

The truck coughed to a stop outside. Danny dried his hands, turned, and waited. He heard the truck door slam, and he heard voices and knew that Felix had Larry with him. They came up the steps and entered.

Larry Besser was a slender man of twenty-nine, with a wiry masculine body and eyes and a mouth like a girl's. He wore a dirty tee-shirt, blue jeans, and two days' sandy beard. In the winter he taught school; in the summer he worked part time at a fishing pier and bummed around the beach. Just inside the door he halted, throwing out his arm in a Fascist salute. "Hail, toothy chief." Danny saw at once that he was drunk.

Then Felix Britt pushed past him, a full bottle of whiskey in one hand. Taller than Larry and about Danny's age, he had a thick, strong torso, tapering to tiny waist and narrow hips. His tee-shirt was dirtier than Larry's and tattered; his blue jeans were tucked into dusty Wellingtons. His face, beneath a full rust-colored beard, was very handsome, deeply tanned, his eyes the bright blue of salt water in the sun. He too was drunk, and there was excitement in his bearing, compressed power, as if he were so full of enthusiasm he might explode. Shoving close to Danny, he clapped a hand on the Chief's shoulder, stuck his mouth almost in Danny's ear. Even his whisper was deep. "Hey, Danny, listen. We got somethin for you, old boy. Boy, have we got somethin for you."

"I see you got a jug, but I done had enough to drink today."

"Hell, no, not this; this is lubrication, that's all. What we got's more important than that."

"Well, what the hell is it?" Danny snapped, irritated.

Felix laughed. "Oh, boy—"

"Will you cut the shit and tell me?"

"Tell him, Felix," Larry said. The undertone in his voice caused Danny to look at him sharply. "The man's waiting out there."

"Man?" asked the Chief with sudden wariness. "What man?"

Backing off half a step, Felix laughed again. "Why," he said, "Peter Hogan, that everybody thinks killed Daisy Canfield!"

Danny Rush's head swiveled as, frowning, he stared at both of them. For an instant he had the crazy idea that Felix had somehow heard him talking to Paula Murphy about Hogan this afternoon and had rigged a joke of some kind. But, of course, that was impossible. "Now wait a minute," Danny said.

"It's true." Larry's voice was slurred but serious. "He's right out yonder in Felix's truck. We been down at Ocracoke the past two days, and we saw him in Jack's Store, and both of us recognized him right away. And the old private eye here"—he nudged Felix—"went right into action. We followed him up to the campground where he had his tent pitched and Felix just flat out introduced himself and struck up a conversation. He was suspicious at first, and scared, you could see it, but when Felix told him about Bubba Dixon and that confession, he loosened up, especially since Felix helped you take it. Finally he admitted that he intended coming back up here. He's been somewhere out west for nearly three years and he's heard nothing about the case since he left here and he said he couldn't stand it any longer, he had to come back and see what's happened and where he stood. So Felix told him we'd bring him to you and you'd do what you could to help him."

Danny realized his hands were still wet; he groped for a towel without taking his eyes off the two men and, not finding one, rubbed his palms on his pants. "I can't do nothing to help him and you know it."

"Oh, come off of it, Danny," Felix snorted. "Judas Priest, this might be the break we been waiting for. The one we thought we had when Bubba Dixon sang."

"He's not here to confess, is he?"

"No," Larry said. "He still swears he's innocent."

"Then what can I do?" His voice rose. "You know what happened to me with Bubba Dixon. I stuck my neck out and Bristow and Jordan damned near chopped it off. I already got troubles enough without trying it again, and besides, I don't *know* anything. *Nobody* knows anything but Bristow and the SBI. You go tell him to talk to Bristow."

Felix looked incredulous. "Danny Rush, you don't mean that. You're not gonna throw an opportunity like this right down the drain?" He seized Danny's wrist, lowered his voice. "Don't you see? If we can get him talking, he can fill in an awful lot for us. He might spill something this very night to give us the answer, something Bristow don't know. You leave it to me, I'll get everything I can out of him." He was whispering. "Listen. If we can get him to thinking we're on his side, I'll stick with him and before I'm through I'll get the truth out of him. But first we got to git his confidence, and this is our chance."

Danny pulled his wrist away. Ever since his stretch in Vietnam, Felix Britt had found it impossible to settle down. He lived by cutting timber for the lumber companies on the mainland, working on fishing boats, running fur traplines in the swamps, and even catching live rattlesnakes and water moccasins for a laboratory in Virginia, meanwhile staying as far as possible from his father in Richmond, who was in real estate and had money. He read constantly and saw himself as the hero of a thousand exciting plots, a Humphrey Bogart,

Paul Newman, Steve McQueen, or Ernest Hemingway, living on wits, courage, and by his own code. Half a dozen schemes a week for excitement, fame, riches bubbled from his mind; and some of them were even sound, but always too much effort, capital, or time was required, or they were downright unlawful. It was impossible not to like Felix, even love him, but it was dangerous to let him carry you away.

"No. I just don't want to get mixed up. You go ahead and do it, but leave me out of it."

"Oh, God damn it, Danny. What kind of policeman are you? All right then, throw it away! Throw away what may be your big chance. Let Bristow have him, and Bristow'll be Sheriff for another hundred years and you'll never get a sniff—"

"I can wait until Bristow retires."

"And run against Bud Farnum, his chief deputy? Danny, face it, Daisy Canfield's your only chance. Otherwise Bristow'll just pass it down to Farnum and— Look, I don't know that this will come to anything. But don't make me look like a fool. I told Peter Hogan you'd talk to him. You can at least do that right now and *then* make your decision. And if nothing comes of it, what've you lost?"

Slowly Danny looked at Larry, whose judgment was usually good, drunk or sober. "You think I ought to talk to him?"

"I don't see how it can hurt."

Still Danny hesitated. Daisy Canfield . . . She was dead, but Sheriff Claude Bristow was still possessive of her. He remembered the cool and icy way Bristow had made it plain to him the night he had presented Bubba Dixon's statement: "You've wasted our time and yours, Rush. You stay in your own jurisdiction and tend to your own knitting." And, Danny thought, he had troubles enough. Yet— This had been a strange, significant day. For the first time in he could not remember when, he had met a woman about whom he had been able to fantasize an entire future. He knew it was fantasy, and yet— Maybe his luck was changing; maybe the signs were coming right. At last he nodded. "Okay. Tell him to come on in."

It had been three years since he'd last seen Peter Hogan, and while he waited, Danny remembered that hot July day under the bridge across the Sound. He saw again the men lugging the canvas-wrapped thing from boat to shore, seemed to smell once more that harsh odor that grabbed his throat and closed it, saw Bristow's deputies turn away, one gagging violently.

The two Styron brothers, who had found her with one hand and wrist entangled in their gill nets, laid down the burdened tarp. Only the doctor and Claude Bristow showed no emotion as newsmen with handkerchiefs tied around their faces readied their cameras. Bristow, medium-sized and thin with a lean gray face, taut lines at his mouth betraying the ulcer in his stomach, stood there impassively in panama hat, starched white shirt, tie and slacks and polished shoes.

Then they heard the siren approaching from the town. The County Sheriff's patrol car stopped and two men got out. Bud Farnum, khaki-uniformed, thick-bodied, stayed very close to the young man in tee-shirt, khaki chinos, and sandals, and he kept one hand on his holstered pistol. Danny Rush, in the cool shadow of the bridge, watched, as did every other man there, the face of Peter Hogan.

Hogan was twenty-two then, his body brawny, hard, his features sharply chiseled, like those of an oldtime movie star; and the wind ruffled his long brown hair. He must have walked full into that terrible smell, but his expressionless face did not change, although Danny saw a convulsive movement

71

in his throat. He did not look like a killer; there was nothing sullen or surly or brutal about him or the way he bore himself, but Danny had been in police work long enough to know that looks meant nothing. Farnum, coughing, pushed Hogan until he stood directly over the folded canvas. Danny moved in closer, fascinated, so he could see. Bristow had not called him, but he had heard the news and come on his own initiative, and since he was a law officer, Bristow could not order him away.

The Sheriff looked at Hogan with eyes like ball bearings, and wordlessly Hogan met his gaze. Then Bristow bent, pulled back the canvas. "We think this is Daisy Canfield," he said. "Can you identify the body?"

Cameras clicked, somebody vomited copiously into the water, and Chief Danny Rush, staring down at the black swollen obscenity on the canvas, felt rage rising in him like the hot green bile that clogged his throat. He stared at the swollen face, teeth shining in its darkness, the wide eyes, the waterlogged black hair, and the bloated nakedness clad only in hitched-up skirt around her waist, revealing panties split with water rot and the increase of girth that they enclosed. This had once been a girl, not yet twenty, lovely, vital with life, hungry for love, the seeds of increase and happiness in her belly. Now she was a promise brutally violated, broken, she had become a senseless waste, a ruination and a mockery. An ancient primeval outrage that caught him by surprise rose up in him, an anger that the strong could so abuse the helpless, a shame that a human of his sex, because of his sex, could do that to another human. He felt that rage, and he felt a kind of terror at the world and how naked everyone was in it against chance and death; and he swung his head toward the man who, if he had not killed her, had failed his man's duty to protect her, and for a moment he was, quite by instinct, ready to spring at Peter Hogan and take his throat in his hands.

"Is it Daisy Canfield?" Bristow asked.

And still, looking down at that which once had been a girl he had held and kissed and laughed with, Peter Hogan showed no expression. "That looks like the skirt she had on," he said, his voice deep and even.

"*Is it Daisy Canfield?*" Bristow pressed. He was like something carved out of granite, only he was sweating.

"I think it's her." Still no change of tone.

"We need positive identification," the Sheriff snapped.

Even he gasped as Hogan bent a little closer. "She had on a high school ring," he said. "It was gold and blue. On her right hand."

The doctor squatted, took a tongue depressor from his shirt pocket, lifted the fat black hand. The fingers were like sausages, But Danny caught the glint of gold and blue.

Hogan straightened up, looked directly at the Sheriff. "It's Daisy Canfield," he said.

The sun was very hot and bright, reflecting from the sand. The pines on a point up the Sound shimmered in the heat waves, and yet for nearly five seconds every man there seemed frozen. On the highway a car slowed down and stopped, a hearse. Bristow's face was set and angry, his eyes fixed on Peter Hogan. Hogan did not move.

Then the tension went out of Bristow. He put one hand on his stomach as if it hurt. He swallowed hard. "Thank you," he said thinly. He bent and pulled the canvas back as men with a stretcher came down from the road. "Thank you," he said again. "Farnum'll take you back to town."

Hogan stood there for a moment more. He said two words then: "I'm sorry." It was impossible to tell whether he addressed the Sheriff or the dead girl in the canvas. Then he turned and went up the bank, alone at first, shoulders very straight; then Farnum scrambled heavily after him.

Bristow watched as they got into the patrol car. Farnum made a savage U-turn and it roared down the road. Bristow spat thickly into the sand. "All right," he said. "Take her on in."

One of the reporters, staring after the speeding car, only a glinting blot now in the sun, said it for them all, for every decent, normal man among them who had ever loved a woman. "The bastard." If Hogan had killed her, it was Hogan he meant. Then they rolled her on the stretcher and took her to the hearse. . . .

Felix opened the trailer door and Peter Hogan entered.

The three years had aged him; although he was now only twenty-five, he could have been a decade older, more than Danny's age. Before, there had been something not quite fully formed about those finely chiseled features; now they were set and solid. His face had endured a lot of weather, but it was not the weather that had put the deep lines at the corners of his mouth. His body seemed leaner, lighter, as if all the excess fat had been burnt off of it. It was strange, Danny thought, but he was dressed exactly as he had been on that day by the bridge: tee-shirt, brown chinos, leather sandals. Only his hair was worn differently—very long, it was pulled back behind his head and tied in a peruke fashion. He was still impassive, guarded, as he said, "Hello, Chief Rush." The hand he put out was almost freakishly enormous; Danny had not noticed that about him before. The palm was wide, the fingers very long and nearly pointed. His grip was strong. A wisp of a smile flicked at his lips. "I guess you remember me."

"I sure do," Danny said, and he was all business now. "Sit down."

Felix pulled up the one loose chair in the trailer as Hogan slid in on one side of the table and Danny on the other. Danny heard Larry Besser wrenching ice from the refrigerator and knew he would be making drinks. He decided not to touch his; he felt remarkably cool and sober and clearheaded and did not want to change that. But maybe Hogan would drink; maybe alcohol would loosen his tongue. Danny said, "How can I help you?"

Peter Hogan's laugh was bitter, and his big hands on the table moved restlessly. "God, can anybody help me?" He looked tired and almost explosively nervous. "Maybe I shouldn't be here at all, but— It's not the murderer returning to the scene of the crime, either." All trace of a smile vanished. "Let's get one thing clear, I didn't kill her."

"All right," Danny said.

"But I had to come back here. I had to find out what was going on and whether or not I'm still a suspect or if they've maybe got somebody else or— These two guys picked me up on Ocracoke. I'd been camping down on Portsmouth Island and . . . okay, trying to get up my nerve. Felix told me that somebody had confessed, Bubba Dixon, was that it?"

"He confessed, but it didn't hold water. Bubba's kinda simple-minded, you know."

"I don't know. I didn't know many people on Harriot, just the Theater crowd. What happened?"

"Well, Bubba said he was hanging around town that night when a kid named Chet Hollister picked him up. Chet was cruisin for a girl, and he had some moonshine whiskey and was pretty drunk, and he told Bubba to come along, they'd get some ass. They cut down old Hays Road toward Oystertown, maybe figuring on some nigger pussy—"

"That's where she would have been walking!" Hogan said, emotion, rising excitement, in his voice for the first time.

"The shortest way from my place to hers."

"Yeah, he said they saw her on the road, stopped the car and dragged her in. Hauled her off to the old Quarry Road and Chet parked in the woods, told Bubba to sit on her head in the back seat while he raped her—"

"God." Hogan breathed the single word.

"But she fought too hard, he couldn't quite get it in, and then it went soft on him. They rassled around and finally Chet hit her and knocked her out. Then he realized what he'd done and he drove out to the bridge across the Sound and pulled up on the turnout on the draw. Got her out and up against the railing and she was awake again and he slugged her hard and tossed her over, that's what Bubba said."

Hogan was silent, mouth thinning. Then: "Well? Well, you took the confession to the Sheriff?"

"The Coroner's report said she was strangled with a rope. Bubba said there wasn't any rope. The Sheriff and the Mayor and the SBI figured Bubba was trying to get a little attention. He'd testified for the Sheriff in a coupla breakin and enterin cases and his testimony helped Bristow get convictions. I guess he sort of got a taste of blood, you see what I mean."

Peter Hogan let out a gusty breath. "I see what you mean. Then you think he was lying?"

"Well, Bristow questioned Hollister and he didn't come up with anything that I know of. I thought it was a good confession until I found out about the rope, and then— Well, I wouldn't want to go to the gas chamber on testimony from nobody like Bubba Dixon myself."

"So . . . dead end." There was despair in Hogan's voice. Then: "What about other suspects? Any others surfaced?"

"I don't know," Danny said. "There's rumors. This island's been alive with rumors for three damned years. Everybody but the Presbyterian preacher's been tagged for it one time or another. Bristow and the SBI claim to have questioned over a hundred people that might have done it. But as far as I know, you're still the best bet." He paused as Larry set glasses and the bottle before them, then slid in beside him. "I'll tell you the God's truth," Danny added. "I don't know much more than you do. What I know I get from newspapers and gossip. It's the SBI's baby and Claude Bristow's, and they don't tell me doodly squat."

"So everybody thinks I still did it." Hogan rubbed his eyes. "Well, I don't know. I just don't know what to do."

"If they ain't got you yet, there's nothin for you to do but go on about your business and hope for the best." Danny felt a certain sympathy for Hogan, but it was tempered by the recollection of the man's impassivity on that day by the bridge. He could have shown *some* regret, Danny thought. "It's been three years. Unless Bristow comes up with some damned hard evidence, he's not likely to do much more about it. It's an embarrassment to him, the only unsolved murder he ever had, and after all the play it got in the papers, he'd as soon let sleeping dogs lie. To tell you the truth"—he knew this would enrage Felix—"if I was you, I'd get outa here tonight and go back where I come from. Just bein here, you're liable to stir the whole thing up again. But if you go, it'll stay quiet."

Hogan nodded, reaching in his pocket for cigarettes. "I know. That's what I ought to do. I guess I will. Only—" He broke off. After he lit the cigarette, he sat in silence.

"Only what?" Larry asked.

"Only I don't know whether I can stand any more of it," Hogan said, despair heavy in his voice. "Not another three years like the last three. Christ, I was hoping by now that . . ." He shook his head.

"I reckon it's been rough," said Danny.

"It's been rough." Hogan raised his head. "You don't know how rough. Do you realize"—his voice rose slightly—"I've been scared to go with a woman for damned near three years?"

"You don't mean you gone—" Danny began in disbelief.

Peter Hogan laughed harshly. "Oh, I've had my one-night stands, the wham-bam, thank-you-ma'am kind of thing, where they don't even want to know your name. And two doses of clap that penicillin cured, as a bonus. But I mean— For God's sake, suppose *you* met a girl you like and you didn't even dare get to know her, get involved with her. Because you knew that if anything happened to her—if she got hurt or killed somehow just from mischance or bad luck or her own stupidity or a jealous boyfriend or anything—and the cops took you in and you had something like Daisy Canfield in your background . . ."

"I see what you mean," Larry interjected. "They wouldn't look any farther, would they?"

"No. And even if that didn't happen, how do you tell a girl you like that once you were suspected of raping and murdering another girl? Even if she believes you're innocent, it's like . . . like a drop of poison in a pool of water, you see? Just enough to ruin it, keep it from being perfect. And, of course"—his mouth twisted—"and, of course, if you've misjudged her and she's the wrong kind, jealous, crazy, whatever . . . well, you've put your life in her hands. If she thinks you've done something she's entitled to get even for— No matter what weird things she says, the cops will believe them after Daisy Canfield."

He paused, finally took a glass, splashed some whiskey in it, poured a little water, drank. "When I came down to Harriot, I thought it would be the best summer of my life. I'd worked my ass off at Juilliard, it had been a lousy winter, my father had just died, I was broke, and then this job cropped up, and it was like a godsend. All this space and sand and sun and water. After New York it was like . . . crawling out of a rathole. And then I met Daisy and that capped it. Did you know her while she was alive?"

"I saw her on the street a few times. She was mighty pretty," Danny said, and he remembered the thing on the canvas and sipped the whiskey Felix had set out for him.

"She was more than pretty," Hogan said, big hands looped around his glass. "She was . . . sweet. That's the only word. Just sweet and gentle and so excited by all this. For her this was a whole new world and—" Breaking off, he drank again. Then he looked at Danny, and his face was full of misery. "Jesus Christ," he said. "I couldn't put a rope around her neck and kill her with it."

Chapter 5

There was silence then in the trailer as the three men looked at Peter Hogan. His eyes begged for belief; the misery on his face touched a chord even in the Chief, who could wear a professional cynicism like armor. But Danny's sympathy was fleeting; he saw Daisy Canfield's body in the sun and Hogan looking down, unmoved, at the corpse of the girl he had just called "sweet."

"All right," Danny said. "Maybe you didn't kill her. But you sure as hell set her up for whoever did."

"You think I don't know that? You think I won't remember that till the day I die?"

"Maybe," Danny said. "But if you want my frank opinion, anybody takes a girl out and don't see she gets home safe deserves everything he gets. A man should look after his woman."

"I know that too. And I meant to. But . . . something

happened."

"You mean you went to sleep." His contempt sounded in his voice. "That's some excuse."

"There's more to it than that," Hogan said. "But I can't tell you about it, unless"—he blurted the words—"unless you can help me. Felix said you could."

"I don't know what Felix meant by that. This is the SBI's case, and Bristow's. If you got anything to say, you say it to them."

"Danny," Felix said, upset, "now wait a minute—"

"I been told to keep out of it. That's what I aim to do."

"Danny, listen. Let Hogan talk."

"Sure. But sooner or later he'll have to talk to Bristow." He turned back to Hogan. "Go ahead. Say whatever you want to say."

After a moment, so softly that Danny had to lean forward, Hogan went on. "I just feel like the time has come when I have got to . . . somehow, get out from under this. For nearly three years now I've been in a kind of limbo."

"Where's that?" Danny asked sharply.

"Between heaven and hell," Larry said. "Nowhere. Go on, Hogan."

"Well, out west, really. Montana, Idaho, Utah, Wyoming, all the lonesome places where I hoped to God they had never heard of Harriot Island and Daisy Canfield. Just . . . going from place to place, stayed alive by playing the piano in bars and roadhouses or maybe the guitar in campgrounds and passing the hat. And the whole time this thing has hung over me like an ax, and . . . I've lost three years."

He sat up straight. "I'm a musician, or was. I had some promise once, they took me at Juilliard on a scholarship, piano and organ both, and"—he raised his great hands—"you see these? They can reach an octave and six." When he dropped them, there was now an intensity in his eyes. "My head used to be full of music. It's not just playing it, you see, but writing it too, and up until the time Daisy died, it just flowed out of me. Everything I saw or felt, experienced, turned to music in me. But now it's gone. It's been gone ever since that summer. Oh, I can play other people's, but I don't have any of my own. That sounds corny, I guess, but . . . who the hell knows where the stuff comes from and where it goes? But it's been gone for three years—" He broke off. "I've got to get it back," he said.

"I don't know nothing about music," Danny said.

"He's right," Larry said. "I know what he means. It's the same with writing."

"Anyhow," burst out Hogan suddenly, "that's why I came back! Because I can't stand this much longer." His eyes met Danny's. "And Britt here promised me the three of you could help me."

Before Danny could speak, Felix cut in desperately. "Now, hang on, Danny, you hear me out. I didn't make him any hard and fast promise. But I told him this, he wouldn't get any help from Bristow, but maybe the three of us could do him some good. That would depend on how honest he wanted to be with us and the way you felt after you heard his side of it. After all, we've never heard his side, except what Bristow told the papers. I told him the matter'd be in your hands, that you were the old pro up here, nine years in police work, and you knew the score. And that Larry and me could help you."

"Well, you told him—"

"I said *wait*." Felix clapped his hand over Danny's wrist. "I'm not tryin to get your ass in a sling. All I'm tryin to do is see if there's an opportunity here for you, for all of us. If there is, like I said, Larry and I'll do the leg work. All you have to do is lie low and give us directions. But, then, if we find out anything, anything we can *prove*—that's when you come in. You and this." He touched the badge on Danny's shirt.

"Look at it this way," he went on, straightening up. "The three of us make a damned good team. You've got the experience and Larry's got the imagination and I got the Goddamn brass. And between the three of us we know everybody, just about, on these two islands. Now, if Hogan didn't kill Daisy Canfield, there's a a good chance whoever did is still right here. Maybe when he finds out Hogan's back, he'll get nervous and do something to tip his hand. Anyhow, this is the last, best chance we'll have. I think that if Hogan can tell us anything important at all and if he'll help us, we might do some good. If we luck out, you're a cinch for Sheriff next election. If we fuck up, you're protected, nobody can fault you. But, damn it, I just can't *stand* to sit on our tails, with Hogan here asking for our help, and do absolutely nothing!"

He broke off, breathing hard. Once again they all were wordless. Then Larry shifted in his chair. "Danny."

"Yeah." Looking at him, with his mouth and eyes so much like a girl's despite his beard stubble, Chief Rush had, not for the first time, a feeling that disturbed him. Things ran deep in Larry Besser; for all his mildness, he drove his sports car like a demon and could drink most men off their feet. When he was very drunk, he was wilder, more daring and reckless than either Danny or Felix, and yet he never lost touch with the real world, could will himself back to earth out of alcohol immediately.

"I think Felix has got something," Larry said. "But I think he's missed the point. I don't think it makes much difference, really, whether you make Sheriff or Felix gets his picture in the papers; maybe it doesn't even matter whether Hogan gets his music back. I think the point is that it matters that Daisy

Canfield's dead and the man who killed her is still free."

He paused. "I may be wrong. Maybe one death in the middle of all the thousands every day doesn't make a damn. What the hell, one bomb can kill a hundred Daisy Canfields. But I think it ought to matter. I think if we're at the point where it doesn't, all of us, we're in trouble."

His thin fingers, locked together, twisted nervously, and he looked down at them. There was bitterness in his voice when he went on.

"So far, it hasn't mattered. Anyhow, the worst part isn't her being dead, it's what they did to her after she died. Alive, at least she was a person. But dead, they turned her into a . . . a Goddamned commodity. First for Bristow and the SBI she was a chance for headlines and easy glory—Hogan. Then when that fell through, she turned into an embarrassment. To Jordan and the promoters here, though, she's a tourist attraction. To you she's a sheriff's badge and to Felix she's a chance to . . . to be Philip Marlowe or Lew Archer, and maybe even I've thought about how much money a detective magazine would pay for a story on the case. We've all got our dirty little reasons for feasting on her body like so many hungry buzzards—"

"Besser," Felix said, "you're plastered."

"Shut up," Larry said. "She had rights when she was alive; I don't think she should lose them all because she's dead. I think she has the right to be avenged. I think if we're all human, we ought to be concerned about even this one little death. And if we're not enraged about it, then maybe we've lost something we can't afford to lose. Maybe nowadays it's impossible to keep it, I don't know. But I think somebody, finally, instead of sitting on his ass, ought to try to find out who killed her."

Danny sat quietly playing Larry's words through his mind

again. He thought once more of the deep rage he had felt that day beneath the bridge when Bristow had pulled back the canvas. Now Larry's speech stirred it in him again.

The trouble was, he thought, he had forgotten what murder really was. The headlines were so full of death, body counts, traffic statistics, it was on television and in the movies all the time—German soldiers burning up in *The Dirty Dozen*, John Wayne shooting Indians . . . Death, these days was like money with the silver taken out of it. And yet it was important. That was his job, to make it important, to be perpetually enraged at it, enough to try to balk it or to avenge it when it happened. That was why he wore this badge and why he had bought the Magnum. Neither one of them was more than a toy if he did not hate the fact of Daisy Canfield's death and translate that hate into action.

He shook his head as if something buzzed around it; his thoughts really were not that clear, they swirled and merged, and yet he had the thrust of them. All at once the last vestige of the elation of the afternoon and evening vanished, and he felt tired and grim and businesslike.

Larry picked up his glass, drank deeply. Danny turned back to Peter Hogan. "Well," he said, "it might be possible. I don't know. I don't know what we can do at all. First, anyhow, we got to hear what you got to say, Hogan. Is there anything you didn't tell the Sheriff you think you want to tell *us*?"

Hogan's face and eyes turned cautious as he looked from one to the other. "Clear this up for me. What can I expect, after all this talk, if there is?"

Larry and Felix were staring at Danny now, waiting. "I make no promises," the Chief said. "I'm an officer of the law and I carry out my duties within my jurisdiction. All I can tell you is that if it looks like there's a reasonable chance you're innocent and somebody else did it, Felix and Larry, under my direction, will poke around and see if they can find out who."

Hogan looked down at those enormous hands. "I guess it's more than I can expect from Bristow. I guess it's the only chance I've got. I guess there's not a whole lot I can add, but there is one thing."

"Go on," Danny said.

"Three years— Christ, it seems a hundred. I was such a kid then, only twenty-two. I just freaked out on the whole scene down here, the beach, the ocean, all this space. I was freaked out on Daisy Canfield too. There were fifty girls out there, but she stood out like . . . like . . ." He groped for a comparison, could not find it. "She made the rest look like dogs."

"Anyhow," he went on, "from the minute I saw her I wanted her. I fell for her at sight. But at first she seemed so proud, so . . . touch-me-not. So pretty I was almost afraid of her. Later I found out she was just shy and kind of out of it, that was all."

He sipped from his glass. "So the first full night off, I asked her for a date and she said yes. The night before, a bunch of us went out to the beach and drank beer all night, and I hadn't had much sleep. But that didn't matter. I was all keyed up just at going out with her. Anyhow, we went to Carney's and I had some beer, and we went to Fat Willy's and I had some more and she didn't drink anything but a couple of Pepsis. I took some beer and we went out on the beach and sat and watched the ocean, but we didn't do much, you understand? She was friendly, she let me kiss her, but not . . . not . . ."

"Deep," Felix said.

"No. She was like somebody out of last century, not this one. She talked about the Indians and how drunk they got and how set against liquor her father was and how things were so different here, and there was so much she still had to learn.

86

She was afraid that people thought she was a stick-in-the-mud, that's what she called it."

His mouth thinned. "Oh, I was pretty sure I loved her, some, anyhow, by then, but with all that beer in me I was getting horny too. The more she held me off, the more I wanted her, and after about the sixth or seventh beer, it just seemed to me I couldn't get through the night without scoring with her."

"You knew she was a virgin," said Danny coldly.

Hogan looked at him and nodded. "I pretty well guessed it," he said bitterly. "It didn't seem to matter just then. Anyway, we walked up on the pier, and while we were there and she watched the fishing I bought some marijuana."

"Oh," Felix said, a sharp explosion of sound.

"Yeah. Pot. I was just stupid enough and drunk enough to think that even if she wouldn't drink, I might get her to blow some grass and maybe that would loosen her up. A Theater guy I knew moonlighted on the pier after hours, and he was the connection. I was pretty heavy into pot that year anyhow; everybody was."

"Go on," Danny said.

"Well, I had a room upstairs in a house out on Hays Road. Two other guys had the downstairs; they didn't work at the Theater. Anyhow, they were asleep when we went upstairs. When we got there, I put some music on the record player, kissed her again, tried to warm her up, got nowhere, and I broke out the pot, lit a joint myself, and tried to talk her into smoking too."

He shook his head. "That was a scene she didn't dig at all. It turned her off completely; she started lecturing me about dope. I tried to shut her up, sort of groped and fumbled at her a little, but— Maybe you know how it is when you smoke a lot, one joint'll do it. That and the beer and lack of sleep hit me all at once, and suddenly I didn't really give a damn about sex any more. I was just too spaced out. I told her I'd take her home, and she said she was scared to ride with me, to take a nap first and sober up and she'd wait. I didn't argue, just flopped out on the bed, and I was gone. Like that."

He drained the whiskey glass. "When I woke up near noon the next day, she wasn't there. I felt rotten, and I had this big dread inside me, knowing what a fool I'd made of myself, and I was more relieved than anything else. I assumed she'd waited until daylight and walked on home. Anyhow, I didn't want to face her right away, so I got some chow and waited till the last minute before going to the Theater."

His voice stumbled. "But she wasn't there, which was strange, because she loved the Theater, and she was always early. At ten minutes to curtain and she hadn't showed, her roommate and the director asked me about her—everybody knew we'd been out together. Well, it had already hit me, if she was in some kind of trouble, I'd be the first one grabbed and my pad the first place they'd look. And it was full of pot. I could have got twenty years for the ashes in the tray alone. So that's why I lied at first."

"You told 'em you'd brought her home, let her out in front of her boardinghouse," Felix said.

"Right. That stalled them for a while, and during the first act when there was a half hour with no music, I slipped out, dashed back there, flushed everything down the john and rushed back to the Theater. At intermission she still hadn't come, and I knew it was bad and they'd have to have the truth to look for her. So I went to Crawford, the director, and gave it to him. I told him everything but about the grass. That I didn't dare tell him or Bristow either. Because even if they hadn't got me for Daisy Canfield, I'd have done twenty years on a marijuana rap."

He paused and during that interval he lit a cigarette with a hand that trembled slightly. "So there it is. The whole thing sounded phony—six or seven beers and I go straight to sleep. Who'd believe that? But the marijuana made the difference. But I didn't dare mention that. That's why I passed out, though, and let her go home alone."

Suddenly he slammed the table with one big fist. "God damn it! If I hadn't been such a horny fool—"

"All right," Danny said. "All right."

"I'm sorry. But that's what drives me crazy. My own damned grossness."

"Well," Felix said, "that accounts for a lot. That's what nobody believed, that you just went to sleep."

He turned to Danny. "It make sense to you?"

"Maybe." But Danny was still seeing Hogan's face looking down at Daisy Canfield's corpse. "You're pretty cut up now," he snapped, "but I saw you when they found the body. You looked at her then and you never batted an eye. All these regrets come later, huh?"

"Good God, man," Hogan muttered, "when I looked down at her, I wanted to scream. But I didn't dare show a thing. Why do you think Bristow brought me out there right away? He was waiting for me to break. And if I had, in any way, he'd have charged me. Put yourself in my position. You're a stranger down here, a long-haired hippie Yankee kid from New York, you're broke, alone, and the whole state on its ear, yelling for blood. You think I didn't know by then who the pigeon was?" His voice went flat. "But I still see her in my dreams like that sometimes and I wake up sick."

He drew in a gusty breath. "Anyhow, I knew my only salvation was to play it absolutely cool. I finished out my contract and they had an SBI agent in the audience every night, with no assignment but to stare at me. I tell you, they were just waiting for me to break. And if I lost my cool, I was dead."

He paused. "That's it. That's all I know to tell you. You can't get me on the marijuana now, and anyhow, I understand they've changed the law. That's all there is."

After a minute Danny said, "If I was you, I'd go to Bristow and tell him about the marijuana. It might change his thinking."

"Danny!" Felix almost squalled. "You promised—"

"I didn't promise anything. I'm just thinkin of Hogan's welfare. If he cooperates with Bristow now, maybe he can get him off his neck."

"I don't think it would work like that," Larry said. "And that doesn't do much for Daisy Canfield."

"It don't do much for you, either, Danny," Felix said forcefully. "You want to just hand Bristow everything on a silver platter?"

Peter Hogan looked exhausted, confused, and helpless. "I don't think I could stand going through another round with Bristow. He worked me over three times that summer—"

"Not physically?" Larry snapped.

"No, but there were times when I wish it had been."

"He's tough, all right," Danny said. "Excuse me a minute." To gain time to think, he went to the bathroom. Leaning on the sink in the tiny cubicle, he stared at his own face, its darkly circled eyes, not knowing what he was searching for. He was not thinking about what Hogan had said, he was thinking, the trouble is, you don't have faith enough in yourself. There was a time when you thought you could do anything. Right up until the time you married Ruth. It was her, he thought. It was her stomped that out of you. Cutting you down all the time, telling you what a fool and ass you were, what a lousy man . . .

He could see it plainly now, the point at which he had changed. Maybe it was because his father had died so early, because he had been raised to put too much dependence in women's judgments and what they said about him. But he had trusted Ruth's appraisal of him too much, taken the guilt and sense of incompetence she had planted in him as gospel. She had made taking chances for the big payoff seem so foolish, so improvident, that he had forgotten how to do it. She thought small—hell, she thought tiny—and she was always terrified of life and chance, and she had infected him with her ailment.

And then suddenly he knew. It was not the whiskey, it was not the checkbook, it was none of that that caused his constant misery; it was because he no longer dared to nourish any sort of dream, no longer dared, like Felix, to reach as far as he could reach. He was unhappy because he had tried to warp himself into a mold that would not fit him, was too small to hold him.

What he had to do was break out of that. Today he had already begun: Paula Murphy. She wanted him back tomorrow. But a woman like that would not want a worthless man. And she had not thought him worthless.

And he was not; his luck had been bad, but luck could change. Until he had married Ruth, he had made his own luck anyhow. Suddenly he thought about the gun; that had been the last try, the last flurry of reaching out, and that was why the Magnum was so important. But a man could not settle for nothing but a pistol. He could be a damned good sheriff, and even the prospect of that gave that much more solidity to the wild dreams he had begun to build around Paula Murphy. He stared at his face. It had been a long time since his eyes had looked back at him like that.

Chief Rush straightened up, left the bathroom. In the trailer Felix paced; the other two sat quietly.

Danny said, "Hogan."

Felix jerked around, staring.

"Can you stay around awhile?"

"I don't know; I don't have much money—"

"He can put up with me in my shack," Felix said.

"All right," said Danny. "This marijuana thing makes just a little more sense out of your story. Enough, anyhow, so we'll take a gamble. You're to lie low awhile, stay under cover. You'll answer any questions any of us put to you, and do it straight. If you agree to that, we'll at least poke around a little and see what chance there is of opening this back up."

Hogan's big hands spread and closed like sea fans. "I'll do anything," he said. "If I can just be free again and get my music back—" He paused. "But I'd better tell you, I can't pay you anything."

"Nobody's asking you to. And we don't guarantee a thing. Felix and Larry's amateurs and while I've handled some killins, they were the kind with witnesses. But like Felix says, we know everybody, and if we can bring this off, we all stand to gain a little something. So we'll try."

"That's the ticket, Danny!" Felix almost shouted.

Danny turned on him. "You listen too. We're all in this together, but somebody's got to be in charge. I got the badge, and I'm the one puttin his job on the line, so that's goin to be me. Agreed?"

Felix's grin faded slightly, but he nodded. "Agreed."

"Okay. We'll give her a whirl. You take Hogan with you. Keep him under cover so Bristow don't get him away from us. Now, I'm tied up tomorrow—"

Felix frowned. "Tied up?"

"That's right. Tomorrow's my day off, and I've got somethin important already planned that I can't cancel. But I'll see you Monday evenin. Meanwhile, see if you can pick anything else important out of Hogan's brain. And, Larry."

"Yeah?"

"You're in this?"

"Yeah," said Larry.

"See if you can put it all in order, so we can go over it from the start. Everything about the Canfield case y'all can remember, includin the rumors, what happened as nearly step by step as possible. You're good at that; you can make a kind of story out of it and then we'll have it at our fingertips."

"Right," Larry said.

"And for God's sake," went on Danny, "don't spill a word of this. If Bristow hears I'm messin in it again, he's just as likely to go to Jordan and git me fired."

"They can't fire you for—" Felix began.

"There's a lot of things they can fire me for if Claude Bristow thinks I'm shapin up to run against him. I mean it, Felix."

"Right." Felix nodded.

"Now," Danny said, "it's late. I'm dead tired. Why don't y'all go on, and we'll talk more Monday."

"But we got to—" Felix started.

"Danny's right," Larry said, sliding out from behind the table. He picked up the bottle. "It's nearly three. Let's cut out."

Felix looked disgruntled but he nodded. "Come on, Hogan."

Hogan rose. "Chief," he said, "if you could—"

"I said we promise nothin," Danny told him gruffly. But when they had gone, he made himself a cup of coffee and drank it slowly, feeling marvelous, full of hope again and making many promises to himself.

Chapter 6

But the next day at one, knocking on the door of Paula Murphy's cottage, he felt self-conscious and apprehensive. Her car was not there. Maybe she had not picked it up yet. Even so, waiting for her to answer, he knew a sickening fear that she had forgotten or changed her mind, decided she wanted nothing more to do with him. Maybe— Then he heard her footsteps. When she appeared, he drew in a quick breath of admiration.

She wore a yellow dress, rather short, scooped low in front, its fabric crisp and fresh. She had done her hair, and there was makeup on her eyes and mouth and she had put on earrings. There was no doubt now that she was a very hand-some woman indeed, and, Danny thought, confidence re-turning, *she had done all this for him!* "Man," he said as she opened the screen door. "You sure are pretty."

Paula smiled. "Thank you, Danny. Come on in."

He wore civilian clothes; last night after the three had left, he had washed underwear, socks, a drip-dry sportshirt, and put a pair of slacks under the mattress to press. Nevertheless, he felt rumpled in comparison to her. Nervously he smoothed his hair.

Fresh wind blew straight through the open windows of the living room, and from the record player came the kind of slow music he had never cared for, classical, but this was not too bad. Following his eyes, she said, *"La Mer.* Debussy. 'The Ocean.'"

"Kind of sounds like it."

She smiled. "Corny, maybe, but I've never believed in letting too much sophistication limit my pleasures." Then she came to him, presenting her lips for a kiss, and when their mouths came together, hers reaffirmed their connection of the day before. But it was she too who broke from the embrace. Her smile had a different quality and there were glints of green in her blue-gray eyes. "Danny," she said. "Danny, Danny." Then: "Have you had lunch?"

"Didn't wake up till late. I just had breakfast."

"I'm not hungry either. Want a drink?"

"Sure."

"They're made and in the fridge." She gestured to the sofa. "Sit down."

While she was in the kitchen, he was surprised that he felt no impatience. Partly that was because he knew that she would be available in bed whenever he wanted her; partly it was because he was still a little fatigued and nervous from last night; but mostly, he thought, it was because he looked forward to a repetition of yesterday's pattern, which had suited him exactly: first the good talk and the drinking, and then the lovemaking, unforced and unhurried.

When she returned with pitcher and glasses, he was

surprised when she sat down across the coffee table. She crossed her legs. She was wearing stockings now, and he liked the effect of taut nylon on her flesh. "How's the sunburn?"

"Much better. I'm not so tender now." She poured.

"That's good."

"Umh-hmh." She raised her glass, looked at him a moment, then drank. "Tender or not, I enjoyed last night."

"So did I."

"Good." Paula laughed slightly. "Well, that's out of the way."

"Huh?"

"Sometimes it can be so awkward afterwards. The next day, I mean. When you just sit and look at each other in a kind of hangdog way. I didn't want it to be like that today, so I thought I'd tell you. It was fun, and I'm glad it happened exactly like it did, car and all. Speaking of which, can you take me to pick it up?"

"The car? Sure."

"Maybe after we finish this drink. I called and it's ready. I thought perhaps we could use it to drive down to Hatteras or somewhere. It's such a gorgeous afternoon, and I still haven't really seen anything of the Outer Banks, and you promised to be my guide."

"Well," Danny said, but he was disappointed. There was more than that too, more than having his plan for the afternoon disrupted. The way she had talked just now, as if there had been so many Sundays when she had faced men with whom she'd made love for the first time on Saturday night . . .

As if sensing something of what he felt, Paula said quickly, "We could be back by dark. Then I'll cook a good supper for you."

He still had nearly ten dollars in his pockets. "I'd like to take you out to eat."

"Well, we'll see. I've got everything we need right here."

"All the same, I'd like to buy it for you."

She hesitated, then nodded. "All right, Danny." She rose, came around the table, ruffled his hair. "Go ahead, finish your drink and I'll make a Thermos of martinis to see us through the day." He reached for her, but she was gone.

She paid for her car with traveler's checks off a thick sheaf, and they left Danny's at the station and drove southward in the Mustang through an afternoon bleached bone white with sun. Presently they left Shoal Island, crossed a long graceful bridge over an inlet, the campground beneath it colorful with tents and vehicles. Gulls and fish crows, pure white and purple-black juxtaposed, took flight from the bridge railings at the car's approach. They whizzed across a smaller island and presently, after another bridge or two, were on Hatteras. Paula had put on sunglasses; Danny never used them.

Now the road was narrow, a tricky ribbon of asphalt through deep sand; and the traffic was heavy, their progress slow. Dunes rose on their left, tufted with grass, occasionally netted with wooden sand fence; to the right, marshes stretched toward the Sound. The sun reigned over all with brilliance; even the numerous beer cans on the shoulders had their spurious jewel-sparkle.

Then Danny pulled off the road into a parking lot on the seaward side. Beyond it a wooden ramp stretched across a barrier of dunes. "What's here?" Paula asked.

"You wanted to see a shipwreck. Well, this here's what's left of an old wooden barkentine."

They crossed the ramp. Then they were on the beach, which stretched endlessly away, without sign of house or boardwalk or habitation. There were humans on it, dozens of them, but their numbers were swallowed by immensity. Here, with nothing between them and another continent save the last hundred feet of white sand and thousands of miles of sea, the wind hit them squarely; and the surf rolled in with constant anger, stirred by underwater shelves and reefs. To their right, like the ribs of a huge picked chicken carcass, the bones of the sailing ship jutted from the sand, children like bright insects swarming over them.

They walked down to the wreck, wordless in the wind and the constant dull roar of ocean, while sandpipers skittered and nattered in the foam, gulls formed themselves in pompous ranks around trapped pools, and foam scudded along the sand like something frightened and alive. The air was charged with salt and iodine, as always, stirring Danny. The body of an excited woman, he thought, smelled like that. He looked at Paula keenly.

Deep in sand, she stood by the ruined ship, beside the dark tarred timbers arching out, feathery hair whipped and ruffled, skirt plastered to every line and curve of body. "My God," she said as Danny came up behind her. "There's so much of it! Does it run on to the world's end?"

"It's full of people now. You ought to see it in wintertime."

"I don't think I could stand it. It almost frightens me as it is." She fingered a rusted bolt. "How many died in this wreck?"

"None in this one, I don't think. She just drove up onshore and they climbed down and walked away."

"I'm glad nobody died. Oh," she said, head raised, "how nice it is. How nice to see how much there is of the world. I think I understand now why people cling so close together. Imagine—imagine a time when it was all like this for thousands of miles. How frightening, how awesome. No wonder they felt that they had to conquer it."

Danny kicked a dead horseshoe crab, its tan carapace drifted over with sand. "I just wish they'd left it like it was."

Paula laughed, squeezing his arm. "Atavist," she said.

"What?"

"Throwback. Primitive man. I can see you now, ten thousand years ago, squatting hairy and naked in the surf, sucking your nourishment out of shells."

"Paula . . ."

"Or myself. Dangling dugs, a child on either knee, foraging in the ocean with the gulls. Probably covered all over with hair."

"You're a crazy girl. Hair?"

"You'd need it to keep the sand from blasting you."

"Maybe so. But if you was hairy *all* over, I wouldn't be here with you now."

She laughed, slipped off her sandals, ran across the strand, and waded in the surf. Danny followed her, keeping outside the line of water. She had conjured up something in his mind that his thoughts chewed on: the two of them, the only two people in the world, naked, living here alone forever in the water and the sun and sand. Like Jane and Tarzan, he thought, and no Goddamned body to bug you at all. Not even clothes to bother with. . . . Something in the thought stirred him, and not only in his genitals, and he laughed softly at himself, remembering how cold and ugly it could get down here in winter. You'd have to have a lot of hair, he thought.

She came out of the water, loped up the shore looking for shells; he hurried to catch up with her. "We better go on back to the car; we haven't even started good yet."

"All right." She took his arm. They stood for a moment looking down the beach and Danny said, "Right down yonder about half a mile is where I seen some whales commit suicide."

"Whales do what?"

"Kill theirselves. They come up on shore and die."

"Really?" She frowned. "You mean they're injured or something, and—"

"I don't know," Danny said. "It was a whole herd of 'em. Six or eight. Back when I was about fifteen. They wasn't real big, but they was fair-sized. They come in across the shelf and tried to drive onshore, the whole herd. Folks spotted 'em and went out in boats to drive 'em away; when they die on the beach they stink up things for miles around. But there wasn't any way to turn 'em back. They had made up their mind they wanted to come on land, and that's what they did. They just drove right on through the boats, stranded theirselves, no way to get 'em off, and they all died. Deliberately."

"Why would they do that?"

"I don't know. Old folks say they do it now and then. A whale or a herd of whales gets tired of living and kill theirselves that way."

"Hmm . . ." Paula stared into the distance. "I wonder what's in the ocean that drives them to such despair?"

"Nobody knows," said Danny.

"Maybe it's evolution," she said. "Maybe people have it all wrong. Maybe that's where the dinosaurs came from, the whales came up on shore and some of them lived—"

"You sound like Larry Besser. He always likes to take things and turn 'em hindside to." He took her arm. "Come on."

In the parking lot each drank another martini. The car raced on down the long narrow island. As they passed through a gray ramshackle town with motels and neon signs superimposed on it like crayon marks on a weathered board, Danny said, "This here's Rodanthe. It's where Old Buck lives."

"Oh, I read about it. This is where they keep Old

Christmas. Celebrate on January sixth."

"Used to," Danny said. "All the kids would gather at the schoolhouse and they'd beat the drum and Old Buck would come in bouncin and bellerin, shakin his horns, a kind of wild ox and wild deer both. Nobody knows where he come from; they say he lives out in them woods yonder. They been doin it for hundreds of years, I reckon; it was the high time on Hatteras when I was a kid."

"I'd love to see it. It sounds so . . . Druidic."

"I don't know nothin about that. But they won't have him next Christmas. Not enough kids showin up to make it all worthwhile, and nobody's got time to bother with it. Besides, there ain't no tourists here in January." He drove on.

The gin fingered through him and he was having fun, sharing his own island with Paula Murphy, seeing it through her eyes, the commonplace coming alive for him again. He showed her the tiny post office, hardly bigger than a phone booth, at Salvo; it was the country's smallest. They whipped through the ancient fishing towns of Avon and Buxton and he took her to the old lighthouse. Striped like a barber pole, it thrust high into the scalding blue, only a relic now, with people lined up to climb the five hundred steps to the iron-railed platform below its lamp. Now there were offshore platforms to serve its purpose, and loran and shoran. They did not climb it but drove down to the beach below it, where people from a campground swarmed. There they looked out across the cruelest part of the American coast, white lines of surf making jagged patterns, fishermen wading to their waists, and in the warm bright afternoon it did not look so savage. But this, he told her, was where Wahab Rush had died.

Then they got back in the car and he took her to the house farther down the road in which he had grown up. It sat, all gray boards and weathered wooden shingles, at the end of a sandy driveway in the midst of treeless dunes; and no one lived there any more. Doors and windows were boarded up. Danny circled it, surprised at how little emotion he felt. He was old enough to know now: Everything changed and died, nothing stayed the same. The whole country, everywhere he had been, was like that, transforming itself every five or ten years, so that no matter how well you knew a place, you could never come back to it and find it as you had left it. Everybody, it seemed, outgrew the shell of home five or six times in his lifetime and made or found another one. Like sea creatures, they moved from reef to reef, from shell to shell, shucking off the old, forgetting it, re-creating themselves a dozen times during their existence.

Paula examined the house curiously. "What's that pipe coming off the roof, into that concrete thing?"

"That's the cistern for the rain water. Its where we got our water for drinkin and cookin. I never drunk nothin but rain water until I was fifteen or sixteen."

Paula stared at him strangely, the wind whipping around her. "You drank the rain?"

"Everybody did it."

"Maybe that explains it. Come here."

When he did, she reached up, ruffled his hair sternly. "Not there."

"What?"

"Faun's horns," she said. "I thought only fauns and butterflies drank the rain."

He blinked. "You mean like baby deer?"

She smiled. "I guess so."

"That's a crazy thing to say. I ain't no baby deer."

"No," she said, "I guess you aren't." She was serious. "I guess it was a hard life here."

"Not so bad. We had the pension from the Coast Guard. And plenty of fish and crabs and clams, and sometimes after a wreck there'd be things we could hide and sell later on. You could get an awful lot just for lumber. Of course, things come dear too, like coal oil and canned stuff. But we made out all right. A man still can, if he ain't afraid of the ocean and he wants to work. That's why folks come down here to retire. But it was awful borin sometimes too. I remember how my mama used to cry sometimes, just from the wind and the sound of the ocean. Sometimes she couldn't stand it any more and she would just sit down and cry. After they brought the electricity in, she used to keep the radio on from the time they cut on until they cut off, just to shut out them sounds, she said. And, too, there was the hurricanes."

"Well, you didn't stay here during hurricanes?"

"Most often we did. It all depended on what folks thought they'd be like. If it was bad enough so the Coast Guard said we'd better really move, we might go up to the schoolhouse or somebody's house up on higher ground and board up ever'thing and just have a hurricane party until the blow was over. I've rid out many a one down here."

"They didn't evacuate you?"

"Evacuate us how? With no bridges and no paved roads?" Paula shook her head.

"They come every year. You get used to 'em after a while."

"God," she said. "What people." Then she said, "What happened to your mother?"

"I got one brother, he moved to Charlotte. He's doin well there with a service station. When I went to the Army, he took her to live with him, but she died about a year after she moved there. It was too high and the air too different, I reckon."

"I see," said Paula as they walked back to the car.

At Hatteras Village automobiles were lined up for more than a mile waiting for ferries. "That's the way to Ocracoke," Danny said. "It's the last island of the Banks with any people on it, the last one there's still no bridge to. Only way to get there's by ferry, from here or from Cedar Island on the mainland."

"It's supposed to be rather unspoiled, isn't it?"

"It's nice. All the big oak trees and little sandy roads there in the village, and Silver Lake, that's the harbor. There don't as many tourists go there, on account of waiting for the ferries and because there's nothing to do but just roam the beaches and sit in the sun. I mean, there ain't no beer or whiskey sold, no movie, no outdoor play, nor nothin. But it's part of the National Seashore too, and I guess they'll put in a bridge ere long."

"And then there's Portsmouth," she said. "The place with the ghost town."

"That's right." Danny started to back the car around.

Paula said, "Wait." She clutched his wrist. "Danny, I've got an idea. Couldn't we take the ferry over to Ocracoke and spend the night?"

"We'll have to do it another time," Danny said. "I got to be at work come seven tomorrow mornin."

"Well, we could drive over now—"

"We'd never make it back. Last ferry'll be jammed and— No. Another time."

"But you only have one full weekend off a month, you said so."

"Well, I'll work it in. Anyhow, you can't find a place to stay without no reservations. And we . . . got no baggage."

"You know those people. You could find us a place. And we wouldn't need baggage if we paid in advance."

Danny looked out across the glimmering blue water of the

inlet. From where they sat, he could see a ferry, rails colorful with people, chugging across the inlet, trailing a faint smudge of diesel smoke. It would, he thought, be a damned nice thing to do, but . . . His face reddened. "Paula, I'll tell you the truth. I don't have that much money with me and they probably wouldn't take my check."

"They take traveler's checks, surely. I've got fifteen hundred in those in my bag."

"Fifteen hundred—" Danny stared at her, amazed by the magnitude of the sum. She shrugged.

"Three confession stories, and I can always write another: 'I Danced Naked for the Fishing Fleet.' Danny—"

He watched the ferry. Presently he made his decision and shook his head. "I can't. I tell you, I've got to be at work tomorrow."

"Couldn't you phone in?"

He shook his head. "You don't know, honey," he said softly. "Word travels up and down these banks faster'n telegraph. If I layed out of work to stay with you on Ocracoke, everybody on Harriot would know about it before I got home. Besides, I don't lay out of work. I can't. I'm the Chief."

"I see."

"I got to pull my duty, and I got to set a good example."

"I see." She smiled. "All right, I won't pressure you."

"I'll swap some days and get an extra weekend. Then we'll come."

"Sure," she said. "Well, there seems to be plenty to see this side of Ocracoke anyhow. Shall we go on back?"

Danny bought their dinner—broiled bluefish, potato, slaw, and coffee—at a restaurant halfway up Hatteras. It took almost all his remaining money, but he knew the cook and it was worth it. The fish had been caught fresh that morning, the portions were enormous, and both of them were very hungry. It was nearly dark when they reached Harriot again. "I want a swim," Paula said. "I'm healed now and the sun's gone in."

Danny had no trunks with him. He left her alone while he raced back to his trailer, got some. When he returned, she wore a modified bikini, neither as naked as those of the young girls nor as modest as the two-piecers of the older women. He thought she looked wonderfully sexy in it. They went down to the beach beneath the pier, wrestled in the cold crowded water. Once something hit Danny's shin with cold clamminess; he reached down and picked it out, a used and sodden Kotex. Shivering, he threw it far down the surf, into darkness. Back at the cottage they dried each other, drinking martinis as they did so, and collapsed laughing on the bed and came together. . . .

Later, she said quietly, her cigarette a glowing redness in the darkness, her head on his arm, "I've had so much fun today."

"So have I."

She reached out to crush the cigarette. "Only . . . you present me with a problem."

"What kind of problem?" He felt unexpected apprehension tear the pleasant fabric of his mood.

"The disposition of my summer." She sat up, reached for another cigarette, lit it. In the match's glare, he saw her, breasts swinging downwards, only two faint small rolls above her belly: normal, voluptuous, relaxed woman softness. Then she put out the match. "I can't keep this cottage longer than two weeks. I thought two weeks would be enough to see everything here. Then I was going on south, maybe to Florida."

106

"You can't do that!" Danny sat up quickly.

"That's what I'm trying to decide. Can I or can't I? Should I or shouldn't I?"

"I thought you were gonna spend the whole summer here." His voice was aggrieved. "I was lookin forward to—"

"To screwing me all summer long."

"That ain't it!" he snapped.

"I'm sorry, that was a cheap shot. I'll apologize. On the other hand . . . two weeks or two months, in the long run, what difference does it make?"

"It makes a lot to me," said Danny hoarsely. "I mean—" He broke off. There was no way he could tell her what he meant without either sounding silly or exposing his own vulnerability. But something within him felt as if it had just been stepped on and was dying of the weight upon it. "I just wish you would stay," he finished lamely.

"That's exactly why it might be better if we both decided now that it would be better if I went." She got up, padded across the room, went to the high window, pulled up the blinds, and leaned her elbows on the sill, looking out across moon-silvered low scrub and the echeloned blank walls of other sleeping cottages. The light slanted in and fell across her buttocks, outlining their broad soft curves. "There's no point in having too much fun together, Danny," she said in a different, harder voice. "It just makes it rougher when the fun stops."

"It's not a question of fun." He sat up, groped for the cigarettes.

"It can't be a question of anything else." Paula was silent for a moment while he lit the match. Then she said, "I told you. Remember? Yesterday. I told you that I had everything arranged just the way I wanted it. I have my job, I have my sideline, which maybe I'll parlay into something more significant later on, and I have my box of pills to keep my womb nice and sterile. For over thirty years now I've been the cat that walked by herself in the wild wet lone, and I am too old to change now. So, whatever we do, whether for two weeks or two months or even more, it all comes out the same. The problem is to minimize the risk of you getting hurt. Or even me, for that matter. That's why I think it might be better if I just go on."

"That's the damnedest thing I ever heard," said Danny furiously. "I don't want you to go on."

She turned, moonlight falling across breasts and torso now, face still in darkness. "Tell me why."

"I just don't, that's all. I . . . . I already feel like I know you better than any woman I ever met. I want to know you better even than that. There's a lot of things I want to show you around here and—"

"That's what I mean," she said. Another pause. "Would I be conceited if I said that you are already thinking about more than two months?"

He said nothing.

"You see? I know. I've thought about it too. You, with your duty and your rain-drinking and . . . your ghost ship. There are not a great many people like you, Danny Rush, and that's why I want to be kind to you. And to myself too. I'll be frank. You're a threat. You frighten me. And believe me, I'm not playing games with you when I say that. I've seen all the games in one marriage, the one I grew up in, that I want to see. What I'm trying to say is, Danny, why stick our necks out? You don't know me, don't ever deceive yourself that you know me. I would tell you all about me if I could, but I don't even know all about me myself, and anything I said might be a lie tomorrow. All I'm saying is, don't be deceived. Don't think I want things that I don't want and that I value things that I don't really care about. Sometimes I think I do, some-times I may seem to, but underneath . . ." Her voice dwin-dled off. She turned back to the window. "There's no way you can explain it to a male. He can't think a woman would place that high a value on just simple freedom."

Danny said nothing, trying to repeat her words in his mind and discern what they meant; and he could not grasp them.

"I'm trying to warn you, Danny; I don't want you to be fooled."

Still, he could not make sense of what she said. He thought he understood, but even if he did, it was not believable. All he knew was that the time had come, much earlier than he had anticipated, that arrived with any woman in any affair. She drew away, wanting to be pulled back. If he could pull her back, if he could keep her, this phase would pass.

"Look," he said, and he got out of bed and came to her, pressed his naked body against the softness of hers, his geni-tals riding high and lax in the slice between her buttocks. "Look, I know there's a lot of difference between the two of us. I know there are so many things you know all about I don't, like there's things I know about you never dreamed of. I guess the way I say high tide seems funny to you, and—"

"Oh, Christ," she said angrily, "that's not it."

"And you're used to havin all the money you need and I'm always broke, what with Ruth and the kids to support. But it won't be that way forever. If I can just find out who killed Daisy Canfield—"

Her naked body stiffened against his own. "What?"

"You know, the girl got raped and murdered. I told you—"

"Yes."

"If me and Felix and Larry and Peter Hogan can—"

Paula pushed him away and turned around. "Peter Hogan? Wasn't he the one they think did it?"

He had not expected her to remember the name, mentioned only once or twice while both were full of gin, and he wondered again at how quick she was. "Yeah. He's here on Shoal Island. Felix and Larry brought him by my trailer last night after I left you. He wants us to help him—"

"Help him how?" She strode across the room, got another cigarette, lit it off the end of the one she had. Her whole bearing had changed; she sat down, back straight, on the bed, crossed her legs. "Help him how?" she said again.

"Well . . ." Danny sought words, and when he found them told her about the conference in the trailer last night. "And . . . and I thought Felix was right," he finished. "I have got to do something to get out of this rut. I got to think more positive. I . . . I think there's more in me than bein a police chief of a two-bit town and I . . . got to give it a chance. I believe we can really do it, I think we can. And if we do, if I can make an arrest and git a conviction— Well, Bristow's had things sewed up down here a long time. But there's so many new people come in and this is such a famous case— There's no reason why I can't. I got the badge and the authority. I just been scared to use 'em, that's all, but now—"

"But now you're going to reach for glory."

He could not tell whether she mocked him or not. "I'm gonna reach for somethin. I made up my mind last night. If they had come to me before I met you, I mighta felt different. But now—"

"I see," Paula said, and she switched on the lamp. She took the cigarette from her mouth, held it low, stared at its swirling smoke. "I see. I'm your . . . inspiration."

"I just wanta prove—"

"You don't have to prove anything to me."

"It sounded like I have to prove a lot."

"Damn it, I tell you you've missed the point." Furiously,

110

she ground out the cigarette. "So you've made your decision, eh?"

"I give 'em my promise, yeah."

She sat there wordlessly for perhaps a half minute. Then she nodded. "Yes," she said. "I see. Well. This sounds very exciting." She raised her head. "It really sounds very exciting. How long do you think it will take?"

"I don't know, I got no idea."

"I see," she repeated again. She sighed. "Well, I certainly would be a fool to leave early, then, wouldn't I? With something like this going on? And I with a ringside seat? I've never been in on a murder investigation before."

"I'd bet you'd be a lot of use to us in this one," Danny said quickly. "I mean there's four men, but a woman's viewpoint would be good, a smart woman's, like you are. You wait'll Larry and Felix meet you, I'll bet they'll say the same. You could be in on it with us, Paula, and we sure could use you. I mean, there are a lot of girls down here at the Theater, for instance, that were here when she got killed, and women too. You could talk to them ways we couldn't and . . ." In addition to wanting to keep her, he recognized the validity of what he said. "You might be the one to get just the piece of info we'll have to have."

"Oh, sure," she said. "I might, that's very true. You never can tell what I'll bump into."

"And when I'm workin, you got all the time in the world—"

"Yes, I'll have that too." She laughed softly. "Well, nobody in Florida's offered me a murder yet."

Danny tensed. "You mean you'll stay?"

"There are a lot of reasons," she said, "why I hardly have any other choice."

"Oh, that's good," he said, coming quickly to the bed. "I'm glad to hear you say that. I think you'll be a lot of help to us."

"One way or another," she said, "I'm sure I will be. All right. If you can get me declared into this investigation as a full partner, then I'll stay."

"Don't worry about that," Danny said with jubilation. He began to kiss her. She turned her face away. "Let me go to the bathroom," she said. "You make us two more drinks."

Chapter 7

"So this is where you live," Paula said the next day, looking around the trailer curiously. "You're a very meticulous housekeeper. I suppose it's the Army training."

Danny had got off shift at four and had spent most of the intervening two hours working on the trailer. It still smelled of drying soapy water from the scrubbing he had given it. "Yeah, they learn you how to keep things neat," he said, determined that henceforward he would GI the place every day. He would not let her think him a slob. He glanced at his watch. "They ought to be here any time."

"How did they react when you told them you were bringing me?"

"Well, they were a little surprised at first," he hedged. Which was, he thought, putting it mildly. Felix had called him at work. "Listen, Larry and I been busy. We've got some stuff put together and we need to talk. You be home around six?"

"I'll be there," Danny said, "but before you come, you call me. There's something I want to tell you, but not on this phone."

"You're not going to flub out on us?" There was dismay in Felix Britt's voice.

"Just the opposite. I got us some more help."

Then Felix had called him at the trailer, where he could talk freely. "Danny!" Felix had said at once, angrily, when the Chief told him. "This is too important to have some feather-headed broad you picked up in a bar—"

"She's not featherheaded and I didn't pick her up in a bar. She's a schoolteacher and a writer, and she's got a mind just as good as yours or Larry's. She'll be a lot of use to us. I don't know whether she will really work with us or not, but I've told her all about the case, and I want her to sit in this evening. Now, you fellows'll be doin me a big favor if you don't raise any fuss and treat her right. Anyhow, I say she's to sit in." There had been some more arguing, but he had cut it short.

Now he was worried, hoping Felix and Larry and Hogan wouldn't embarrass him. "You want a drink?" he asked Paula, turning to the pint he had bought with the last of the check he'd cashed at Finley Harbor.

"No, thanks. Have one if you like."

"No," he said, a little surprised at his own answer. "This is serious business. I reckon I'll wait until afterwards." He looked at her in the dim light raying through the trailer's drawn blinds; she wore a blue dress that was mate to yesterday's yellow one, and it was hard to keep his hands off her. He just wanted to reach out and touch her. He did, lightly, stroking her cheek. She smiled, turned away, but there was no rejection in it. He knew that she was afraid he would go farther, and she did not want to be mussed when the others came.

"You'll like old Felix and Larry," he said. "They're about my closest friends. Only, you've got to take Felix with just a little grain of salt. He gets carried away sometimes. I mean, once he gets hitched onto something, he goes like a house afire, and he don't always stop to double check. Like the time he canned the bear."

"Did what?"

"Last fall, word went around some feller up in Virginia would pay five hundred dollars for a live black bear cub. Felix took a notion he was gonna earn that money and he made a trap. Cut one end each out of two fifty-five-gallon oil drums, hinged 'em together and welded carryin handles on 'em. Then he carried it down in the swamp. Way it was set up, one drum laid on the ground and the other was cocked up in the air. Bear crawled into the first one to get the bait, tripped a trigger, and the top one would come down, slam him in the ass, knock him in, and lock behind him."

"So what happened?"

"The durn thing really worked. He come boilin out one Saturday, got me and Larry to help him fetch it up to his truck. Man, that was somethin, luggin those two drums with a live mad bear inside two miles through the swamp. Then we took him up to Virginia, found the feller, and learned that it was fifty he was payin, not five hundred, and he had already bought a bear and didn't need another one. So we carried it over to the Dismal Swamp and turned it loose. Felix was disappointed, but he was kinda proud too. Said it was probably the only time anybody ever canned a hundred and ten gallons of live bear."

Paula laughed. "And this is the man that's going to help you catch a murderer?"

"Help *us*, he said. "You're in this too."

"We'll see—" She broke off as, in the dusk, there was the grind of Felix's truck's failing transmission, the roar of Larry's sports car.

"Here they are," Danny said.

At least, he thought, they had put on decent clothes. All three wore clean sportshirts, and while Felix and Hogan were in jeans, Larry had on neatly pressed slacks. Entering, they halted packed just inside the door, looking soberly and tentatively at Paula. Quickly Danny performed introductions.

Their greetings were reserved, and she sensed that, and she moved quickly to break the ice. Casually she perched one hip on the table, one leg swinging free, and Danny had a quick vision of her sitting that way on her classroom desk, facing a new class, a yardstick in her hands. She combined quiet authority and total poise with outgoing friendliness.

"I hope I'm not intruding, although I suppose I am to some extent. But I'll try not to be any trouble and possibly I can be of some help. Danny's told me about this case and what you're trying to do, and I do wonder if maybe someone who could apply a little feminine psychology—and, if it comes to that, maybe draw information from another woman that a man couldn't get— I wonder if such a person wouldn't be useful to you. I've never done any detective work, but I've taught school and done some writing, and I think I have a feel for people and situations. Anyhow, I've got the whole summer free, and if I can help you, I'm perfectly willing to stay here; and if you decide I can't, why, I'll move along and no hard feelings."

Then, quite concisely, again as if addressing a class, she reeled off biographical data—where she had taken her teaching degree and her master's, her sales of confession stories— which made Larry's eyes light—and finished, "I've been on my own for a long time and I've been around a good deal. You don't have to make any concessions to my delicate feminine sensibilities; I'm perfectly aware of the facts of life. And I've made the same bargain with Danny that I understand you have; he is the boss, and what he says goes. If, on that basis, you want me to sit in, I'd like to, but if you'd rather not, I have no desire to break up a team with my presence."

But even before she had finished, they were captured, especially Larry. Expecting some honky-tonk floozy Danny had become infatuated with while drunk, they had found a mind as good as theirs and maybe better, and a presence to match it. Danny felt a thrill of pride as he saw the sullen doubt leave Felix's face, and even Peter Hogan's tense body relax, his big hands unclenching.

"Well," Felix said, laying a file folder on the table, "this might be a stroke of luck. Maybe the woman's angle is what we need."

Larry said nothing, but he looked at Danny with surprise and new respect. "Hogan?" Danny asked.

Hogan shrugged. "I need all the help we can get."

"Okay," Danny said, and his relief was in his voice.

"Then let's get to it." He took Paula's arm and squeezed it a little. "Slide in," and he motioned to the bench on one side of the table. He took a seat beside her, Felix and Larry sat down opposite, Hogan dragged up a chair at the end, and then he said crisply, "Shoot. What you got?"

He was pleased when Larry's tone matched his own, wholly businesslike. "Well, the newspaper on Manteo was closed, so we couldn't check the files. So we went to see Jared Struther." He turned to Paula. "Struther's an old-timer down here, a retired newspaperman who's still stringer for a lot of papers further west. He filed a lot of stories on the Daisy Canfield case and he let us use his file. He gave us some pictures of the body too. Meanwhile, Hogan's been laying low at Felix's shack; I doubt that anybody knows he's here yet. What we've done is this: We used Struther's records as a basis, and then Felix and I questioned Peter Hogan. I mean, we put him through the wringer just like Bristow would. Picked his brains for every scrap of information and made him level with us, and I think he has. We combined all this with what we got from Struther and that was more than we'd dared hope, because he and Bristow are good friends and fishing buddies. Besides, Bristow sort of used him as a consultant when they were looking for the body." He turned to Paula. "Jared used to have a pretty raunchy specialty back during the Second War. He was assigned to roam up and down the Banks and take charge of the bodies washed ashore from torpedoed ships. Photograph, identify, and bury them. He's an expert on the currents around here and, I guess you'd say, corpse flotation. Anyhow, Bristow confided in him, even some stuff that never got in the papers."

Danny stiffened. "You didn't tell Jared what we were up to?"

"Hell, no. I told him I was thinking about doing an article for a detective story magazine. He said he'd kind of thought about it too but had never got around to it and probably never would, to use his stuff and good luck."

"Smart," Danny said.

Larry grinned at Paula. "Some advantages to having everybody know you're a failed writer."

"Maybe this will be your breakthrough."

"Maybe. Anyhow, we took all this, plus what Felix and I knew about other suspects and all the rumors, and I constructed a kind of narrative that tells all we know about Daisy Canfield's death up until now. Felix and Hogan have both checked it, and so far as we know, nothing's been left out. Bristow, of course, knows a lot more and so does the SBI, but we can't go to them."

"All right," Danny said as Paula took notepad and pencil from her handbag. "Go ahead, Larry. Let's see if we can get this whole thing together."

"Right." Larry began to read, voice low but full of expression. As, piece by piece, the entire narrative of the death of Daisy Canfield fell into place, illuminated in some way by Larry's skill, Danny felt a rising excitement. Now he was comprehending wholly something which until now he had never been able to grasp entire, people coming alive, seemingly, before his eyes. He leaned forward, listening closely.

For Daisy, it was like an invitation to a feast after long starvation. One quarter Sioux herself, she had yet been set aside from the Indians on the Rosebud Reservation where she had grown up by her father's edict. Most of the Sioux were mired deep in poverty and many in vicious drunkenness; her father, the Episcopal missionary, feared even more her infection by their pagan religion, to which in despair, as well as pride, increasing numbers of tribesmen turned, so that the drums of secret sacred dances beat at night again deep in lonesome coulees and canyons. Elsewhere there were the white ranchers' sons and their cowhands; but she did not want to be a rancher's wife. She had in her a quick intellect and a secret hunger; and when she had escaped by winning a scholarship to the junior college so far away in the South, she found satisfaction for it at last.

The college was a place of great white-columned buildings and sweeping oak-shaded lawns, a century-old factory for the creation of ladies of education and refinement; but now it was fighting a losing battle. The girls would no longer tolerate the restrictions of only a decade before. Within twenty minutes' walk there was a state university jammed with young men; attracted to it were the hippies and flower children and heads, living in crowded warrens that had once been proud old houses but had fallen into decay. There were bars and night-clubs and topless go-go places, weird boutiques and dim pungent beer halls. Daisy was plunged into a world that made her head swim, her eyes widen, her pulses beat faster, and, sometimes, her stomach turn. But one thing she understood immediately: She was never going back to South Dakota.

The college had a small drama department, and the city a good Little Theater. Daisy signed up for classes in the former, and immediately she realized she had found what she'd been seeking. She knew suddenly that she was no longer limited to one personality, one fate; onstage she could be anyone she chose; a thousand different lives beckoned to her. She won a part at the Little Theater, and when summer came, instead of going home to Mission, she tried out for a role in an outdoor drama, was successful, and was assigned to *Blackbeard!*

By now she knew how far behind she was, how much she had to learn to catch up. The life she had chosen was not wicked—she convinced herself, although her father would have claimed otherwise—but it was fast and loose, swinging, as they said. The greatest sin was to be dull and Out of It, and she, for all her beauty, was almost that; but she hoped to gain ground, become more acclimated, at the Outer Banks.

She had never been near the sea before, and in this differ-ent kind of space—blue, sun-dazzled, swarming with sun-bronzed nudity, and, at the same time, still enmeshed in what she thought of as the glamour of the Stage—she was a bit over her depth. But she had a tutor; her roommate, Gerry Morse, helped her strike the necessary rhythm, make the first tenta-tive steps toward fitting in.

120

Gerry was from Atlanta, blond, pretty, a year older than Daisy, and with one season at the Theater already, a veteran in more ways than one. She was also the luck of the draw, assigned by the management to share with Daisy the room in the downtown boardinghouse. And since Gerry had a car, transportation was no problem. And since Gerry knew all the men, that was no problem either.

Except that Daisy was not yet ready. She wanted to be, she longed to be, but there were inhibitions bred too deeply in her bones to be shed so quickly and so easily. Her changing would not take place overnight; she must change slowly, gradually; and in doing so, she determined, she would not forsake all the old values which were still good. She would at least continue to respect and place a value on herself.

There was not much time for fast living anyhow at first. Seven days a week the cast and crew prepared and rehearsed, and this went on for almost a month. Dizzy with exhaustion and strain, they were not released at night until just before closing time for bars and taverns. The few parties were short and hurried, attended mostly by the group's hard core of swingers; Gerry was a regular, always staying late. Daisy went a few times—Hogan had seen her at one or two—but she missed a lot of them, and so far as he knew, she did not prowl the beach or piers late at night, as many did. She held back, making sure of her ground before she moved an inch. This gave her an aspect of hauteur which he had found forbidding at first; later he learned that it was only shyness, naïveté. And there was some quality in her—sweetness was the only word he could find for it—which, despite her refusal to enter the swirling mainstream, bound people to her in friendship, liking, respect, and even love. She was one of the few women in the cast who had no enemies, backbiters, or rivals; and, considering her beauty, that was a miracle.

●　●

After beer at Carney's and Fat Willy's, they had been sitting on the beach in the shadow of a dune, watching the roll of ocean, listening to its dull, sullen grumbling, and he was drinking more and in a fog of weariness, alcohol, love, and lust. He pulled her to him, squeezed her breast, feeling soft flesh under the crisp white blouse and the bra beneath it. He tried to get his hand into her neckline. She pushed it away. "Peter, don't—"

"Daisy, I—" He was full of boozy love and pent-up desire, and it seemed to him he would explode if he did not have her. He got one arm around her and tried again with his other hand, his lips driving for hers.

She was a strong girl, used to riding horses, walking, and a full share of housework, and she writhed free, holding the wrist of the hand grappling for her breasts. "Peter, now— Please!" Suddenly there was something new in her voice, disgust and fear, a terror incommensurate enough with what he had tried to do to cut through his fog of beer and amorousness. "Please don't be like *him!*"

Hogan blinked. "Like who?"

"Like—" His grip had slackened and Daisy pushed him away. Free now, she jumped to her feet, grabbed her sandals. Panting slightly, she pushed at her hair. "Peter," she said, "I think we'd better go. Let's take a walk or something."

Hogan rubbed his face. With her out of reach now, he got reluctantly to his feet. "All right," he said.

Larry's voice paused for a moment, with a special significance. "There it is," he said. "There's what we picked out of Hogan's brain."

Danny looked at him uncertainly. "What?"

"Don't be like *him*. What she said when he tried to feel

her. Hogan only remembered it when Felix and I dragged it out of him."

"I'm still not sure—"

"No," Hogan said. "No, you couldn't be, unless you'd heard her say it. But what she put into that one word."

"It seems to us," Larry said, "that what it indicates is this: Before Daisy went out with Hogan, she must have had some kind of experience with another man. A rough one, bad enough to scare her. When Hogan tried to feel her up, she thought of that and hit the panic button."

"It ties her to somebody else," Felix said. "Somebody who was close enough to her, knew her well enough, to have come on mighty strong with her. Strong enough to scare her silly."

"Who would that be?" Paula asked.

"We don't know," Larry said. He shrugged. "Maybe it wasn't even anyone here, maybe it was somebody where she went to college or back in South Dakota. But it's a lead of some kind, maybe—and it's one Claude Bristow doesn't have."

"I didn't even remember it," Hogan said, "until yesterday. It's funny, I've been over that night a thousand times in my own mind, but— Maybe it was coming back to Harriot."

"Well, it's something to consider," Danny said, unconvinced. "But a girl doesn't get to be nineteen years old without lotsa guys making passes at her."

"Well, whoever this one was, he scared her," Hogan said. "She didn't have any reason to be that afraid of me."

"Didn't she?" Danny asked and looked at him narrowly. Then he said, "All right. But go on now; what happened next?"

The house, built especially for rental, was on a dirt road just beyond the fringe of Oystertown. It was divided into three small apartments, two below and one upstairs. When Hogan and Daisy got there, the lower floor was wholly dark; two cars were parked in the drive, and it was obvious that Fred Austin and Conley Justice were home and asleep, so he and the girl were silent as they went up the stairs.

It had not been easy to get her to agree to come here with him. Realizing how badly she was upset, Hogan had modified his tactics, although the desire within him would not let him modify his aims. A walk down the beach and out on the pier had calmed her and restored him to her good graces. Still, she had been dubious when he had suggested that she go home with him. But he had talked music to her and engaged her interest; she knew little about the classics, but she was hungry to learn, as she was hungry for all new knowledge. "I'll play a few records and make some coffee," he had promised.

Once upstairs, he put the *New World Symphony* on the record player, hoping its intimations of vast spaces would strike a chord in her. He was still quite drunk, but excited too at having her alone, and with woozy shrewdness began to map what seemed a feasible campaign. When she returned from the bathroom, they sat together on the daybed, and she leaned against him with eyes closed, listening intently to the music.

"I like it," she murmured presently. "It's funny, it kind of makes me think of home." She was much calmer, more receptive now, he thought. Without any particular preliminaries, he took out two marijuana cigarettes bought on the pier and lit them both and held one out to her. "Here. This'll heighten your enjoyment."

She sat up, looked at it wide-eyed. "You know I don't smoke, I—" Then she said, "Oh."

He filled his lungs with smoke and felt an immediate effect. "Go on," he said. "It won't hurt you, and you'll appreciate the music much, much more."

She edged away. "No thanks. I don't need it to appreciate the music. I just told you, I liked it." Then she stood up. "Actually, Peter, I think you better take me home."

He could not remember exactly what he answered. Between drags on the cigarette he made his pitch, a heavy sales talk. She refuted all of it, began to lecture him. She knew marijuana itself wasn't dangerous, but what about the next step? Concerned for him now, she was almost preaching while he smoked. It was about then that he felt it happening; suddenly he was disengaged. The aggression drained from him; all at once he felt pleasantly relaxed and passive. He still wanted her, but without that terrible urgency. Suddenly, instead, he was listening to the music, engaged with it. The cigarette he had lit for her burned unheeded in the ashtray. He put out the tiny tip of his, reached for the stub of hers. Then he heard a theme: *Going home* . . . "I'd better take you home," he managed.

"No," she said. "I don't think you're in any condition now to drive." She was not disapproving so much as stating fact.

"I'm fine." He stood up and knocked the ashtray on the floor. "Except—" It hit him now. Fatigue, smothering him like a heavy blanket. "Only tired. So damned tired."

Daisy took his hand. "Come on, Peter." She slipped the roach from between his fingers and stubbed it out. "You'd better get some sleep and clear your head. Then you can drive me home . . ." She helped him stretch out on the daybed.

"Just a nap," he murmured. Ah, the music was so good . . . He turned his head. "I'm sorry," he said, looking at her. "Just a little nap."

"That's right," she said. "I'll wait. I don't mind waiting." She picked up a magazine and sat down at a table across the room, smiled at him, and then began to turn its pages. That was the last time he saw her.

Once more Larry halted. "Some time after that she left," he said, looking around the table.

Paula's chin was on her hand, as if she were deep in thought. "What about the two men downstairs?" she asked.

"Fred Austin worked on a fishing boat," Peter said. "He was really a merchant seaman here between trips. Drank a lot, but quiet. I didn't know him very well. The other one, Conley Justice, was from Georgia Tech. He was up here doing work for his master's degree, something about controlling dune erosion with special beach grasses. We got along all right, he seemed a nice intelligent guy."

"Yeah," said Felix. "But tell her what he did next day." He looked at Paula. "Next morning, early, Justice got up early, drove to Norfolk, and he traded cars there. Swapped in his Chevy for an Oldsmobile and went on to Maryland. When Bristow questioned him, he swore he'd arranged the swap days in advance, and the trip to Maryland was to see a girl. Only, the way I understand it, she wasn't home, so he had a blast on his own in Baltimore." He turned to Hogan. "There's no reason why he couldn't have heard Daisy come out, maybe followed her, and— And maybe she left some mark on his car so he had to get rid of it in a hurry. And, of course, when the SBI checked it, the dealer had already cleaned it up."

Hogan shook his head. "I told you, Felix. Justice had already mentioned to me that he was swapping cars before I even went out with Daisy."

"All the same," said Felix. "All the same . . ."

"Did you have a phone?" Paula asked. "Could she have called someone to come and get her?"

"No," Peter Hogan said.

"Would she have waked up one of the men downstairs and asked for a ride?"

"Hell, no!" Hogan said.

"She might have thought that preferable to walking home alone at that time of night."

"She wasn't afraid of that." Hogan said. "She would have been afraid to wake up a strange man, afraid she was imposing, but she wasn't afraid of the night. She was a country girl and—"

"It seems peculiar all the same that a girl like that would dare to walk—"

"These girls'll dare anything," Danny said. He thought of Deborah Stern in Grover's Pleasure Palace. "We find 'em out at all hours in every kinda place. It's a wonder more of 'em haven't gotten killed."

Larry said, "According to Struther's information, Fred Austin, the sailor, testified that he was asleep and heard and saw nothing. Justice said he was sleeping too, but he woke once and heard music upstairs. Then again later, and he said he thought he heard footsteps coming down the stairs, the door open and close. Then he said he thought—but he was so groggy he couldn't be sure—he heard a girl's voice and a man's, and a car engine start."

Paula turned slowly to Peter Hogan. "If that's the case, then I should think you're lying."

Hogan's face paled. "No," he said. "I'm not."

"Go on, Larry," Danny said. "What else you got?"

"Well, everybody pretty much knows the rest. How this island was combed from stem to stern for nearly two weeks. It was on about the tenth day that the first evidence was found. Lincoln White, a colored man who's groundskeeper for the golf course, brought a wallet to the grocery store in town. Link couldn't read or write, so he didn't know what he had.

But it had Daisy Canfield's name in it. The storekeeper called the Sheriff right away. Link took them to where he said he'd found it, walking back to Oystertown after he put his tractor away. It was on a side road about a mile and a half from Hogan's house—not the route she'd have taken to get home. They found her handbag in the ditch, with most of her belongings scattered around. It was right by an old sand pit—"

"A what?" Paula asked.

"A borrow pit, a kind of quarry, where they'd dug out dirt to use for fill to build roads. The pit was full of water, a small lake, you might say . . ."

"So they called me," Felix said. "I've got a full skin-diving outfit. I combed that lake good, but there wasn't anything in it."

"The next day more of her stuff appeared, and in a different place. A gardener at the Buccaneer Theater found a paperback novel with her name in it, a lipstick, and a comb in the shrubbery about a hundred yards from where the Theater drive meets the highway. He called Bristow and the SBI—"

"That's only about a mile from the bridge across the Sound," Larry continued. "So they just went down the highway to the bridge on foot. And that's where they found her shoes. And the plot thickened. One shoe was right at the bridge approach, leaning very neatly against a phone pole, in plain sight. The other was in the grass just beyond the ditch on the other side of the road. Just inside the golf course rough. That, Bristow said, was when he knew she was in the water."

"The thing about it is," said Felix, "there ain't any *pattern*. The handbag a mile and a half from Hogan's place, the book and other stuff at the Theater another mile away, and then her shoes right at the bridge. Nobody's made any sense of it yet. Was she raped beside the sand pit? At the Theater? Why were her shoes found at the bridge? Who leaned one up against the pole, and after he did that, why did he throw the other on the golf course?"

"Anyhow, they concentrated on the water after that," Larry said. "The SBI made dummies about her size and weight and threw 'em off the bridge at all hours to see which way they'd drift. But when she was found, she was in the opposite direction. The dummies drifted south; she was in found north of the bridge. The Styron brothers, they're fishermen over across the Sound on Shoehorn Point, had gill nets set out in the Sound."

"What's a gill net?"

"You set a good solid stake in the bottom," Danny explained, "and then you take a net about twenty feet long, maybe three feet wide, it's got a mesh just big enough to let a fish's head through. You float it at the top and weight it at the bottom, and it's like a fence across the channel. Fish pokes his head in, can't get out, hung by his gills. A lot of people around here keep 'em out, especially when the blues are runnin'."

"She was in the third one they checked," Larry said. "At first they thought they had a shark. But when they pulled it in, she was caught by her wrist. They anchored her so she couldn't float away and brought Bristow to see her."

He reached into the file. "Struther had a paraphrase of the Medical Examiner's report. They sent her to Norfolk for an autopsy." He began to read.

"'The pudenda were bruised and gorged with blood. The annular hymen had a quarter-inch tear at four o'clock. The insides of the thighs and the left ankle were severely bruised; there was a large bruise on the right jaw. She had been strangled with a quarter-inch braided rope doubled twice, but she was not quite dead when she entered the Sound; her lungs contained a small quantity of water. There was a residue of brownish fluid in her stomach, coffee, beer, or cola; apparently no drugs or alcohol in the bloodstream. Death was, in the last instance, by drowning, but first she was raped and brutally beaten.'"

"Ugh," Paula whispered. For a moment there was silence in the trailer, as if each were seeing it: the frightened girl struggling in darkness, battling for her life and knowing that it was hopeless.

Danny in that moment felt his own mortality and knew that each of them had the same sense of the awfulness of death.

Almost as if to combat that, Danny spoke. "Well, that's about it, ain't it, Larry?"

"In sum. We all know about Chet Hollister, the object of Bubba Dixon's concern. He admits to having driven around town that night, but his mother swears he was home in bed before one-thirty. They checked his car and found no evidence that she'd been in it."

"Don't forget Harold Krause," said Felix.

"Right," said Larry. "Of course there's Harold Krause . . ."

In his late thirties, the lawyer was prosperous, married, and a father. He was also a drunk. Once Harold Krause had been a handsome man, but now a bloated belly swayed before him and his face was flushed and red, his eyes watery. He missed more appointments than he kept, and some of his arguments in court had become irrational. None of that could go unnoticed in a small town; everyone knew he drank enormously and most knew about his trouble with his wife, who had begun to be afraid that he would kill her.

Lately he had become, with or without reason, insanely jealous. By nine or ten at night, half blind and maddened with

130

drink, he would roar and stumble and rage about the big house on Shipsbell Road, threatening to beat her to death for her betrayals. When he was like that, she would take their two small children and run away, seeking refuge wherever she could find it, hiding from him until the fit had passed. Lately, when she did that, he would go looking for her, roaring around the island in his Cadillac, hammering on doors, raging under windows, or simply parking his car on the shoulder of the highway and screaming her name. More than once Danny Rush had taken him home from Carney's, the downtown tavern; and Bristow's deputies did the same when they found him in the county. Somehow, though, he was never charged; he was, after all, a potent member of the island's political structure. For the same conduct, a drunken fisherman would have lost his driver's license and probably have gone to prison; Krause remained at large.

On the night that Daisy Canfield vanished he lurched into Carney's just before closing, standing unsteadily in the doorway, sullenly surveying all the women in the room. Everybody knew his wife had run away again. Not finding her, he turned wordlessly, went out; then the Cadillac roared off into the night.

That was the last of Harold Krause's drunken binges. For two weeks he remained completely sober, drawn and pale and shaky. On the day after Daisy's body was found he was in Midyette's barber shop, where the sole excited topic of conversation among the loafers was the murder. Krause remained absolutely silent. Finally the barber dusted him, and, trembling, Krause got out of the chair. Something about the way he stood there damped all chatter, and the silence was complete.

Krause looked around, red face redder from the steam of the hot towels after his shave. His eyes were deep sunken and

131

full of misery. Everyone stared at him.

"Goddamn it," Krause whispered hoarsely. "I didn't do it. I *know* I didn't!"

Only that, no more. Then, spilling change which he did not bother to retrieve, he crammed money into the stunned barber's hand and went out, leaving behind a taut, charged silence that exploded suddenly into excited supposition.

Chapter 8

"Dreadful," Paula Murphy said. "Absolutely dreadful. I thought— I didn't know it would produce this effect on me. It's like . . . like a stopped-up toilet overflowing. Just from listening I already feel like I've been . . . smeared."

"I know what you mean," said Larry. "Well, you might as well have the full dose. Look at these." And he took two glossy photographs from the file and shoved them to her.

"Oh, God," Paula said. She turned her head away, then forced herself to look again.

In one, Daisy lay in the boat that had brought her to shore, skirt hiked up over her abdomen, split waterlogged pants white against dark flesh. The other was as Danny remembered her, on the canvas, with Bristow's shoes visible.

"She's so *black*," Paula whispered.

"Normal after two weeks," Larry answered softly. "The walls of this fleshly temple crumble very swiftly."

Paula turned them face downward.

Nobody spoke for a moment more. Then Larry said briskly, "Well, that's what's *known*. I mean what we know, not what Bristow knows. The suspects so far are Hogan, here; Justice and Austin, who lived downstairs; your old friend Chet Hollister, Danny; and Harold Krause. And, of course, every other male on Harriot and Shoal that night who wasn't home in bed or in a wheelchair, say about five thousand, give or take a thousand. Now the only problem is how to check them out." His smile was a bit sardonic. "I'm open to suggestions."

No one said anything. Larry rose, went to the kitchen, and got a glass of water. "You know what I think?" he said. "In my ignorance, I think we've bitten off more than we can chew. I don't want to howl calamity, but there are certain facts we have to face. How do you solve a murder that's gone stale, that's over three years old? Especially one where you can establish a connection between only one man and the victim—and he's the man you're trying to clear?"

"We're not tryin to clear nobody," Danny said, a sinking feeling in his stomach. "We're just tryin to find out who done it."

"Well, I still want to know," Larry said. "To begin with, most of the suspects we've mentioned have left the island. Chet Hollister's gone, you know. Fred Austin doesn't seem to be around; he may be on a ship in the Indian Ocean right now, for all we can guess. The other guy—Conley Justice, who traded cars—where the hell is he? At another college, on another beach planting grass? Working for the government? How do we locate and question them? How do we check their stories?"

He drank. "Of course, Bristow and the SBI know all that. But if we go to them, your tail's in a crack, Danny." He set down his glass. "I think we've been deceiving ourselves. A case like this isn't a penny-ante game, especially coming in this late. It takes money and it takes the authority to question people. And we got no money and the only authority we have is Danny's badge, which, with all due respect, doesn't carry all that much weight. I mean, Bristow and the SBI, they're on the *inside* and they've got nowhere. And we're . . . outsiders. In every sense of the word."

Felix jerked his head around. "You cooled off mighty fast. You were hot enough the other night. All that big talk about caring about one dead girl."

Larry nodded. "I still care. I still care very much. And I'm not saying we should give up. But where do we start? What kind of handle do you get on this thing when you don't have money for travel and phone calls and a badge to force people to talk and—" He broke off, shrugged.

"I don't know," Danny said.

"Well, I think," Felix said, "that Larry's full of crap." His voice was angry, desperate. "We could start with Krause."

"That's true. Krause has been sober for three years now," Larry said. "He divorced his wife, remarried, and he hasn't touched a drop since. So all we have to do is go out and question him. Tell him we want to take a statement from him, and we don't want Bristow to know."

"Larry," Paula said. "Danny? Felix? Peter?"

Larry broke off. "Yes, ma'am."

Paula hesitated. "Would it be out of order for me to make a few suggestions? Observations?"

Larry grinned. "I think we need all of both that we can get."

"Excuse me, Danny, I think better on my feet." He let her out, and she faced the table; and now it was as if she were in a classroom again.

"I'm a late comer to this," she said, "and I don't know all

these things like you do. I don't know Sheriff Bristow either or any of the . . . the intermingling of personalities. But on the assumption that neither the Sheriff nor your State whatisit people are absolute incompetents, wouldn't you be wasting your time going back over the same old suspects anyhow? And doing it in the same old way?"

"That's what I mean," Larry said.

"Obviously you don't have the resources to beat them at their own game. So you'll just have to play a different game, one that is small enough for you to handle. You ought to pick a suspect and concentrate on him. And if it doesn't pay off, you haven't lost very much and nobody's the worse for it."

Peter Hogan made a sound in his throat.

"And use imagination," she said. "Take chances in your thinking. That may be where you have an advantage over the others. After all, most policemen aren't noted for their imagination, are they? They have to be sure and methodical." As if to mollify Hogan, she added, "Look at the way they picked you. Because you were so obvious. No imagination at all. And that's another advantage. Because the others are sort of dazzled by you, they can't see past you. But if we make up our minds that you're innocent and proceed steadfastly on that assumption, at least we won't be wasting valuable time and energy."

"Almost, you make me believe again," Larry said wryly, but with a rising excitement. "What you're driving at is coming back to *him.*"

"That's right. The mysterious him who grappled at Daisy's bosom before Peter Hogan did. After all"—she smiled—"the others belong to Sheriff Bristow. But *him* is up for grabs."

"I told you!" Felix snapped. "I told you that was the most important thing."

Danny himself felt a response; this was common sense. A

moment before he had been depressed, now his spirits rose, and he looked at her with warm admiration. "I think you're right."

Paula shrugged.

"Go on," said Larry. "Any more suggestions?"

"I have a few, but I feel like I'm presuming—"

"No. No, you've got a fresh outlook. Let's hear 'em."

"Well," she said and reached past Danny to pick up the photographs. "I hate to look at these again, but—" She turned them over, laid them on the table. "I would like to ask a question. She's naked to the waist, but she still has on her pants. How do they account for that?"

"Nobody has," Felix said. "She had on a bra and blouse that night but they've not been found."

"Well, doesn't that seem rather strange? he—the murderer—took off her blouse and bra and didn't replace them, but he raped her and then put her underpants back on her?" She smiled. "I've never been actually raped, but I always thought the pants were the first things they went for. I mean the ravening, lustful kind of rapist. . . . What's the old saying? Seduction is for sissies, but a strong man needs his rape? That sort." She looked at them. "You'll have to tell me. If you were raping a girl out of sheer sexual necessity, and one who was fighting at that, what would be the first move?"

"Well, you're right," Danny said. "You'd grab her panties and pull 'em down."

"The voice of experience," Larry murmured. Then he was serious. "That seems a fair enough assumption. If it was somebody like Chet Hollister or even one of those two guys downstairs or a kid cruising the island—somebody so horny he had to have a receptacle for it in a hurry, needed it so bad he'd grab a strange girl off the road— Why, as a tentative assumption, you could say that almost eliminated that kind of

137

suspect."

"It's a working hypothesis anyhow."

"Wait a minute," Danny said. "You mean it was somebody she already knew?"

"Let me put it this way," Paula said. "Now this part of it I know a little more about. I've written dozens of scenes that took place in parked cars, and they've always followed the same dreary scenario. First, the usual kissing and neck nibbling and ear blowing, with everything getting a little hotter all the time, and maybe now she lets him put his hand on her breast—with two layers of cloth to guard it, of course. One thing leads to another, and finally she might take off her blouse and bra and give him free access to what he seems to want so badly. Of course, she'd probably put the clothes in the back seat where they wouldn't get rolled on and wrinkled."

They were all staring intently at her now.

"For a nice girl, that's quite a concession. But it usually turns out to be counterproductive. She thinks she's given him enough to satisfy him, but all she's done is arouse him so he's even harder to stop. And you know what the next step is."

Danny blurted, "He tries to git his finger in it!"

"The magic maneuver." Paula's mouth quirked. "At first he pretends he's not really doing anything, but all the time that hand creeps lower. Sneaks under the skirt, up the thigh, and finally pushes aside the panty crotch, gouges, shoves." She was wholly serious. "Believe me, that can be rough, it can hurt. In fact, it can bring a girl to her senses in a hurry, especially if the man's brutal about it. And suddenly she's got to make a decision. Either he's gone far enough or she's got to let him go the rest of the way. And by then, if she closes up, he still might not stop. Not everybody's as considerate as you, Peter."

138

"By then," Felix said, "he'd be like a stick of dynamite, primed to explode!"

"That's right. They're in a car, she's naked to the waist, he's touched home base, as the saying goes, and now she's decided. She clamps her legs together, pushes his hand away, and she says, 'I think you'd better take me home. Now, stop it, please stop it!' But he's not about to stop. He's got that hand going, and he's strong and it's strong, and he rams it in, using all the force he's got to get her legs apart and behind those pants. . . . And what was it? A quarter-inch tear in the hymen. A penis would have obliterated it. But a finger—"

Danny's eyes shifted to Peter Hogan. His big hands were clenched on the table.

"And now she's more than outraged or reluctant, she's afraid. She screams and fights rather than give in. After all, she's a preacher's daughter and from a place still not completely in this century, much less the sixties or seventies. So he wrestles with her and when she won't stop screaming—then he hits her."

"It fits," Felix said excitedly. "He knocks her out, and by then he's already bruised her legs. And then he comes to his senses. Maybe he can't tell whether or not she's breathin, maybe he thinks he's killed her! So he quits thinkin about anything except What now?"

"That's right," Paula said. "Even if she weren't dead, he'd know that he might be charged with attempted rape. Assault on a female, whatever the charges are, Danny. Enough to send him to jail or ruin him or both."

"So he decides to kill her," Felix said. "He's got some rope, hell, everybody down here keeps rope, anybody that's got a boat. He strangles her to make sure she's dead, and by then it's four in the mornin, hardly anything movin on the island. So he runs her out to the bridge, makes sure nobody's comin, and dumps her over."

"And what about the shoes?" Larry asked quietly. "He takes her shoes off and leans one against a phone pole and throws the other on the golf course? Why?"

"Bristow thought the one shoe by the phone pole was a half-assed attempt to make it look like suicide," Danny said.

"Half-assed is right," said Felix. "He props one there, throws the other across the road, sprinkles part of her stuff at the Theater, then tosses out the rest by the sand pit? Miles apart? Some suicide evidence."

"Well, he may have been rattled," Paula said. "But it doesn't fit very well, does it? Of course, the shoes. . . . She might have been walkin barefoot when he met her. When she got in the car, she might have just dropped them on the floor. Later he found them . . . I don't know."

"Got in the car, wasn't pulled," Larry said.

"I don't know that either. I'm just conjecturing." She paused. "The most pathetic thing about it is," she said, "was it worth it? How much better off she would have been if she hadn't been so stuffed full of that old-fashioned morality. If she'd been promiscuous, easy going, she'd still be alive today. Why, if she'd just yielded to Peter here and spent the night with him . . . What harm would that have done her?"

"That's a kinda cold way to look at it, ain't it?" Danny asked, something about the speech disturbing him.

"Maybe." Paula smiled faintly. "Personally, I'd rather be violated than dead. But maybe I look at things in a different light. Anyhow, those are just a few ideas that have occurred to me. I'll have to leave it to you to judge whether they make sense."

Danny was silent for a moment, but it was as if some irresistible force drew his gaze to Peter Hogan.

The young man met his eyes, then looked away.

"Hogan," Danny said.

"For Christ's sake," Hogan said. "Do you think I did that?"

"Those big hands of yours coulda done a lot of damage to her crotch. And . . . maybe you wouldn't do it in your right mind. But the way I've heard it, people stoned on beer and pot might do anything."

"And come back here? Do you think I'd be fool enough?"

There was in that moment in Danny Rush an upwelling of disgust, almost rage. He saw Hogan looking down at her corpse impassively; he thought of Hogan offering her the marijuana.

"Why not? Whether you killed her or didn't, her death fucked up your whole future. If you're guilty, you still need to know where you stand."

"I said I didn't kill her!"

"Do you even know or not, spaced out like you said you were? Maybe you did start to take her home. And maybe you decided to try again on a lonesome road. And maybe you had better luck at first this time—"

Peter Hogan sprang to his feet. "Hell," he said thickly, "I won't stand for any more of this." He strode toward the trailer door, but Chief Rush was there before him, blocking it. The two men confronted each other, and Hogan raised clenched enormous fists. Danny looked coolly into Hogan's swirling eyes with the hard impersonal glare he had used on countless soldiers, fishermen, sailors, actors, students, beach bums. It worked; Hogan's face began to show uncertainty. Danny had expected that. The difference between the civilian and the officer in such a situation of impending violence was that the civilian had to make a decision; the officer's was already made.

"Wait a minute," Paula said. "Danny. Peter. Wait. Sit down, both of you. Peter . . ." She took his arm. He relaxed a little. "Come on, sit down."

Hogan let out a long breath, let her push him back into his seat, but he still glared at Danny.

"What good will this do?" Paula asked. "Don't you think the Sheriff's followed the same train of thought? Didn't we agree that the only approach was to assume that Peter Hogan's innocent?"

"She's right, Danny," Felix said.

"Maybe," Danny said after a moment, but that stubborn dislike for the young man was still in him. Long hair, fancy music . . . and the marijuana and that impassive face looking at poor black, swollen Daisy— When Linda's grown, he thought fiercely, if somebody like that ever comes around her— He relaxed. "Okay," he growled. "So Peter Hogan's innocent. So what then?"

Nobody spoke.

"Look," said Larry finally, "before we go any farther, let's run back over the other suspects. Those two guys downstairs—"

"She didn't know them," Hogan said. "Never met them." His voice still shook a little.

"It doesn't seem reasonable," Paula said, "that any sane young man, even if he were very wrought up, hearing a girl leave a house in the middle of the night would leap out of bed and follow her with rape on his mind. That's pretty far out, unless one of them was a psychopath."

"They weren't," Hogan said.

"Then Chet Hollister—"

"Well, we put Bubba's confession up against his alibi," said Danny heavily. "The alibi won."

"It couldn't have been Bubba Dixon himself, trying to throw suspicion on someone else?"

"He's got no car," Danny said.

"And the lawyer?"

"Theoretically it coulda been him," Danny said. "He was searchin for his wife and he was mad enough to kill her. He might have seen her in the dark and mistook her. She was about the same size, only a little thinner. But drunk as he was, I just don't think he could have handled her. I think she could have outrun or outfought him."

"Besides, you've already given us his profile," Larry said. "He was somebody who knew her at least as well as Peter Hogan and maybe better." He turned to Hogan. "Who else had she been close to, do you know?"

"I wish I did. She was so damned beautiful, and yet there was something so . . . so above it all about her that I think I'm the only one in the Theater who really approached her. There were plenty of other girls ready and willing, and the fellows kind of shied away. They didn't know that she was just a little timid." He shook his head. "Anyhow I don't know of anybody. I know she went to a few parties, but— Like I said, that was our first real night off. Anybody else she saw, it would have had to be in the morning or late at night. She might have dated somebody else then."

"Well, of course," said Paula, "there's one person who would know. Her roommate. If they'd lived together for a month, they'd know all about each other's love life. What was her name?"

"Gerry Morse," Larry said. "She was from Atlanta."

"Yes. Well, it seems to me she'd be the place to start. If somebody could find and question her—"

"Atlanta's a long way off," Larry said. "I wonder what it would cost." He looked dubious.

"Wait a minute," Danny said, something stirring in the back of his mind. "Say her name again."

"Gerry. Gerry Morse, maybe short for Geraldine."

Danny frowned, groping for a wisp of association. Deborah Stern, that wasn't it. The other girl, Frances something. . . . For a moment he was in the apartment in the Canfield Complex once more, with the drunken girl sprawled in the chair and—

"What the hell's going on out there?"

"Nothing, Gerry. Go back to sleep."

"Larry," Danny said. "You don't happen to have a this year's Theater program in your file?"

"Yeah, as a matter of fact."

Felix was reaching for it, but Danny already had it. He withdrew the thick slick-paper publication with its colored cover of the same design as the poster in his office. He thumbed through it until he found a listing of the cast. Slowly lips working, he ran a thick finger down the tiny type. "Well," he said, triumph in his voice, "here it is. She's back. She's at the Theater this year. Why, I even know where she's staying. In the Canfield Complex, Apartment Four."

The others looked at him, then bent to stare at the program.

"Why, you son of a gun," said Felix, a little awed.

Danny looked at Paula. "Now," he said proudly, "you know why I'm in charge."

Chapter 9

The clash of steel on steel chimed savagely through hushed darkness. On board the pirate ship, young Lieutenant Maynard pressed Teach back and back again, both men sweating, crouched. The audience was wholly rapt.

"God's blood, Maynard!" Blackbeard roared, teeth gleaming in his raven whiskers, "I'll feed your guts to the fish crows and the gulls!"

On Danny Rush's left a little girl whined, vaguely frightened. "Mommy—"

Maynard leaped in. "Easier said than done, Teach! Ha! Ha!" He parried, thrust, ducked a swinging roundhouse of a stroke from Blackbeard's cutlass, recovered, thrust out a foot. Blackbeard stumbled, turning from the audience. "Now!" Maynard yelled and, with both hands on the saber grip, raised it high. Blackbeard, braced on the ship's rail, looked up and screamed. Maynard, body swinging to block the view, struck downward.

From the stage came a sound like a melon being split. The child beside Danny screamed. "His head! Look, Mommy, his head!"

The thing bounced into view, wide-eyed, teeth still gleaming in the beard. Simultaneously, as Maynard stepped back, the body slid headfirst over the ship's rail. Maynard raised a bloody sword in triumph. The corpse's legs kicked wildly, then disappeared. From behind the stage there was the sound of a splash.

"Thus ends Blackbeard!" Maynard shouted.

A wild cheer went up from the victorious sailors on the body-littered poopdeck. Then one, staring over the rail, let out a cry. "Lieutenant! Look! Our Father in Heaven," the sailor shouted. "The body! Look at the body! It's swimming! It's swimming around the ship!"

A horror-stricken hush gripped the amphitheater. Then Maynard stepped back, lifted the severed head by its hair. "Well," he said, "I wager he won't go far without this."

Laughter. Maynard held it higher.

"And thus be it with all buccaneers and enemies of the freedom of the seas!"

The little girl's breath was sobbing with excitement. "Good heavens," Paula Murphy said sickly on Danny's other side.

"Phillips, take charge of this." Maynard passed the head to a subordinate.

"Aye, sir, I'll salt it down." He peered over the rail. "It's gone, sir."

"And good riddance. Now, the captives?"

"Here, sir," and a cabin door opened. Four women in the flowing dress and lace of another day rushed out screaming with relief. One, a blond in golden taffeta, threw herself into the Lieutenant's arms.

"There, there, Doña Maria," Maynard said. "No need to cry. You're safe." His voice rose. "You're all safe. Our coast is safe now, every inlet, creek, and harbor. No longer will these scoundrels block America's destiny, our country's growth."

The girl in Maynard's arms turned toward the audience, stretched out her hand. "Yes," she said, voice soaring, if a touch brassily. "Yes, I can see it. I can see it now, Lieutenant. Where the pirates skulked, the merchantmen will come, the clipper ships, the schooners, the brigantines, and barks, with their cargoes of peaceful commerce. Where these dark buccaneers drank, caroused, and tortured victims, great cities shall spring up. Where—"

"Oh, my God," Paula murmured helplessly. "I don't believe it, I simply don't believe it."

"Yes." Maynard's voice rang out in finality, to match her tone. "One country, under God, with liberty and justice for all." He thrust out his saber, they stood poised, and from the night on either flank the chorus swelled, nearly half a hundred voices, as, save for the spotlight on Maynard and Doña Maria, the stage went dark. "Oh, beautiful for spacious skies, for amber waves of grain. . . ."

And then it was over, the last organ note dying, the last curtain call taken, the exhausted child beside Danny nestling in her father's arms. "Daddy, did they really cut the bad man's head off?"

"No, honey, I don't think so. That was just a dummy."

"What's a dummy?" The voice faded. All around them the audience rose.

"Well," Paula said, dusting at her bottom, "Shakespeare it ain't."

"I thought it was pretty good," Danny said. "I liked that sword fight."

"This is the first time you've seen it?"

147

"I told you so." He laughed a little self-consciously. "I don't know. It's here all summer every summer and you know you can come any time you want to, so you never git around to it. I guess they'll still be playin it twenty years from now, like *The Lost Colony*."

"I daresay they will. There's enough bloodshed in it to run forever, if the taste of Americans doesn't change."

"You didn't admire it much."

She laughed, squeezed his arm. "It was all right. Very stirring in spots. A sort of primitive appeal. Anyhow, we've seen her now and we'll know her when we see her again. Maybe I'll even tell her that there were no clipper ships in the days of Blackbeard. Or send the playwright a note. If he can read."

They left the theater and wandered along woodland paths to the parking lot where they had left Paula's car. "I reckon it was a little farfetched," Danny said.

"Maybe not. We don't have any Blackbeards, but there's a man named Calley alive and well in Georgia."

Danny did not want to comment on that. A soldier had his duty— He opened the door for her.

"And there was Daisy," she said as he slid behind the wheel. "Have you ever thought about how strange that is? It was Blackbeard's violence—and the fact that it was salable—that brought her here. In a way, he killed her too."

Danny thought about it and found it true. She always had new angles from which to see things; that was part of what was so fascinating about her. It took a long time to work through the outflowing traffic. Halted once, he saw the lights of the Canfield Complex gleaming on his left.

"I guess this is a kinda roundabout way to do it," he said, "but I really think it'll be better if I brace her while she's in my jurisdiction. If I come out here, I'd be in Bristow's territory and she might clam up. Anyhow, Carney says she's in every night after the show."

Once on the highway, following the stream of traffic across Harriot Island toward the town, he was silent. To himself he admitted that he was a little frightened. In a way, this was his first move in opposition to Claude Bristow, and Bristow was bound to hear, for he heard everything. How much importance he would attach to it, Danny couldn't guess; but he knew this: Claude Bristow ruled Midyette County with an iron hand, and Danny Rush would not be the first flare of competition he had pinched out like a match's flame.

All the same, he told himself, glancing sideways at Paula, it was worth the risk. He knew now he loved her as he had never loved any woman or believed it possible to; and somehow, he had vowed, he would hold her and marry her. He was not fool enough to think it might not take the rest of the summer to achieve winning her love totally. He understood that she was used to freedom, set in her ways, as the old folks said. She would not easily give up the life she had made for herself, and why should she to marry the Police Chief of a one-horse coastal town? But if he could prove to her that he was more than that, if he could, in his way, make the name for himself that Wahab Rush had made, become a man of consequence and power— He had, he thought, wasted so many years. All his carousing with Felix and Larry, the bitterness with Ruth— But he would make up for that. His mind leaped ahead, building plans and fantasies in a way it had not done since he had met Ruth, and these were fantasies of a greater magnitude. Back then the most he had been able to conceive was enough to honky-tonk all Saturday night and screw all Sunday, a kid's dreams. But he was a kid no longer, and his dreams now were a man's dreams: prosperity, comfort, important work to do, a big house on Shipsbell Road, and a woman in it who was equal to it. "Outsider," Larry had said. It was true, he had been an outsider ever since leaving Hatteras. But bring this off and he'd be one no longer. His name would be in every newspaper in the state. He would be famous. He could use his name and the name of Wahab Rush—for he would not be ashamed to invoke it then—and there was no reason why he could not unseat Bristow, who had been around too long anyhow, and take his place.

But first he had to keep Paula here long enough to demonstrate what he could do. He was almost grateful to Daisy Canfield for getting killed and giving him this chance. He thought of what Larry had said: everybody using her. Well, that was true. But at least in using her he would avenge her.

Carney's was long, dim, narrow, smoky, seething with young tanned flesh, brain-numbing with the smash of hard rock from the jukebox drowning the shrill babble of voices and laughter. The Theater and beach crowd came here to drink, and in the summer the islanders shied away, preferring Fat Willy's on the causeway. Paula and Danny found a table and Danny managed to get a couple of beers at the crowded bar. In silence then they searched the crowd and watched the door. Danny wondered why people had to have so much noise. Even Ruth. Today after depositing his paycheck, when he had gone out to give her almost all the money she had coming, the television set had been turned up full blast. What were they trying to keep away with all that racket?

Then, beside him, Paula stiffened. "There," her lips formed the words. "There she is."

Danny frowned. The girl who had just come through the door with a crowd of young people had the same great yellow mane certainly, but otherwise she looked nothing like the dignified Spanish lady on the stage.

But she was something to take a man's breath away. In the full skirt she had not seemed tall, but the one she wore now barely covered her rump, with an incredible length of sleek nyloned legs below, ending in chunk-heeled sandals. Her torso was very short, her breasts small yet definite beneath her clinging blouse, and that proportioning emphasized the illusion of height. Her neck was long, her hair magnificent, thick on the crown, falling heavily to her shoulders, and framing the small face of a baby tart. Whether it was theatrical makeup not yet taken off or what she usually wore, he did not know, but her eyelids were painted silver with greenish arches above, her lashes were long and obviously artificial, her brows darkly penciled. If impact was what she was seeking, she achieved it; the whole effect was of fit, vital youth and an innocence wantonly spoiled. Sex radiated from her like heat from a well-stoked stove. Contrasted to her, Paula and most other women in the room looked old and stodgy.

She strode to the bar, smoking a cigarette very jerkily, short deep puffs, and put one arm around a boy sitting on a stool. She rubbed her breasts against him, laughing, showing good white teeth in a small red mouth, and, face close to his ear, whispered. He signaled to the waitress. Danny thought, I bet she ain't bought a beer for herself since she was old enough to drink.

The beer came while she laughed with the boy. She took it and, as he was about to close his arm around her, saw someone farther down the counter and cried out. She dodged his grasp and moved along, slid gracefully into a niche between stools, one leg pressing hard against this youth's jean-clad knee.

He said something that made her laugh; she ruffled his hair. Slowly Danny got to his feet. "Well," he said, the word almost lost even to himself in the uproar, and he went to her.

As if she were conscious of every man in the room, where he was and what he did at every moment, she saw him coming. Sucking deeply on her cigarette as if it were a pacifier, she half turned away, trying to ignore him. He tapped her on the shoulder. "Miss."

Slowly she faced him. Her eyes, enormous, hazel, met his with elaborate innocence. "Oh, Chief Rush."

"You know me?"

"I've seen you around." Now her eyes held a latent invitation, but the rest of her childlike whore's face was still wary. "Something I can do for you?"

"I'd like to talk to you a minute or two. Can you step outside with me where it's quieter?"

She paled beneath her makeup, although she laughed slightly. "What am I charged with?"

"Nothing. I just need a minute of your time."

"All right." One more deep drag on the cigarette and she put it out; he saw that her nails were bitten to the quick. Her hand shook a little. "Let's go."

They threaded through the room and Paula followed. Out on the street the quiet was blessed. Gerry Morse halted close to Carney's doorway, as if ready to dodge inside at the slightest alarm, looking warily at Danny and at Paula.

"This is Miss Paula Murphy," Danny said. "She and I would like to talk to you about Daisy Canfield."

"Daisy?" The girl relaxed, then laughed. "Oh. Is that getting hot again?"

"You might say so," Danny told her. "I may conduct a new investigation. Anyhow, I need some information from you if you could spare an hour where we could go somewhere and talk. Miss Murphy here will chaperon." He had to smile a little at that.

She smiled back. "Well," she said, "if you think you need

one." Then she was serious. "Honestly, I told Sheriff Bristow and those SBI people everything I know ages ago. Why don't you just talk to them?"

"This is a separate investigation."

"Well, fine, but I just finished a performance, and I had a beer—"

"Well, this won't be too formal," Danny said. "All we need is a quieter place. Why don't we run out to Fat Willy's on the causeway and talk there? They ain't so crowded and their jukebox ain't so loud."

Gerry toyed with the long strap of the leather handbag slung over her shoulder. Her tiny red mouth pursed. At last she nodded, yellow hair gleaming in the light from Carney's. "All right," she said. "I guess I can't get in any trouble with the Chief of Police and a chaperon too."

"Then let's go," Danny said.

The more he saw of her, the more Danny had the feeling that the plastered-on sex appeal was illusion; at twenty-three, alcohol was already her thing. He could tell by the speed with which she put away the first beer and worked into the second as she sat across from them in a booth in the tavern on the causeway, long earrings and brass bangles on her wrists winking in the muted glow of the neon in the window. The place was like a barn, easily accommodating its fifty or so patrons without crowding, and although its record player too went endlessly, the country and western it played did not drown out all conversation.

"Well, she was a funny girl, y'know? She used to ask the weirdest questions. At first I thought it was a put-on, but then I realized she just didn't know, she'd never had a chance to learn. She was immature for her age, you understand? About three years or four behind herself."

"I think we know that about her," Danny said. "What we want to know is about the men she went with."

"Well, there was Peter Hogan, you know, the night she—" The tiny mouth pursed and Gerry turned her beer bottle around and around.

"We know about him too. What we want to know is about any other men she might of had to do with while she was down here."

"Well, I told Sheriff Bristow all that."

"Yeah, but—"

"I wish you'd ask him. Anyhow, I don't remember it all exactly."

"You can if you try," Danny said.

"I don't know. I don't want to get anybody else in trouble anyhow." She pouted, looking down at her glass.

"Well," Danny said, but Paula cut in, leaning across the table, voice soft. "Gerry. Look at me."

Reluctantly the girl raised her head.

"Listen," Paula said, "Daisy was your friend. And somebody murdered her brutally, and that somebody hasn't been arrested. For all we know, he's still at large on this island, and maybe he'll kill again, maybe another of your friends, maybe even you. Raped, strangled with a rope, thrown off the bridge in the dead of night. As long as he remains free, no girl can really walk this island day or night or date a stranger without running the risk of— Do you see what I'm driving at? You owe it to Daisy, but you owe it to all your friends in the show right now too; you owe it to yourself."

"But I don't know who killed her. Maybe it was Peter Hogan."

"Maybe it was. We're not asking you to tell us who killed her. All we're asking you to do is answer a few questions. For Daisy's sake, and for the sake of all the other girls in the show.

You don't have to accuse anybody, you don't have to get anybody in trouble; all you have to do is tell us the truth."

The girl did not answer.

"Did you and she double-date?" Paula pressed gently.

After two very long seconds Gerry said, "Yeah. Twice."

"With whom?"

"I went with George French, a boy I knew. She went with a man who'd picked her up on the pier."

Danny sat up very straight. "Who was he?"

Gerry ignored the question. "It was about a week after we got down here. We were still tied up almost every minute, but she used to get up early, borrow my car, and go out to the beach to swim. She was standing on the end of the pier one morning letting the wind blow in her face when he came up and asked her if she was a gypsy."

"Who—" Danny began again, but Paula signaled him to silence.

"He was some operator," Gerry said. "She really fell for him, came back and told me all about him. To her it was a big adventure. He'd asked her for a late date, after rehearsals, but she was scared, you know? Didn't want to go out alone that late with somebody she'd just met. So we double-dated that night, George and I and Daisy and him. No big deal, we just had a swim, then we messed around the pier. Then George took us both home in his car. We did the same thing two nights later."

Her beer was running low; Paula nudged Danny, and he comprehended, signaled for the waitress. "Did she keep on seeing him?" Paula asked.

"Until they broke off about a week before she went out with Peter."

Tensely Paula's leg touched Danny's beneath the table. "What sort of relationship did they have?"

155

"Ha," said Gerry. "You tell me." The waitress brought the beer and Danny poured it. Gerry took a long drink. "Thanks. Well, she thought she was in love with him for a while, until he turned her off."

"Turned her off?"

"She never would go out with him at nights, that late. But she saw him in the morning before rehearsals and in the afternoons if she wasn't on call, and for the first several days, you know, she was in a kinda romantic fog. She'd come back and tell me everything they did and fill the Goddamn room up with seashells they'd found, you know? They'd walk on the beach or swim or he'd drive her around to see the sights and buy her lunch somewhere; like I said, for her that was a very big deal. Heavy stuff."

"And then?" Paula asked.

Gerry drank again. "Well, like I said, he tore it." She laughed harshly, yet with sadness. "It was in the afternoon. I was just getting ready to go out to the Theater and wondering where the hell she was, and she slammed in looking like the world had ended. We were late for rehearsal because I couldn't get her to stop crying." Gerry paused. "To tell you the truth, I never found out what he did to her. But as near as I could understand, he took her up to his apartment over the art gallery and tried to lay her."

"The art gallery," Danny repeated. And then he comprehended.

"Gordon," he said. "Wallace Gordon."

Gerry Morse raised her weary child-tart's face. "Yeah," she said, "that's who it was."

Shoal Island was dark now at two in the morning as Danny Rush and Paula Murphy drove north along it. Only the fishing pier, its double row of lights like twin strings of jewels spread out across the water, was still open, for fishermen, like drunkards, went home only as a last resort. Paula leaned back against the seat, staring upward, throat a smooth curve pale in darkness. "I should be very excited," she said. "But mostly I'm awfully tired."

"Me too. But I promised Felix and the others I'd come by and tell them what we found out. They'll be waiting up."

"You must be tireder than I am," she said. "You were up so late last night, had to go on duty this morning. You must be absolutely dead for sleep."

"I am, but I'm wound up too. I git like this sometimes. So nervous it takes me a long time to throttle down."

"Poor Danny," she said and put her hand on his thigh. "I hope this all comes out just right for you. I hope it comes out exactly the way you want it."

"I hope so," Danny said. She did not know how vital to that she was, but he would make her see before long. He put his hand on hers.

It was strange, he thought, the difference between love and lust. Tonight, automatically, he had lusted after Gerry Morse, with those long legs, pert fanny, little red lips that drew on a cigarette as if it were a— But if she were with him now, merely touching her hand would have no significance, give him no fulfillment in itself, be important only as it led toward sex. But with Paula every touch, every moment, had meaning, compensation, apart from sex; simply being with her was as good in one way as sex was in another. "You know what?" he asked. "Compared to you that Morse girl sure was pitiful."

"Compared to her I look like a plow horse." Then she laughed. "But I know what you mean. Scared little kid, hiding in her mama's makeup, daring life with her ass poked out from beneath that miniskirt, hiding from it in her beer.

Maybe I'll use her in a confession sometime." She withdrew her hand. "But thank you very kindly for the compliment." She paused and, as if she wanted to change the subject, said, "Tell me some more about this Wallace Gordon."

"Well, I've already told you most of what I know. He's about my age, maybe a little older, owns the art gallery about a mile up the beach, and another one at Virginia Beach, I understand. Lives in Virginia, he's only down here for part of the summer every year. Anyhow, I can see where he would have swarmed all over Daisy Canfield; he looks like a damned movie star. You remember one called Dana Andrews?"

"Yes," she said.

"Somethin like that. And that's the main thing I've heard about him, that he really lays the women waste. Of course, he meets a lot of 'em, they come in his gallery. That's his reputation, anyhow, what they call a cocksman. Snappy dresser, seems to have plenty of money. They say he's been married and divorced. He lives upstairs over his gallery when he's down here."

"Is he down here now?"

"I don't know." He broke off as he reached the intersection he wanted, turning left toward the Sound. This road too was paved, but narrow and full of chuck holes, and he drove carefully.

It led through a desert of sand and and scrub, the larger, more expensive beach houses giving way to little weather-beaten cottages with the marks of permanent dwellings: their yards littered with junk, nets piled on their porches, pickup trucks parked in their drives. "This is Old Shoal Village," he said, "the original settlement on this island." Ahead, where the road ended, in what was hardly more than a shack, lights shone through windows, and Felix's battered truck and Larry's car were parked out front. Danny pulled up behind them, and when he and Paula got out, they could smell fish and the stench of brackish water from the pools trapped in the sound-side sand flats; she probably would not notice it, but indeed, to Danny, the whole island had had a characteristic stink for over a year, sign that development had outrun its sewer system.

They went up the uncertain wooden steps, knocked, and at Felix's growl entered. In the tiny cluttered living room Larry and Peter Hogan were playing gin rummy; Felix, on the sofa, was sharpening an ax. All three were naked to the waist.

The players put down their cards, and Peter Hogan scraped back his chair. "Well?" His eyes shone in the yellow light from the pigtail socket.

"Well," Danny said, "you're not all by yourself any more. We got a brand new suspect, Hogan."

"Gordon!" Felix exploded. "That slick son of a bitch! Hell, I should have guessed. I've known him for five years, and he's worse than I am when it comes to women. Go on, Danny."

They were sitting around the table drinking instant coffee.

"All right," Danny said. "Well, according to Gerry Morse, he and Daisy dated pretty steady in the daytime for two weeks, and she was gone on him, you understand? And then one day she comes back to the room all in tears and as nearly as Gerry can tell, what happened is that Wallace Gordon must have taken her upstairs over the art gallery and got down to cases with her. Apparently she had to fight like hell to get loose at all—"

"But he didn't lay her," Larry said.

"How could he have? The Medical Examiner said she was a virgin up to that night," Felix said.

"All the same, he did something more than try to kiss her and give her a squeeze," Danny said. "From Gerry's account,

159

he got pretty close to home base before she stopped him, because afterwards Daisy began to blame herself. She kept carrying on about how it was her fault for letting him go too far, which probably means she got somewhat carried away herself."

"My guess," Paula put in, "is that it was a premiere performance of what could have happened in the car the night she died. Probably she let him undress her to the waist, but when he tried anything beyond that, she balked. And then, apparently, he got rough with her and that frightened and revolted her." She paused. "The more I think about our Daisy, the more I think she must have been a bit neurotic herself. I suppose she had reason to be, with that beauty of hers, and dropped into a society completely strange. . . . She must have felt like a pork chop in a pack of wolves."

"Go on," Hogan said tensely. "What else is there?"

"Well, there's considerable," Danny said, "and how Bristow and Gordon kept it under cover so long I don't know. Apparently Daisy told Gordon she never wanted to see him again; and apparently Gordon wasn't about to take no for an answer. He called her up, both at her room and at the Theater. And he and George French—Gerry Morse dated him, he's the one that sold you the marijuana, Hogan, right?—seemed to be good buddies. Because French called Daisy a couple of times on Gordon's behalf, and he asked Gerry to use her influence too."

"Actually," Paula put in, "it would seem that Gordon fell in love with Daisy himself."

Felix laughed shortly. "You don't know Wally Gordon. Oh, he's a smooth romantic cat, I reckon. But he never loved anybody or anything in his life but that dong of his. To tell the truth, I really believe he's a little crazy. Score, that's all he can think of. How many can I rack up this summer? All he wants to be is the fastest gun in town."

"How'd you get to know him so well?"

Felix's grin split his beard. "I told you, I make it my business to know *everybody*." Then he was serious. "No kidding, you oughta hear him talk about women. He hates 'em; honest to God, he really hates 'em. He talks about how you have to treat 'em rough. slap 'em around, that's what they love. That's why his wife divorced him, he beat on her too much."

"He certainly must have confided in you," Paula said, her voice almost suspicious.

"I've taken him rattlesnake hunting twice."

"Rattlesnake hunting?"

"Yep. There's a lot of 'em on the mainland, and a lab in Norfolk pays good money for live ones. Well, a couple of years ago I accidentally killed a couple instead of taking 'em alive, so just as an experiment I skinned 'em and tanned the hides. Then, just for the hell of it, I made wristbands out of 'em and barged in on Gordon and asked him if he could sell 'em. He thought they were great, asked me how I got 'em, and I told him about snake hunting. He offered me ten dollars if I'd take him someday, so I did. And I'll say this for him, I have never seen anybody quicker and colder than him in all my life. He's the only man besides myself I've ever seen pop a snake's head off."

Paula's mouth opened. She stared wordlessly.

"Nothing to it if you know the technique, you're strong enough, and you got the guts. Grab a rattlesnake by the tail and snap him like a whip. First crack breaks his spine anyhow, if you're good enough, in two or three cracks you can pop his head right off. Of course, he can't be no six-foot diamondback thick as your leg."

"Good heavens," Paula whispered.

"He was proud of that," Felix said. "Proud enough so we sat around and talked, and I tanned the skin for him; you'll see it now if you go in his gallery and look in the office. Anyhow, we went twice, and afterwards we sat up in his apartment and got flat drunk and talked, and that's how I know about his divorce and how he feels about women."

"Well, he is a love, isn't he?" Paula asked.

"He's a Goddamned arrogant overbearing self-centered son of a bitch," Felix said. "But go on, what's the rest of it?"

"Completely in consonance with what you said," Paula answered. "He called and called her and she wouldn't talk to him. One night at the Theater she left her pocketbook hanging at the back door in the dressing room, the same bag she was carrying when she was killed, a big tote. When she came back after the performance, there was a gift-wrapped package sticking out of it. Inside there was a gold and enamel necklace, no card, nothing to show who it was from."

"So he just crept up and put it in her handbag?" Larry asked.

"That's not the least of it. Gerry took Daisy home from the Theater one afternoon, let her out at the boardinghouse, and went on downtown to do some shopping. When Gerry came home, Daisy was sitting on the bed all wrought up. It seems that when she came upstairs and entered her room, she found Wallace Gordon sitting there."

Peter Hogan asked tensely, "What happened then?"

"Apparently nothing. The landlady was right downstairs. Gordon made another pitch, but he didn't get physical. But he kept calling after that and Daisy kept hanging up on him and . . . And that was the end of it until the night she went out with you."

"Well, Jesus," Hogan said in a strange voice. He stared down at his big hands, "Well, Jesus."

Nobody else spoke. After a moment Hogan said, a little shakily, "That could have been the way it was, you know. Gordon was hot after Daisy, and George French was his friend. Suppose . . . Suppose Gordon had asked Daisy for a date on that first free night and she'd hung up on him? Suppose after French saw us on the pier, he called Gordon and told him who Daisy was out with? Suppose . . . Gordon hung around her house waiting for me to bring her home, and when I didn't, suppose he went looking for her? Maybe he drove to my place, waited outside. And when she came out, he was there."

"When he was after a woman," Felix said, "he wouldn't give up. No more than a bulldog will turn loose."

"And so he took her somewhere," Hogan went on. "Either out by the sand pit where they found her bag or to the Theater—or to both. And got her undressed to the waist, and she fought after that and he hit her and . . . maybe had some rope in his car, and he finished her with that. Threw her off the bridge—" His voice was suddenly ferocious. "God damn him! God damn the man."

"Easy, Hogan," Danny said. "We don't know yet that he did it. He's bound to have an alibi, probably a lot stronger one than yours"—his tone was acid—"or Bristow wouldn't have let him go."

"If he does, it'll be a woman," Felix said. "I'll bet on that."

"Is that all?" Larry asked, playing with the cards on the table before him.

"No. There's one macabre little footnote," Paula said. "After Daisy disappeared, but before her body was found, Wallace Gordon asked Gerry Morse for a date. Nothing, she said, ever scared her more terribly than that."

Larry's eyes gleamed as he looked up. "What did she do?"

"She went with him," Danny said harshly. "Because she

knew there wasn't any other way to git rid of him. He took her to his apartment over the gallery and they got drunk and she let him screw her. He never mentioned Daisy Canfield the whole time and he never bothered her again."

Larry shook his head incredulously.

"I told you, he's kind of like a rattlesnake himself," Felix said.

"Yeah. Well, I'm goin by the gallery tomorrow and size him up again. Meanwhile, I don't want anybody else hangin around there to make him suspicious, gogglin at him. I don't want him to get the notion that anything is up." He was beginning to realize now how tired he was, muscles trembling slightly with fatigue, eyes grainy. "Because we got a long way to go with him yet. I been through this once with Bubba Dixon and I won't have it happen again. We got to have evidence, hard and fast, that'll stand up in court. Until we git it, we're just spittin in the wind. We got to find out what his alibi was and see if there's any way to crack it. And I hope there's some way we can do that without Bristow and Jordan findin out, or I'm liable to get my ass fired before we get started good. I already stuck my neck out tonight talkin to Gerry Morse, and I'm just hopin she won't feed it back to the Sheriff." He stood up. "Anyhow, that's all for tonight. Y'all can chew it over all you want, but lay low; Hogan, especially you. We'll see you tomorrow sometime. Come on, Paula."

"Yes," she said rising. "We'll all be like Scarlett O'Hara and think about it tomorrow. Good night, gentlemen."

When they were outside, Danny said, "You drive, you don't mind. I'm kind of bushed."

"Sure." Paula slid behind the Mustang's wheel, turned it nicely, drove in silence until they were on the main road again, purring along the sleeping beachfront. Presently she said, "When you go to the gallery tomorrow, stop by and pick me up."

"No," Danny said.

"But I want to see him for myself."

"You keep away from him, you hear?" Danny said. "I don't want you going near him."

She smiled. "You're afraid for me? You think I'm that seductive?"

"I just don't want you near a man like that."

She was silent for a moment. He added, "Remember, I'm in charge of this investigation. I expect you to do just like Larry, Felix, and Hogan—follow my or— my instructions."

"Yes," she said. "I made that promise, didn't I?"

"You did."

"Well," she said, "I suppose in that case, that's that." She turned into the court, pulled up before her cottage, where Danny's car was parked, and they got out. "It's been an exciting evening," she said. *"Intensely* interesting. Do you want a nightcap?"

Danny said, "I'm so tired I'm walking in my sleep."

Paula smiled. She reached up, pulled his head down, and kissed his mouth solidly, if not passionately. "Well, don't drive in it. Be careful, Danny. Good night."

"Good night," he said and stood there until she was safely inside with the lights turned on. Then he drove back to his own trailer. When he opened the door, he found an envelope on the floor. In it was a notice reminding him that his trailer rent was ten days overdue. He threw it on the table and went to bed. For only a moment he lay awake, fireworks of fatigue exploding behind his closed lids. Then he slept.

Chapter 10

Well up Shoal Island and away from the honky-tonk atmosphere of the piers, in a place where a gap in development actually provided a view of the ocean, the Seafront Galleries were housed in a solid brick two-story building, itself and its large parking lot enclosed by an old-fashioned rail fence. Danny parked his car and got out, raising his eyes to glance at the curtained upstairs windows; then he went through the gallery's double doors.

He found himself in a spacious air-conditioned room, its walls hung with paintings and etchings, a table in the center bearing handicrafts and art books and volumes about the Coast and Outer Banks, a long showcase near the door filled with other gift items. There were planters full of greenery, and the quiet, uncrowded atmosphere was restful, luxurious, and attractive. A few people ranged the walls of this room and another leading off of it, but the only employee in here was a girl behind a cash register. Danny, in civilian clothes, looked at the paintings as he edged toward the rear, where an office door was partly open.

Mostly they were seascapes, old piers, old houses, boats at dock, and always the sand and ocean and the sky. He liked them because they were full of realistic and recognizable objects, but was astounded by the prices: two hundred, three hundred and fifty dollars for a *painting?* Who had that kind of money to throw away? Edging closer to the office, he peeped in, but it was empty. Working his way around the other wall, he wondered if Wallace Gordon was even on Shoal Island now; and he was trying to decide whether he should ask the girl behind the register when the man and woman came out of the other room.

She was in her thirties, her blond hair streaked with dyed-in silver, her body good in a white belted summer dress, her legs excellent, and her face, which was perhaps very pretty, obscured by great sunglasses. Danny could tell at once that she had money and that she was on the loose; it was the way she walked, the way, as she laughed, she overdid it just a trifle. "I don't really believe it; you didn't!"

"I certainly did," Wallace Gordon said. "It was an old leatherette-covered card table and we just set the paint buckets and turpentine cans on it while we were redecorating. There were plenty of cigarette burns and drink stains too. Anyhow, when we got through, one of the workmen said, 'Mr. Gordon, I'll swear if that thing don't look better than some of those crazy pictures you sell.' And that gave me the idea. I took the cover off the card table, stretched and framed it, gave it a title, Dead End Number Four, and put a price of three hundred dollars on it. Sold it the second day to a dealer from New York. That's why I say art is in the eye of the beholder."

"Well, really—"

He took her arm. "Incidentally, before you go, there's something here I want you to see." Drawing her to the table in the center of the room, he went on: "There's an old woman down on Ocracoke who knots these handbags out of old fishnets; I really think they're very good, genuine, not like most of the made-in-Japan junk that floods the market now. This is the old-fashioned kind of craftsmanship."

He was a tall and ruggedly handsome man, his brown hair graying at the temples and his face deeply tanned. His eyes were deep-set, a vivid intense green. His voice was deep too, and smooth, bereft of all but a faint softness of Southern accent. He wore a light houndstooth sport jacket and sharply creased gray slacks in such a way that the clothes looked even better than they were; his body was designed to make the most of clothes, wide in the shoulders, flat in the stomach, trim in waist and hips, and long in legs. He bore himself with the ease of an aging athlete who meticulously keeps in shape.

"Anyway," he said, picking one of the bags from the table, "here." He thrust it into the woman's hands. "Compliments of the establishment."

"Oh, I couldn't—"

"Oh, yes you can. Just carry it and use it and tell people where it came from and . . . think of Seafront Galleries and Wallace Gordon on occasion."

She looked down at it, then up at him, as he towered over her. "Yes," she said. "Yes, I'll do that. It's very kind of you. Really, it's lovely, it's a very lovely thing. I'll tell everybody where it came from."

"Fine. Of course, if you'd like another color . . . But it seemed to me this one went with your hair, and if I remember correctly . . ." He reached out, tilted back her glasses. "Yes. Your eyes."

She looked up at him, lips slightly parted; she seemed breathless. Finally: "I . . . hardly know what to say."

Wallace Gordon smiled, a slow, easy, somehow intimate quirk of lips, and Danny, from this angle, could see the amazing way his eyes warmed as they looked into hers. In that moment the man was so attractive that he even felt some amorphous response within himself. Jesus, he thought, awed.

"Don't say anything," Gordon replied gently. "Enjoy it in good health, show it to your friends, and . . . come back to see me."

"Yes. Yes, I . . . Oh, I will."

She seemed fixed to the spot, unable to move; but apparently Gordon was ready to get rid of her. His hand touched her arm, and he guided her around and she went quite meekly to the door. There she took her glasses off, and Danny saw that she was indeed quite pretty, though she was aging fast; the lenses had concealed deep crow's-feet at the corners of her eyes. Still smiling, Gordon spoke to her a moment more; once he chuckled deeply. Then he opened the door. "Goodbye," she said a little shrilly, and there was the ghost of a nervous giggle in the word. He answered her in a deep, smooth voice, and she went out. Gordon stood there watching her cross the parking lot, absently rubbing the back of his left hand, thickly furred with dark hair, with his right. Once she stopped, half turned, waved, her teeth gleaming in a kind of hysteric grin. Gordon raised his hand and dropped it, nodding, and she went on. When she had got into her car, he remained standing there, taking a cigarette from a pack, clamping it between his lips, lighting it, and blowing two plumes of smoke from his nostrils with obvious self-satisfaction. Then, as if his mind had changed gears, he swung around abruptly, surveyed the gallery and saw Danny Rush. Danny quickly turned his head and pretended deep interest in a painting. Gordon started toward him, then veered away, as if he had read Danny's credit rating in his clothes and knew he was only browsing. Heels clacking on the tiled floor, he went to the office. As he opened the door wider, Danny got a glimpse of the long broad rattlesnake skin mounted above the desk. Then he closed the door.

It was, strangely, as if something had gone out of the air, leaving it flatter and more tasteless. His presence had been so tangible that his absence was too. Danny Rush turned away, aware that his palms were sweating and feeling a kind of mingled nausea and excitement in his belly. Good God, he thought. A nineteen-year-old girl against *that*?

Almost dazedly he went to the door and out into the bright hot sunlight. He got in his car and sat there for a full minute before he turned the switch. He knew now. Evidence had nothing to do with it; this was pure gut certainty. He had just seen the murderer of Daisy Canfield.

It had been his intention to stop at Paula's, but instead he drove straight to his trailer. He was wholly preoccupied now with something filling him that was not yet within his power to identify. But it generated in him a surge of masculinity almost sexual, a strange sense of purpose and new determination. Things vague and formless were taking shape, becoming concrete. It was something momentous, and for an interval he wanted to be alone and let it build, define itself.

At the trailer he made a cup of instant coffee, found a pad and pencil, put an ashtray on the table, all with a new brisk, methodical manner. He sat down, smoking and only watching the smoke drift and curl.

And now he thought he began to understand.

For once he had found something worthy of himself.

All his life, it seemed, he had groped in a fog of

inconsequentialities, not challenged by any of them, only harassed. That whole time he had been seeking something without knowing what it was—more than love, more than prosperity, more than peace and quiet. He had gone into the Army looking for it, and maybe too marrying Ruth had been part of his search; but neither of them, nor even this job here with its little salary and its alloy badge, was it. It was something to match an inner vision of himself, something enormous and important enough to be worthy of the man he had once conceived himself to be. He was not designed to count nickels and dimes and balance check stubs and write parking tickets and dribble his life away in endless tiny details of survival.

He was Wahab Rush's son, and Wahab Rush had not done that. Such things made a man too small and shriveled; Wahab Rush had been a giant, doing a giant's work, contending against the most enormous and brutal force on earth for the lives of men. He had had a purpose, one of such huge importance that his own survival had even ceased to count, another petty inconsequence, and in that purpose, that mission—that was the word—he had known a kind of freedom his son had never tasted, and a joy; and the fact that he had met his death in its fulfillment was not a tragedy but a glory. What he did, he did not for money, not for gain, but because some magnificence within him would accept no less, some power he felt inside himself could find no equal challenge but the sea and death. And, Danny saw now, that was what was wrong with Wahab Rush's son. He had not found his purpose yet; his strength and his magnificence had been frittered away on tiny things, the little concerns imposed by little men, and that was what had caused such profound unhappiness and almost ruined him.

He ground out the cigarette, lit another, sipped the coffee

that was going cold.

Aiming too low, Danny thought. Letting them tie me up. Being bound by all the little things, like running a race with chains wrapped around your legs, and forgetting who you were and where you started to, forgetting how strong you were without the chains. He felt a sense of bursting bonds, and all because he had seen Wallace Gordon plain.

So far he had been uncertain and unsatisfied in this matter of Daisy Canfield's death because it had only been presented to him in and he had only thought in terms of his own gain, and that was not enough. Money, a house on Shipsbell Road, a sheriff's badge, even Paula; none of those was enough; they were smaller things; he had needed something larger.

Now he had it. He had seen today a man of intelligence, strength, and power who had raped and killed a young girl who must have wanted very much to live, and who went on seeking victims. He still could not account for his certainty, but the certainty was there: of calculated evil. It was not as if Gordon were someone like Bubba Dixon, driven to desperation and unable to comprehend his drives. It was not as if he were the lawyer, victim of drink. It was not as if he could not find satisfaction with other women who would give it to him willingly. It was simply that there was in him a malign force, like a storm at sea, and surely it was as important to stop such a man as to bring a sailor from the ocean. If what he was and what he represented were not checked, even eliminated, then it would be as if Wahab Rush had refused to take his boat out.

Beside that thought, all the rest of it shrank to nearly nothing. If he got the Sheriff's badge, well and good; he knew now how he would use it. His purpose could run beyond this Wallace Gordon, there were other Wallace Gordons against whom he could contend. If he made money, fine. And as for

Paula— The certainty in him did not flicker. This was the best way to bind her to him. There was nothing in Danny Rush, the traffic cop and ticket writer, the small man dealing confusedly with little things, to attract a girl like her. There was nothing in money either. That had been the trouble all along, the faint defensiveness he had sensed in her. She had said it—she respected strength and power, and he had displayed none yet. But she would see.

Then he thought, his mind almost clicking like a trap, So damn much for daydreaming. Now get busy. He went back to the table, rolled the pencil in his hand, bent over the pad, and tried to bring his mind from the exultant general to the taxing particular.

Bristow had questioned Gerry Morse, and Bristow knew about Wallace Gordon. It was, of course, not likely that Bristow recognized in him what Danny had seen today; Bristow was a politician, and eighteen years of being one as well as a lawman would have dulled such perceptions in him, if he had ever had them, they were bound to. All the same, Bristow knew his job within the limits in which he had chosen to perform, and he would have checked out Gordon. That he had taken no action and that no word of Gordon as a suspect had leaked out must indicate that Bristow considered Gordon's alibi ironclad. Nor had Gerry Morse spread rumors about him; her silence would have stemmed from fear. Anyhow, the alibi—Felix was right, it had to be a woman. The question was Who?

Danny scribbled a note on the pad. "Felix snake hunt?"

He sat back and looked at it. Maybe Felix could get him drunk afterwards and—

Danny shook his head. Nobody would draw anything out of that man drunk or sober. That would be overmatching Felix.

Maybe Paula could—

173

He abandoned that immediately. He did not want her near the man.

Of course Bristow and the State Bureau of Investigation would know who she was and maybe even where she lived now. But could he get that information out of them? And what sort of backlash would there be? Not that, in his present mood, he was afraid of backlash, but—

He reached for another cigarette, but his hand stopped and he looked around as he heard a car pull up before the trailer door. Its engine was soft and smooth, neither Felix's truck, Larry's sports car, nor, judging from the power of the sound, Paula's Mustang. Danny rose as he heard someone get out of it and knock on the trailer door.

Opening it, he stared at the man in the doorway for a wordless second in complete surprise.

"Hello, Chief Rush," Harold Krause, the lawyer, said. He cleared his throat. His voice was low, a trifle shaky. "Could you, ah, spare me a few minutes?"

Danny blinked and nodded. For a moment he had the quick dismaying certainty that someone had hired the attorney to prosecute him for a bad debt or check. But in his present mood he was proof against that basically inconsequential fear. "Sure," he said. "Come on in, Mr. Krause."

Of medium height, Harold Krause was in his forties now, but looking older. Nearly bald, only a few strands of pale hair lying across a reddened, freckled scalp, he wore thick glasses over bulging brown eyes. His face was thin, but its skin was slack and loose where once it had been stretched with bloat. He had a nervous mannerism of folding both lips inward, then extruding them. As he entered the trailer, Danny became sure that he was not here on any errand of aggression; he was hesitant, almost shy, like, Danny thought, a whipped dog dreading another kick.

"What can I do for you?" Danny asked.

Krause sat down at the table, hand toying nervously with his necktie. Again he cleared his throat. "I understand . . . I've heard . . . that you're starting some kind of new investigation into the Daisy Canfield murder."

Danny tensed. "Where'd you hear that?"

"I don't know exactly. It's just around. Everybody says it." Krause smiled uncertainly. "People have made sure I was well advised."

Danny's mouth thinned. Felix, he thought with utter disgust. I should have known he couldn't keep it to himself. Got to put on his act before the crowd.

"Is it . . . true?" Krause went on, looking up at Danny through thick lenses.

Danny sought exactly the right words. "I'm not at liberty to say."

"Oh." Krause tugged at the necktie, and his shoulders slumped a little beneath the jacket of his double-knit suit. "Well, I guess that means you are."

Danny did not speak. Krause's lips went in and out, and Danny had the feeling he was trying to gather courage. "Well, have you had any leads yet?"

"I'm not at liberty—" It seemed the perfect all-purpose answer.

"Please, Chief. Have you found out anything? I want to know what you've found out. I . . . you know why it's important to me."

"Yeah, I guess I know," Danny said. "You still ain't sure you didn't kill her, are you?"

"Of course I'm sure," Krause answered with a try at spirit, certainty. "That's why I came here. I wanted to tell you that I'm innocent, you don't need to waste your time on me."

"I'm not wasting any time on you."

175

Krause seemed not to hear. "Because," he continued rapidly, words tumbling out, "Sheriff Bristow has already checked me out, and it wasn't me. If it was anybody, it was that fella Peter Hogan and—"

"All right." Danny said. "Maybe it was."

"Then why stir up all this mess again? Why rake up all this old nastiness? Everything's died down now, everybody's just about forgotten, the girl's dead and gone, what difference does it make? I mean, it was an awful thing, but— Nobody can bring her back. And you know this town, you know the way rumors go around, talk . . ." His voice rose. "You'll stir it all up again."

Danny shook his head. "I don't aim—"

But Krause bent forward earnestly. "Chief, you're a drinking man yourself, I've heard that. But I hope to God you're not one like I was. I wouldn't wish that on any human being. But maybe you've got some idea, maybe you can imagine what—"

He sucked in a breath. "I've done pretty good. I made one woman happy by letting go of her, and I've tried to make another happy by taking care of her. I've got my practice back in hand and I've not had a drink of whiskey in just about three years. Do you know what that means?"

"It's something you can be proud of," Danny said, and he felt a certain admiration, even envy.

"Yes, but it hasn't been easy. It . . . the way I did it, I just put it out of my mind: that night I lost, Daisy Canfield, everything up until then. I decided to start over, fresh, but all the same . . . You don't know how much strength it's taken. More, really, than I ever thought I had. It still takes all my strength. Every morning when I get up, I know I'm going to have to fight a battle, and every day I know I might lose, and, believe me, I know the penalty for losing." The hand went to the tie again, and Danny saw that it was shaking. "But . . . I have struck a . . . a very delicate balance, you see? And it can be upset so easy, you understand? And if it is—" He turned his hand over, brought it down all the way from the table to his knee. "Crash," he said reedily. "Crash."

Danny looked at the floor under Krause's hand.

"I'm not out to pin anything on you," he said slowly. "I got no idea you did it."

"That's not it," Krause said. "I mean, you just don't know—" His lips worked in and out for a second. "I haven't made myself clear." Then his eyes brightened, turning suddenly crafty and hopeful. "Of course . . . Chief, I'm not exactly loaded money-wise. But maybe— Would you guarantee to forget this whole thing for two hundred dollars?"

Danny frowned, surprised to find himself not tempted. "Mr Krause, I tell you, I'm not doin anything that's gonna hurt you."

"Chief, I don't think you can judge what's going to— Five hundred." Krause let out a fluttering breath and took a checkbook from his coat pocket. "Five hundred dollars right now."

This was temptation of a different magnitude. This time Danny hesitated for a second. Then he shook his head. "Forget it, Mr. Krause. Five hundred or a thousand. Just forget it; that ain't the point." He tried to make his voice as gentle as possible. "I just don't think you ought to be disturbed about anything. I just think you oughta go on about your business and not worry."

Krause sat there looking at him wordlessly for a moment, those lips thinning and pursing. Then he nodded. "Yeah. Yeah, I guess that's right. Of course. Sure, that's right."

"It certainly is," said Danny.

"I won't worry," Krause said, and he rose. He rubbed his cheek hard, leaving a red spot on the slack skin. "No, I absolutely won't worry. Because I'm in the clear. Well. I suppose now I'd better go. Chief, I appreciate your time. Thank you for your advice."

Danny stood up. "I won't mention this to nobody if you don't."

"Of course I won't." Krause went to the door. "Thanks again, Chief."

"You're welcome," Danny said. When Krause had gone out, he turned away, biting his lip.

"God damn Felix," he said aloud.

Now the beans were spilled. If Krause knew, that meant that Bristow would have heard, and Jordan.

Realizing that, Danny was surprised to feel no fear, only relief. He had to do what he had to do, and he could not have done it anyway bound by the necessity of keeping it from them. Felix had saved him from the stress of making a decision, that was all. Now he simply had to work out the details and borrow Paula's car, for where he would go was a long journey each way, and he was not sure his own would make it.

When he knocked at her cottage door, she appeared, clad once more in the yellow dress that became her so. "Hi, come in." She smiled at him.

Danny entered and took the initiative to kiss her briefly on the mouth, once they were in the living room. She returned the kiss. Then: "It's a little early for martinis, and besides you've got to go on duty. Want a cup of coffee?"

"No, thanks, I'm full of it. Look, I—" He broke off. He was not even facing fully in that direction, but somehow it had drawn his gaze to it like a magnet: the handbag lying on the sofa. Yellow and brown, it was made of knotted fishnet.

Danny went to it and picked it up. Then he let it drop and turned. "I told you not to hang around Gordon's place," he said. "You been out there this morning."

Still smiling, she answered. "Did you really expect me to stay away? After all, I have my curiosity too."

"Did he give this to you?" Danny asked fiercely.

Paula blinked, smile fading. "No. I paid nine dollars for it. I think it's rather nice."

Danny was silent for a moment. Then he gestured; it did not really matter. With great interest he asked. "Did you see him? What did you make of him?"

"Yes, I saw him, but only from afar. He was with another customer. And he didn't ask me," she continued, a faint bite in her voice, "to his apartment or try to put a rope around my neck." Then, very seriously, she said. "But I think he would be perfectly capable of doing either or both. I see now why Gerry Morse kept her mouth shut about him. No wonder she was frightened. He's not something that a girl like her—or Daisy—could possibly handle."

"No, he ain't," Danny said. "And he's the one who did it."

Her brows went up. "You've found some evidence?"

"I ain't found anything. I just looked at him. Compared to him, Peter Hogan is just a little kid. There— Well, I just know, that's all. He's the one we want."

"Well," Paula said and turned away to get her cigarettes. "What will you do about it?"

"Whatever I've got to do to hang it on him," Danny said, and what was in his voice made her turn and look keenly at him. "You can bet on that."

Two tiny vertical lines appeared just above her nose.

"Anyhow, Felix has blown the whistle on us. I figured he would sooner or later. When he gets into somethin like this, he's like a kid with a new toy, he just can't sit still. So I don't have to worry about Bristow findin out any longer; that's settled. What the hell, all they can do is fire me. In the

179

meantime, I'm gonna check out that bastard's alibi."

"How'll you do that?" she asked quietly, her eyes still on his face.

"Well, first I got to find out who gave it to him. And the only way I know to do that is to drive over to the capital and talk to the SBI."

"Do you think they'll tell you?"

"One thing's certain, Bristow won't. But, by God, I'm an officer of the law and they send me bulletins all the time tellin how they want to be of service to me and cooperate with me, and— I'm gonna try. What I'd like to do is borrow your car for a day; you can use mine while I'm gone. It's about a five-hundred-mile round trip and I wouldn't count on that old clunker of mine to make it."

"Why," she said and stubbed out the cigarette. "Why, yes, surely. Of course you can have the car." She added, "But there's a condition."

"What's that?"

"I go with you."

Danny hesitated. He would, of course, like to have her; he could never get enough of having her with him. But the scribbled balance in his checkbook flashed into his mind. Possibly, in fact likely, he would have to stay overnight. Even if he picked the cheapest hotel in town and ate only hot dogs, it would leave him short for the trailer rent.

As if she could read his mind, she said, "And let me pay the expenses."

His face reddened. "I couldn't—"

"Now don't be a male chauvinist pig," she said with amusement.

"I ain't being nothing. Only—"

"Then half. We'll go dutch. That's not too much for your pride, is it?"

Slowly Danny smiled. The trailer rent: a pettiness. He was tired of them, ready for the big reach and the daring gamble; he could deal with details later. "No. My pride ain't that big." But then the smile went away. "All the same, you understand this won't be no pleasure trip. I'm serious about this now."

"Yes," she said very quietly, "you are. I can certainly see that."

"I'll arrange things with the other boys. If it all works out, we'll leave at four this evenin."

"I'll be ready," Paula said.

Chapter 11

When the bellboy left and closed the door, Danny looked around the motel room with awe and pleasure. Motels, yes, he had stayed in plenty of them, but never in one like this. The room was huge, the carpet soft, the bed vast, the color television the largest made, and the bathroom had an adjoining dressing room. He thought about the price and put it from his mind. His new sense of purpose had given him a freedom from worry about such things, the things that twenty years from now would make no difference whatsoever. Besides, Paula's obvious pleasure made it worth it.

The drive from the Banks had been a long one over bad roads made worse by a stream of log trucks from the timberlands, seemingly overloaded and overbalanced, their great burdens of tree trunks lashed in place with chains, their engines straining to move at a snail's pace, their width making passing difficult. Fortunately, the arrangements with the other officers had been comparatively simple, so they had got away earlier than he'd hoped, with plenty of daylight to make the trip and for Paula to see the country: first, the brooding coastal swamps and marshes, the road only a thin lost slice between green towering walls of jungle; the slow blackwater streams; the endless tree farms of the paper companies; the level fields and pastures of the farms; the tiny little towns scattered like beads from a broken string along their way, growing ever smaller as their people migrated from the back country; then the land climbing and the livid broad-leafed gold on the stem of tobacco fields and the occasional mansions of farmers who leased perhaps a hundred acres of allotment and yearly cleared a thousand dollars on each acre.

"My God," Paula said. "All the nowhere. If you could package all this nowhere and sell it by the square foot to the people in New York and Washington who don't have any nowhere, you could make a fortune."

The capital was different, a sprawling modern city with enormous shopping centers, vast tracts of expensive houses, swarming traffic. Even Danny, who had not been here for two years, was startled by how it had grown. They had passed the college Daisy had attended, its shaded lawn and white-columned red brick anachronistic amid the glittering office buildings grown up around it; and then they had seen the new motel, an amazing thing like a piece of clay sewer pipe stood on end with its bell upward, and that a rooftop restaurant twelve stories above the town. On impulse, Danny had turned into its drive. "Let's stay here. It's pretty close to the SBI headquarters."

As Paula unpacked her suitcase and hung clothes in the closet, Danny made two drinks from the bottle he had brought. He gave her one, tossed his own down rather quickly, and made another. "Later on," he said, "we'll go up yonder to that fancy restaurant and see what kinda chow they serve."

She looked at him obliquely. "That's likely to be rather expensive."

"So what, it's on me."

"Danny—"

"Well, damn it, I got a right to take you out and do something nice for you. All I ever did was buy you some bluefish down on Hatteras."

After a second her face changed, softening, smiling. "All right, as long as I pay my half."

"No, this is my treat!" He drank. "It's somethin I want to do for you."

Smile widening, she finally shrugged. "All right; if you're sure—"

"I'm sure."

He sat on the bed watching her as she began to undress. It was good to be like this with a woman, he thought, see her in such intimacy without either self-consciousness or, for the moment, overpowering lust. It was part of a relationship that he needed and felt lonesome for, a closeness. He watched her step out of her pants, and she stood there without self-consciousness, naked. "I'm for a shower. Will you join me?"

Danny grinned. "Why the hell not?" And he undressed.

The bath was large and there was plenty of room in it for the two of them. They soaped each other leisurely, sensually, and intimately. Danny had done this only once before, with Ruth, before they were married; it aroused him tremendously and seemed to have the same effect on Paula; she was almost savage when they had dried each other and she ran to the bed and threw herself on it, waiting for him to mount her immediately and without preliminary. Indeed, she was more explosive than she had ever been before, and he did not think it was entirely the effect of the luxury of the room. He thought she sensed what was in him now and responded to it.

The menu in the restaurant appalled him; he had never dreamed of such prices for a meal, but again he was not overly concerned. But he was touched when Paula insisted on ordering the cheapest thing on the card, freeing him to do likewise. It was the first time in so long that a woman had shown consideration for him, tried to let him off the hook instead of pinning him on it.

The meal was not as ruinous as he had thought it would be, but neither was it satisfying, and he was still a little hungry and considerably outraged at the ridiculous cost of such small portions when they went back to the room.

By then it was quite late and they decided against a sightseeing walk; she could do that in the morning while he was at the SBI. Instead they made love again, but, curiously, this time Danny was a little disturbed afterwards; some of his enjoyment of the aftermath was dissipated in the sense that Paula was still not quite satisfied.

But that wore off as she seemed to submerge her remaining desire in the way that women had. They lay together with her head on his arm again, and he said, "It's funny how it's all come together."

"We came together. What else did?"

"Everything. You, Hogan, the Daisy Canfield case, Gordon. Everything. I got a feeling it was meant to be, all of it. I mean, I feel different from any way I ever felt before. You'd laugh, maybe, and think it was silly if I told you, but . . . I know who I am, really, now, and what I want and how I'm gonna get it. I found that out today." His arm tightened around her. "I'll get it. *We'll* get it."

Paula remained silent, her face on his chest. Presently she

said, "Go to sleep, Danny. You've got a long day ahead of you."

Officially it was the Justice Building, and it was new, a gleaming structure of marble, granite, limestone in a mall of governmental buildings. The last and single time Danny had been in SBI headquarters, they'd been housed in much more cramped space downtown, and he felt a certain pride himself that the importance of law enforcement had finally received such impressive and rightful recognition.

He was on the Bureau's mailing list, and he knew about the recent changes in it. Once a refuge for political hacks, with the vast influx of money made available by the new concern for law and order it had been overhauled and professionalized. New agents had been recruited and trained, a narcotics division established, laboratories expanded, an arsenal of anti-riot weapons set up for use by officers in any part of the state who needed them, a sort of lending library of strange weapons. There was also an intelligence division now which kept personal data files on any potential trouble maker, from students photographed at demonstrations to Ku Klux Klansmen identified at rallies.

In a waiting room not unlike that of a prosperous dentist's office, Danny wondered why the agency had been so unsuccessful at solving murders like the Canfield case. It was not unique; there had been half a dozen equally spectacular killings, unlinked by any pattern, making headlines in the state over the past few years. But while the Bureau announced the breaking of major drug rings with impressive regularity, none of those murderers had ever been caught. But that was just as well for him, Danny thought; their failure gave him his opportunity for success.

Presently a muted phone buzzed and the receptionist stood

up. "Chief Rush, the Director will see you now." Danny rose, a little tense, his palms beginning to sweat. She led him into a large softly carpeted office in which a tall man was rising from behind a desk almost wholly clean of paperwork.

"Chief Rush." The Director was raw-boned, in his mid-forties, his nose a blade, his jaw long, his chin big, his hair red, clinging to his skull in an almost kinky wave. He wore a double-knit gray suit, and massive links glittered in his cuffs as he put out his hand, greeting Danny as if he were an old and valued friend. "How are you? How are things in Harriot?"

"Okay, I guess."

The Director, who was not himself a professional officer, but who had long experience as a governmental administrator, motioned Danny to a chair, smiling. "They seem to keep you pretty busy. I checked our records; you've never been to one of our training sessions."

"I talked to Mayor Jordan about it a coupla times, but the town never could rake up the money."

"That's a shame. We'll have to do something about it. We're working on a program of subsidies right now, and if we get the appropriation through the Legislature we'll have the money to bring in officers from the smaller, poorer areas with all expenses paid. I'll see that your name's at the top of the list."

"I appreciate that," Danny said.

There was silence for a moment. The Director fingered the single file that lay before him. "I understand you wanted to discuss the Daisy Canfield case. Have you got a new lead for us?"

"I don't know."

"Well, suppose you tell me, and we'll arrange for our agent in charge to make an evaluation."

"I'm not in a position to do that," Danny said. "All I want is a little help."

"Oh." Some of the warmth went out of the dark eyes. "Well, of course, that's what we're here for, to assist local law enforcement at their request. What, precisely, do you want?"

"What I'd really like," Danny said, eyes flickering to the folder, "is a chance to go through the Daisy Canfield file."

"Oh, well— I'm afraid that's not a possibility. The Legislature requires us to keep our files confidential. You know, there's always raw, unevaluated data, and—"

"All I want," Danny said, "is for you to let me see the same parts of it you'd let Sheriff Bristow see."

Slowly and methodically the Director took out a pipe and a tobacco pouch. "Has there," he asked casually, "been a change of jurisdiction in the case?"

"I don't know anything about a change in jurisdiction," Danny said. "Daisy Canfield lived inside the Harriot town limits. Seems to me that gives me all the necessary jurisdiction."

"Well . . ." The Director clamped his pipe between his teeth, then removed it. "That's not quite the way it works, Chief. I thought you were familiar with the way we operate. We ourselves have no jurisdiction until the local authorities request us to come in or the Governor orders us to. Now in the Canfield case it was Sheriff Bristow who asked us in. Once that pattern's established, we try to maintain a very definite information flow chart. A sort of chain of command, as it were. We deal with Sheriff Bristow as the officer of primary jurisdiction and . . . So it's not really me you want to see at all. But I'm sure if you went to Claude, he'd be happy to make whatever he's got available to you." He looked regretful. "If only you'd called first, I could have saved you a trip. You wouldn't have had to travel farther than the county courthouse."

"I don't think that trip would have done me much good," Danny said. "You know perfectly well Claude Bristow ain't gonna open his file to me."

The Director sat up straight, keeping his face composed. "I don't see any reason why he shouldn't."

"Then you don't know much about politics in Midyette County."

The Director's mouth thinned. "No, I don't. It's our policy to stay out of local politics. But I can't imagine the Sheriff not cooperating with one of his town police chiefs. Just as I can't"—he chewed the pipe—"imagine a police chief not cooperating with the Sheriff or with us if he had new information in a case."

Danny hesitated. "I tried that once, you might remember. That statement I got from Bubba Dixon. I didn't get very far with that."

"Well, you were in that conference with the rest of us. You know perfectly well why we couldn't use it. We get half a dozen like it every month."

"I reckon so," Danny said angrily.

"However," the Director said, "there's no reason to make a simple thing complicated. If you want me to, I'll just call Sheriff Bristow and get his permission and—"

"I tell you, you won't get no permission from Claude Bristow."

"I'm sorry you and the Sheriff don't have a better relationship. Maybe if you spoke to Mayor Jordan, he could arrange—"

Danny snorted.

The Director cupped his pipe, considered. "Still," he murmured, "if you really do have a piece of information you consider important . . . If you would just cooperate, we have trained agents to assist you. Maybe—"

"In other words, if I give you anything I got, you'll take over and use it. *Then* you'll let me see the file. No, thanks, I'll follow up my own leads." His voice rose as his temper slipped. "I know, if this case is solved at all, you and Bristow are determined to be the ones to crack it. And nobody else is gonna have a chance and embarrass either one of you—"

"Chief, now wait a minute—"

He never knew where the inspiration for his next words came from. His blood was up, his pulses hammering, and there was, too, desperation in him. "All right, sir," he heard himself say with forced quietness, "I guess I'll just have to go around to the newspaper here and tell 'em that you wouldn't even let the Police Chief of Harriot see your file on Daisy Canfield."

The Director sat up straight and put his pipe on his desk. "Don't be ridiculous. You know that paper. It's a muckraking rag—"

"I'll tell 'em you said that too."

"Now, listen, Rush, you don't want to get mixed up with anything like that. You'd only be making trouble for yourself."

"I'm used to trouble," Danny said. "All I'm insisting on is what I'm entitled to. I git your bulletins every week. If I git a lead on a stolen car, you expect me to report it to you. In turn, you give me a list of cars that have been stole. Information going two ways, and you're always offerin your cooperation in that poop you send me. But now— If you don't mean it, why do you put it in your bulletins, that you're here to help any law enforcement agency in the state?"

The man ran his hand through tight-curled hair. "Well, we can't stop you from talking to the papers, no. But we've got a full-time public relations man to explain anything you say and give the public the truth of it. And make you look like a fool, if it comes down to that."

Danny hesitated, mentally drawing back. And yet, he saw, he had scored; the Director was concerned. "Maybe we can compromise," he said. "All right, forget lettin me see the whole file. You give me a few answers to some questions about a suspect and I'll forget about the papers."

The Director's eyes narrowed slightly. "Answers about a suspect? A single suspect? Who?"

"His name is Wallace Gordon."

"What do you know about Wallace Gordon?"

"Not as much as you do. I got nothing that you ain't got, I don't think. I do know that he was interested in Daisy Canfield and that he double-dated her a few times and he wouldn't give up when she turned him down. That's all I got, but it's enough to make me curious and just for my own satisfaction I want to know what his alibi was for that night."

"You don't have any more than that? This is just personal curiosity?"

"That's all it is," Danny said.

The Director relaxed, smiled faintly. "Why didn't you say so when you first came in? Certainly we can accommodate you to that extent." He reached for the file, began to open it, paused. "Although I'll say this, Chief Rush. This case is not closed. Both ourselves and Sheriff Bristow have ongoing investigations under way. And you know the old saying about too many cooks spoiling the broth. I hope you won't get yourself too deeply involved. You might upset some very delicate operations without knowing it."

"They got anything to do with Wallace Gordon?"

"Not that I know of, no."

"Then I won't upset anything." Danny took out a notebook and pencil. "I promise you that."

"Very well," the Director said. "After all, we're here to help you." And he opened the file.

Chapter 12

But it took all of Danny Rush's willpower to survive the blow, the disappointment. He tried to put a good face on it, but nevertheless the drive back to Harriot was made in nearly total silence. All the same, he determined, he would not be balked. The thing to do was keep his eyes high, look ahead to his main objective. Then, somehow, he would find a way to overcome the obstacles. Nevertheless, he still had no idea how as he and Paula faced the others across the table in Felix Britt's front room.

"I told you it'd be a woman," Felix said triumphantly.

Danny could not help venting a little of his disappointment on him. "You told me a lot of things. You sure as hell told a lot of other people a lot of things too."

Above his beard Felix's cheeks reddened. "How do you know it was me? I swear I didn't—"

Danny shook his head impatiently. "Never mind. It don't

make no difference. I'd have had to break our cover anyhow. We never would have got anything done tippy-toeing around. But what we got to do right now is figure out something. New Orleans. Who the hell would have thought she'd be in New Orleans?"

"Are you sure she's really there?"

"No. I couldn't even swear to that. But that's the last place she was reported. Her name's Mona Shelbauer and she used to be a waitress up on Nags Head. She swore that Gordon was shacked up in her house with her the whole night that Daisy vanished. They questioned her and never could break her story. Not long afterwards, she went down there. I got a description of her; they didn't have no picture."

"I wonder how hard they tried to break her story?" Larry murmured.

"Not very," Hogan said bitterly. "Probably wasn't worth the effort when I was such a tempting morsel." He turned to Danny, a touch of desperation in his face. "Well, you can go *down* there, can't you? You can find her and question her—"

"I got to see," Danny said. "I don't know. There's a lot of things I got to see to. I've got my duty here, you know, and there's other considerations. It's not as simple as it sounds. For one thing, I'll have to raise some money. I don't suppose any of y'all have got three or four hundred dollars."

Felix just laughed. Larry shook his head. "I wish I had." And Hogan said, "Christ."

Then Felix said quickly and with hope, "Maybe Paula could—"

"No," said Danny savagely. "No. It's not up to Paula to finance this thing."

"Danny," she said quietly, "I could—"

He turned on her. "No. Anyhow, first I've got to see if I can get the time off, rearrange the vacation schedule. If I can't do

that, I won't need it. And if I can, I think I can scrape it up."
It was a hollow boast, but something in his voice made it
sound convincing. For a moment he half believed it; his faith
was not diminished.

Paula shrugged. "Well—"

"I'll see," Danny repeated.

Felix looked uncomfortable, then brightened. "Well, we
struck one lick while you were gone, Danny."

"What's that?"

"Larry and I've figured out the crazy way Daisy's stuff was
scattered all across the island."

Danny sat up straight. "You have? How? What do you
mean?"

"Yesterday we all went back over the route: sand pit,
Theater, golf course, bridge. And then we caught old Link
White, the guy who found her wallet by the sand pit, on his
way home yesterday evenin. We got the truth out of him."

"You got— You didn't get rough with—"

Larry laughed. "It cost two bottles of Three Bears Port."
He turned serious.

"I applied a little of Paula's inductive reasoning to this
situation. In other words, I brainstormed, and damned if I
didn't turn out to be right. Anyhow, Danny, the killer didn't
throw Daisy's handbag out at the sand pit. Link White put it
there."

"He said so?"

"He did after he came strolling along a back road on his way
home and found those two white gentlemen sitting by the
roadside guzzling wine, his favorite brand. We gave him
howdy in the cool of the day and he gave us howdy right back
and came over and eyed those wine bottles. He wouldn't
profane ours by drinking from it, but he was right amenable
to a slug out of the other one. Old boy was pretty tired after a

hard day's mowing on the golf course anyhow. So he sat down and had a drink and another drink and we started in to talk. And after a while, naturally, we talked about Daisy Canfield, and Link got a little drunk, and anyhow, he'd forgotten what he'd told the Sheriff."

He paused, then went on. "This is what really happened. The day after Daisy vanished, Link was mowing the golf course near the road. He looks down from his tractor, sees two shoes leaning against a phone pole, a big woman's handbag neatly placed by 'em. He crosses the road, gives them the onceover. Finders keepers, he thinks, checks the shoes, sees they won't fit his wife, tosses one away. Grabs up the handbag, but he's kind of wary about it, doesn't want anybody to think he stole it. Caches it till quittin time, then takes it home, shows it to his wife. Neither had heard a word about Daisy Canfield yet. And you know those people, they salvage everything. So she puts it up."

"After about a week," Felix said, "it sank into both of them. Neither one can read or write, but they heard it on the radio. They get scared and Link disposes of the handbag out by the sand pit. Still, he feels like he should do something to get 'em completely in the clear, so he takes the wallet into town. Only he tells the Sheriff that he found it by the sand pit. That way, no complications about withholding things the white law's been looking for all this time."

"You're old, black, illiterate, and broke," Larry said. "So what would you do?"

"Well," Danny said, his mind seeking the implications of this. "What does it mean?"

"For one thing, it's another nail in Bubba Dixon's story. You know he said they parked by the sand pit first. But it seems to me its main importance is that it makes the Theater the likely scene of the crime. Gordon—whoever—picks her up just outside of Hogan's where he's been waiting for her. *Come on, let's talk.* He takes her to the theater and they park. At three in the morning it's dark and lonesome out there, and— In the scuffle or when he opened the door, the book, the comb, and lipstick fell out and he never noticed. But when he's dumped her off the bridge, he's still stuck with shoes and handbag. So he does the best he can. He puts them by the bridge to make it look like she laid them down, then jumped or fell. Probably forgets until too late she's naked to the waist, finds her blouse and bra in the back seat of his car and disposes of them elsewhere."

"It's only conjecture," Larry said, "but it helps to show us what we might be trying to prove."

"Yeah," Danny said, and it was as if he were watching a moving picture now that he knew the actors and the background in the drama. He saw it unfold in flashes, and the rage and determination rose in him again. He was so brisk when he stood up, his voice so undiscouraged, that they looked at him with a surprise he sensed. "Good work. That may be very helpful."

"Where you going?" Felix asked.

"Right now," Danny said, "home to get some rest. I got to pull shift tomorrow and a lot of things to do on top of that."

He already knew what his first step must be, and he knew that it would take all the courage he possessed; he only hoped he had enough.

Taking the early shift next day, he was for a time preoccupied with office work and his patrolman's duties. Jordan came in and chatted with him briefly and to no particular effect, not mentioning Daisy Canfield or the investigation. Still, Danny thought, he's bound to know, and yet, somehow, he was not uncomfortable as he usually was in the Mayor's presence. He no longer felt inferior to Jordan nor vulnerable to charges about his shortcomings. He knew he had them and would probably always have them, but he had found something in himself now that outbalanced them. That made the difference, put them in perspective.

Thus, though he was very tense, he was still insulated from the fear he would have known before when he confronted Marshall at the bank. Marshall was not any older than Danny Rush and managed to look younger, small, quite handsome and always neatly barbered and beautifully dressed. Until now he had always seemed much older to Danny, as if constant contact with money had somehow aged him. He was smooth, polite, and asked only a single question: "What do you need this five hundred for?"

"To catch up on all these personal bills," Danny said. "You could set it up for me on the installment plan and—"

"I think we did that once before."

"Yeah, but—" He had constantly run behind in the payments, and there was no way to make Marshall see that he had changed. Besides he knew in his own heart that he could not keep them up, not if he used the cash to go to New Orleans.

"Well," Marshall said and tapped his pencil on his teeth and swung around to stare at the paneled wall beside his desk; and that was when Danny saw the refusal in his eyes. "Well, I think we would have to have a financial statement. You know what I mean, just a list of your assets and your liabilities. You bring that in, and I'll submit it to the committee at the main office up on Roanoke. You don't need it right away, do you? It'll take a day or two to get an answer."

"No, I don't need it right away."

"Well," he said again, swinging forward, ready to bend over papers on his desk. "Bring it in tomorrow and I'll process it right away. Okay, Chief?"

"Yeah, sure," Danny said, and he went out. Both of them knew that he would submit no such document and that the matter was completely closed.

Danny thought about going to Carney's to have a beer while he considered more carefully his next alternative, but somehow he did not believe he could bear the noise. Instead, he went to his car and drove directly out to Grover's.

The Pleasure Palace had not opened yet. A black man was stacking beer in a cooler, and Grover was arguing with a truck driver delivering salted peanuts, pickled eggs, and pigs' feet. Presently he paid the man, dealing out cash from a huge worn leather wallet. Danny waited patiently in a booth, drinking the beer Grover had given him on the house.

The peanut man departed and Grover, in a flawlessly pressed summer suit that had cost at least the amount of Danny's weekly salary, got a beer for himself and came to the booth. "I ain't in no trouble, am I?" Grover grinned.

"No," said Danny. "I need a favor." Somehow, even though Grover was black, it was easier. Maybe that was because Danny felt a natural superiority to him that eliminated any possibility of total humiliation. No matter what Grover's verdict, decision, Grover could not win. If he said yes, he was pretty good for a nigger. If he said no, he would be acting just like a nigger. That paradox was knowledge, not a thought in Danny's mind.

When he had finished Grover looked at him guardedly, fingering the bullet pucker on his cheek. "This protection?" he asked finally. He sold bootleg whiskey and Danny knew it. But it had never seemed to him worth bothering about, especially since it was one of his own sources in time of need. The idea had not occurred to Danny. Now he considered it. Of course, that could be one solution. But he said, "No. Just a loan."

"You mind if I ask how you goin pay it back?"

"I've got a deal goin."

"Ummm." Grover knew about deals; it was enough explanation for him. For a moment Danny felt triumphant certainty; but then Grover grinned faintly and shook his head. "Chief, I would like better than anything in this world to accommodate you. But I got to tell you very honestly I jest ain't got the ready cash. I might have it next week or week after next, if that ain't too late."

Not that it would ever materialize, Danny thought. He stifled the anger at being refused by his inferior. "I'm afraid that would be too late. You sure you can't rake it up now?"

"No way." Grover shook his head. "Just no way, Chief, much as I'd like to."

Danny swallowed disappointment. "Well," he said casually, "I'll just go see the bank then. I thought this would be quicker and simpler."

"I know." Grover winked. "Sometime it hard to explain a deal to the bank. You come back in about two weeks, Chief, if you still need it."

"Yeah," Danny said and drained the beer. "Well, thanks anyhow, Grover."

"Sho," Grover said and slid out of the booth. "I got things to do. You want some more beer, you just holler."

"No, thanks, I'll be on my way." Danny left, pushing the old car to the limit as it roared out of the drive.

He did something that for him nowadays was rare. He went to the beach. He usually did not consider the beach at Shoal the beach at all; it was more like a big picnic where everybody came half naked. He liked the lonesome beach, uncluttered by people, their possessions, and their rubbish, the beach of his childhood. He tried to ignore the shouting crowd as he walked along the water's edge, hands in pockets, head down.

Well, that ended it, he thought. As far as the bank and Grover were concerned, it was over, and there was nowhere else to go except to— But, he thought, I can't do that. Everything within him rebelled against it. First he would have to admit that he was unable to raise the money anywhere else. Secondly he could make no promise about repayment. But most importantly he wanted her admiration, not her pity. And, of course, there was the dreadful possibility too that she might have reconsidered, changed her mind, and if she refused him, that would throw a barrier of embarrassment between them that could ruin everything he had tried to nurture.

And yet, he thought. He looked out across the ocean. Beyond the bobbing heads of swimmers it was clean and empty, beautiful. But he knew what a fury it could be. It could turn into a churning monster in an hour. Then lives would be at stake, and the men who went out to fight for them would not consider for one moment their personal fears and feelings. Neither had he any right to consider his. If he had to risk even that for the money to take Wallace Gordon, he must do it. It was a burden laid on him.

He went to his car and drove to Paula's cottage. She was not at home, so he went to Fat Willy's and had a beer. He called and she had still not come in, so he had another, nursing it, making it last; he did not want to be drunk when he asked her. He wanted to be dead sober and rational about it all.

Apparently she was having supper out; it was nearly nine when she finally answered. He was not as sober as he would have liked to be, but he was all right, not too bad, either. And the sight of her reassured him. Obviously she was pleased to see him. "Do you want a drink?" she asked.

"In a minute. I've already had some beer. First I want to talk to you."

He was surprised at how tense she suddenly was, and for a moment his resolution faltered. Apparently he faced refusal here too. But now he could not stop. "That money," he said quickly. "The money I need to go to New Orleans to find that woman. I tried at the bank and it's gonna take a while to get the loan through. I don't want to wait that long. I . . ." He hesitated. "Could you see your way clear to lettin me have it if I sign a note?"

Paula's eyes widened and her brows went up.

"A note?" she said. "Don't be absurd."

Danny thought— Could not be sure—

"I'll have to cash some traveler's checks tomorrow. But I won't take any note."

Danny felt tension leave him like air from a ripped balloon. He seemed to deflate with its parting, only then realizing how swollen with it he had been. In its place, though, other emotions surged up within him, but mostly there was joy. Not that he was getting the money, but that she was giving it to him, and giving it to him on faith, on trust, acknowledging that her interest was sealed with his. It was, in its simplest form, a declaration of love.

"Thanks," he said, fighting to keep calm against the currents swirling in him. "I'll pay it back just as soon as I can." The words rolled from him in a burst of confidence, and he moved a step closer to her. "You'll be surprised what I build that five hundred into for us."

"No," she said, shaking her head and smiling faintly, "I don't think I would be. For us, you said?"

"I said that, didn't I? Don't you know by now I'm in love with you?"

"Yes," she said, "I know that."

"Well, then." He went to her and took her in his arms and just held her tightly to him, his face against the perfumed smoothness of her hair. "God," he said, "I've given you so little and I wanta give you so much."

He could barely hear her whisper. "It's not a matter of what you can give me. I'm not your ex-wife; my emotions aren't for sale."

"I know," he said. He buried his face in her hair. "I know. I love you."

For a long moment she was silent. Then her body moved even closer to his. "Yes," she said. "I love you too, Danny. It's all right, I love you too." And now there was a kind of desperation in the way she clung to him. "And I hope you do it. I hope you find all the evidence you need and make Bristow and the others look like fools. I hope it all works out so you can spit straight in their eyes and never worry about them again."

"It will," he said. "Now it will." Then he broke away from her just enough to see her face. But she didn't look at him and he had to tilt her chin up. Her mouth, though, was weak and unsteady when it smiled.

"Now," he said, "I can tell you somethin. I can tell you about a change I have felt comin over me and a new way I look at things that I know you won't laugh at. You and Larry are the only two that I could tell that would understand." And he told her, fumbling for the words. "The thing about it is," he finished, "it was all simple for him, my old man, you see? My people have been in the Coast Guard ever since there was one. It was the only big thing there was to do down here, so they didn't have to make a choice. But me, I had so many other choices I got confused. I had to circle around and stumble before I came back to home base. You understand?"

"I think I do."

"It was Daisy Canfield brought me there. And Wallace Gordon. And now I'm right. I know who I am. And you don't ever need to worry about bein ashamed of me. I'll see to that."

"No, I'll never worry about that," she said. "Come on, Danny." There was urgency in her voice. "Come on, let's go to bed."

Chapter 13

New Orleans was hot, and its heat was different from that of the Outer Banks, which was surprising, because it too was near the sea. But the heat of Hatteras was clean and fresh, mitigated by merciful sea wind. New Orleans, Danny thought, was like having your face buried between the sweaty breasts of a fat woman. You could smother; but it was a fascinating way to go.

He had, of course, been in big cities before, especially during his Army time in California. But there was no doubt that this one was unique, a strange mixture of American tourist trap and surviving foreign gracefulness. In a sense, looking for Mona Shelbauer was combining business with pleasure.

After some inquiries, he had decided on the LaFayette, a hotel past its prime, between Basin and Rampart on Canal, and was pleased to find it not too expensive and adequate to his needs. In his room he stripped off his sport coat and slacks and showered and put on fresh clothes, including the only summer suit he owned. Then he went directly to the address the Director had given him as her last known one, and found it a rickety frame boardinghouse on the very outskirts, near the water of the lake. The landlady barely remembered the girl. "Lord, that was a full three years ago, and she didn't stay but a month. I got no idea—"

"Where did she work? You know where she worked?"

After much mental straining, she dubiously and tentatively gave him the name of a restaurant on Canal Street, directly across from his hotel.

He spent another sizable amount getting back there in a cab. When nobody could remember her at the place, he was still not discouraged. He had expected to have to do some leg work and would have been almost disappointed if it had not been necessary. He went to the main police station. They had no idea whether Harriot was large or small; the fact that he was Chief was enough. But it would take some time to check the records that far back. Give them a call tomorrow morning, if that was not too late.

That left him with an afternoon and night to kill. He roamed the French Quarter on foot, feeling guilty about the waste of time, yet savoring being in a strange place. At the bus stop on the corner of Canal and Rampart, a fat blind woman held out a tin cup and squalled a song he could not decipher in a stirring voice of tremendous range. Nobody looked at her; he gave her a dime.

He had heard of Bourbon Street and worked his way over to it. But at this time of the afternoon most of its places were closed down; a few small bars were open and some leather shops. He went in one of these and bought a small hand-carved wallet for Paula and a carved leather cat for Linda and a dog for Junior. He ambled down the sidewalk, looking at the spectacular photographs of big-busted strippers, and passed on into a district swarming with hippies, leather-clad homosexuals, and what looked like runaway teenage girls. Feeling a certain revulsion, he cut over to Royal and window-shopped the antique stores, but they were not the sort of thing to fire his interest, and besides he felt bad when he saw so many things he would have liked to buy for Paula and could not afford. He had a drink at Pat O'Brien's and watched the artists and the necking couples at Jackson Square and looked at the nearby display of artillery. Then he wandered through the French Market, had a cup of coffee in the strangest coffee house he had ever seen—all marble and mirrors, serving nothing but delicious coffee and doughnuts—the Morning Call. Its name made him grin; his mother, going to the outhouse, had used to say, "Time for my morning call." He bought a pornographic novel and a girlie magazine at a dirty book store, invested a dollar in the peep shows, went back to the hotel and undressed and lay down in the air-conditioning, tired and footsore. He looked through the books and was surprised that they did not stir him; indeed, for the first time he was faintly repelled. He thought of Paula, felt a pity for the poor bastards who must rely on them for kicks, and threw them in the trash. Then he slept.

After supper he went down to Bourbon Street again, finding it transformed. In the velvet night it glittered like a spilled box of artificial jewels, bright with neon, yammering with two-beat Dixieland and the spiels of the barkers outside the striptease joints who passed out tokens good for free drinks to every man. At first he was sure he was in a sinkhole of depravity, but gradually he became aware that the crowds swarming along the narrow street consisted mostly of entire families—men, women, kids—ambling along wide-eyed on sightseeing expeditions. The most depravity he saw was in the eyes of teenaged girls in such groups, full of longing, frustration, and rebelliousness at the restraining presence of their parents in such a pasture of novel pleasures. On a hunch, Danny called the police station, but the men on duty knew nothing of his request. Anyhow, he would have to, they said suspiciously, come by in person. He returned to the hotel. He hung up his clothes after removing his credentials and the Colt Magnum from the jacket pocket and putting them on the bed table. Sitting on the bed, picking his toes, he thought of Ruth.

He'd had to see her before he left, tell her he'd be away, and give her some more money, the thirty dollars he was still in deficit on the child support. Having spent all his own in the capital, he reluctantly paid it to her from Paula's five hundred. When she heard he'd be out of town for several days, she looked at him with the suspicious beady eyes of a starling. "Where would you go?"

"I'm goin on vacation."

"Shoot, you got no money to go on no vacation. You goin with a woman."

"No, alone. It's a kind of business vacation."

"You don't fool me, you got a woman; I done heard." Then shrewdly, "Or is this that Daisy Canfield thing?"

"Who told you about that?"

"Lord, it's all over town. They say you're out to find who killed her and if you do, you'll run against Bristow in the next election. You ain't gonna do any such fool thing, are you?"

"What I do is my own business."

"Mine too! I got to depend on you to feed these kids. You get Bristow set against you, you'll lose your job. Ain't you got no sense?"

"I said," he roared, "it's my own damned business!"

She stared at him, hands folded across the pot belly under the old, now tattered, maternity smock. "Well, there ain't no need to yell at me. Go on with your fool schemes."

"Thanks," said Danny bitterly and slammed out. In the yard he picked up the two almost naked dusty children. "Daddy's gonna take a trip," he whispered, holding them very closely. "He's goin a long way off, and when he comes back, he'll bring you a good surprise. Daddy's gonna have a lot of surprises for you chaps soon."

To his own surprise, there had been no trouble arranging the time off with Jordan. All the Mayor had said was, "You're responsible for the vacation schedule, Chief. Just give the clerk a roster, so she'll know who's supposed to be on duty." And his men had cooperated. That was one thing: he got along well with his men.

He picked the novel out of the trash and read for a few minutes. Then he threw it across the room and went to sleep, one arm around the extra pillow as if it were Paula's body.

The next morning, early, the police had an answer for him. There was one arrest on her record. Indecent exposure; she had taken her G-string off during a period when there was a crackdown on the strip bars. That was over a year ago; they had a home address for her on Bourbon Street down in the hippie-infested section and the name of the club where she had committed the offense, the Double O. She had paid a fine.

He went to the house first, a big three-story place with balconies of wrought iron about to come loose and fall off, and all thronged with longhaired boys and whooping homosexuals and tight-faced young girls in knitted shirts and low-slung blue jeans. It was, he thought, like seeking information in Oystertown. The house smelled worse and the young people clammed up just as tight as Negroes. He got absolutely nothing out of them except the fact that neither Mona Shelbauer nor Shelly Bower, her professional name, lived there any longer. He called the Double O, but nobody answered except a janitor who told him it would open at five o'clock. With an entire day to kill, he roamed a while longer, and then, back in his room, decided to write a letter to Paula. His loneliness, his longing for her was as tangible and as uncomfortable as starvation would have been. He drank two beers while he wrote it, and it got out of control, and anyhow he would be back on Harriot before it was delivered, with any luck. So he threw it in the wastebasket. Somehow the time passed until the Double O opened. There was no barker outside, no dancing inside, despite the photographs of overblown strippers beside its narrow door. There were only a few morose solitary drinkers scattered around the horseshoe-shaped bar. Danny sat down by one of them. "You come in here often?" he asked.

The man was middle-aged, pale-faced, with a briefcase beside his drink. Immediately he nudged his knee against Danny's thigh, gently, tentatively. "Oh, yes, quite frequently."

"They got a dancer here named Shelly Bower?"

The knee moved away. "I really wouldn't know. There are so many bitches capering on that platform—" He indicated a polished slab between the bar wings. Then he picked up his drink and moved away. Finally Danny caught the bartender's attention. Drawing on the expertise of a hundred movies and a thousand television programs, he covered a five-dollar bill with his hand.

She was not here now. She had quit six months before. He didn't know where she'd gone. Danny hadn't meant to release the five so soon, but it had vanished somehow. "Some other joint along the street, I guess," the man said.

"Which one?"

"How the hell I know?" the man said and went off to serve a customer.

Danny cursed, finished his drink, and went to eat.

It was late when he came back to the street, and things were in full blast. He heartened, after temporary discouragement. Leg work. That was the basis of all detective work. She was here somewhere, and if he was persistent enough and clever enough, he would find her. It was a matter of taking the strip bars one by one.

He did that, making full use of the tokens good for free drinks handed out by the barkers beside each door. Learning, he began to reduce his offer to the bartenders. After all, a cop was their natural enemy, and they must have spotted him as one. Anyhow, they told him nothing, so the money was wasted. Meanwhile he saw a great deal of bored and indifferent gyrating woman flesh on the inevitable platforms between the wings of the horseshoe bars. They wore, he thought, pasties, for God's sake! He could see more than that in any topless bar in Norfolk. And most of them looked as if they were about to go to sleep in the middle of their dances. Again he became discouraged and lonely. Sitting in one place called the Purple Nightowl, he noticed one of the strippers, now clad in a low-cut evening dress, come out a rear door and take a seat at the bar's other wing. The stool next to her was vacant, and on impulse he went to it. It was, anyhow, what Humphrey Bogart would have done.

"Hi," he said, edging in beside her.

"Hello." Her voice was cool, and she looked straight ahead, drawing her leg completely away from the space occupied by his.

"Don't worry," Danny said. "I just want to talk to you. I

just want to kill a little time."

She sipped her drink. "I enjoyed your dance," he said. "Likely you had to study a long time to learn to dance like that."

She slowly turned her head, and darkly penciled brows drew together. "Hey, where are you from, anyhow? You a Cajun?"

"A what? No, I'm from a place called Harriot. The Outer Banks."

"Yeah, yeah, I thought so. We got a girl here talks that way."

Danny tried not to betray the way he came suddenly alive. "Is she from up there?"

"Yeah, some place like that. Maybe you know her, she calls herself Shelly Bower."

"Oh," Danny said. "Yeah, sure. She'd be one of the Shelbauers from Nags Head." He grinned at her. "I'd sure like to talk to her. Is she on tonight?"

"As soon as *she* gets off." The girl indicated another who marched somnabulistically through what was supposed to be an interpretation of erotic frenzy. "Yeah, she's got a half hour after her dance. When she goes off, I'll tell her. What'd you say your name was?"

"Wahab. Danny Wahab."

"Wayhab, sure. She'll be excited."

Danny clutched his glass, feeling triumph and satisfaction. He watched the dancer scuttle off to a spatter of applause.

The bartender picked up a microphone. "And now, ladies and gentlemen, the Purple Nightowl presents that redheaded bombshell, Miss Shelly Bower!"

She sauntered out in a dress of lavender chiffon, jaws moving rhythmically on her cud of gum. In this light and with all that makeup on, it was impossible to tell what she really looked like. Her dancing was no better and no worse than the others as she slowly shed the dress to the strains of "Misty" played on a record to three different tempos. She wound up finally squatting, breasts bobbing, pasties glittering, haunches flopping, as she simulated some weird sort of sex. Then it was over; she rose, picked up her discarded dress, and, dimpled buttocks clamped together, minced off to another halfhearted rattle of applause. The girl beside Danny slid off her stool and went backstage.

"Hey," she had said excitedly. "You're a Wahab, huh? My aunt married a Wahab, maybe that makes us cousins by marriage. I get kinda lonesome, you know, sometimes, but Jesus it's good to get outa that place."

She danced seven more times before she was off at three. In between, she and Danny sat in a booth and talked about Hatteras, Ocracoke, and Nags Head. "How'd you wind up down here?" Danny asked.

"Oh, a boy friend gave me the money to come."

"He must have liked you a lot or wanted to be rid of you awful bad."

"Both." She grinned. Danny judged that she was in her late twenties, and up close she looked tired, the powder filling pores like craters on her face. He tried not to drink too much and he bought her more than he consumed, but he thought possibly it was colored water and she got a percentage. He did not know how bars in New Orleans operated. After Paula it was hard to gear down and follow her inane chatter; he had never realized before how different the conversation of a stripteaser and a schoolteacher could be.

When the place was nearly ready to close, she dressed and they took a cab to her two-room apartment up a grubby flight of stairs near the French Market. In the steamy night the area had a stirring smell of river and of fruit and vegetables. Her place was a mess, but she seemed not to notice; anyhow, she did not apologize. She shut the door, faced Danny, came to him and gave him a heavy, wet kiss, her tongue thrusting deep into his mouth. "You know," she said after a moment, backing away, "I usually charge seventy-five. But for an old Hatterasman like you it's only fifty."

"Why not," said Danny, but he felt smothered in the heat and clutter and had a wild desire to break free.

She turned. "Unhook me, huh, and then we'll go into the bedroom." She wore a very simple dress now, with a checkered pattern, and had shed her wig; her own hair, raven black, lay closely cropped and curled against her skull. Danny fumbled with the top snap and got it loose, with the curious feeling he was watching this on television. He pulled down the zipper.

She faced him once more. "Only, you won't take it hard if I ask for it in advance?"

"Why, no," Danny said as she started to lift the dress above her shoulders. But he did not reach for his wallet. He had already decided on his tactics. "What do you hear from Wallace Gordon?" he asked.

The girl froze with the dress draped around her shoulders. Her eyes, the whole quality of her expression, changed instantaneously. She let the dress drop back into place. "Why," she said, "you get out. You stinking cop, you get out of here!"

"No," Danny said. "I want to talk to you about Wallace Gordon."

"Why should I talk to you, you bastard? I've already told that fucking Sheriff all I had to say. You work for him?"

"Uh-uh. I'm Daniel Wahab Rush, Police Chief of the Town of Harriot."

"That fucking two-bit place? Why—"

Danny said, taking out cigarettes, "You don't still love that miserable son of a bitch, do you?"

"Love?"

"That's what I said." Danny passed her a cigarette. "Does he even write you?"

"You damn well better believe he writes me. He came by to see me last spring."

Danny lit her cigarette, then his own. "So he keeps you on the hook, eh?"

"What he does is none of your damned business, you creep. Get out of here."

Danny looked around the little room. Discarded underwear and pantyhose lay on the sofa; scratched records were piled beside a cheap stereo; a poster of Paul Newman, like Felix without the beard, looked down smiling from the wall. On a table there was a conch shell and a sand dollar; she had brought that much sea with her this far, anyhow. He picked up the shell. "You told the Sheriff he spent the night with you when that girl was killed."

"He didn't kill that Indian broad," Shelly Bower said. "He didn't do that, I know. He was with me!"

Danny turned the shell over in his hands. "This one's been drilled. I'll send you a perfect one from back home, maybe, I've got a lot." Then he said, "I want to tell you a little something. You don't have to believe me, but it's true. Do you remember when Daisy Canfield disappeared?"

"About."

"And it was two weeks before she was found."

"Yeah," she said tensely.

"And he was pretty hot and heavy with you then, wasn't he?"

"We were goin steady. He used to come up to Nags Head

every chance he got, almost every night. He was up there with me the night she—"

"Sure," Danny said. "Of course, while she was still floatin in the Sound and they hadn't found her yet, before he needed you for an alibi; but while he was still, what, goin steady? with you, he took Daisy Canfield's roommate up to his apartment above his art gallery and laid her."

"You're a Goddamned liar," the girl said, but both her voice and eyes showed the shock of wounding.

"You know it's true," Danny said. "You know he's a swordsman and he's always been a swordsman."

"And I'm a whore," she rasped.

"You weren't then, were you?" Danny asked and put down the shell. He went to the sofa, moved pantyhose aside, and sat down and crossed his legs. "You can't still love him," he said. "You ain't that stupid."

Mona Shelbauer did not answer. He could only see her back. Beneath the body makeup there were freckles on it. "Maybe you do," Danny said. "I don't know." In this moment, slightly abuzz with whiskey, it seemed to him that he knew everything about love there was to know. He'd had Ruth and now Paula and . . . He felt sympathy for her, not condemnation, but he also thought he knew where her weak spots might be. "But I think if I was you, I would hate him now. A man that loves a woman ought to take care of her. I wouldn't say he had taken very good care of you."

She made a coughing sound. Presently she said, "He's going to open up another gallery soon, down here. Over on Royal Street. It'll be his main one. He's gonna close down the one on Shoal."

"Is that what he told you recently, or is that what he told you three years ago?"

Mona Shelbauer whirled on him, mouth opening as if she

would scream at him. Then she closed it without a word. She straightened up, let out a sighing breath. "Why don't you just get the fuck out of here?" she said at last.

"Because," Danny said rising, "he killed a girl. He tried to rape her and when she wouldn't go along, he hit her and knocked her out and then he strangled her with a rope and threw her off the bridge. And she wasn't but nineteen and she was a virgin—"

"He didn't," Mona said. "It was just that he was out that night on the beach and he knew anybody without an alibi would be worked over—"

"All right," Danny said. "Love him or hate him, it's up to you, but he still screwed her roommate while Daisy's body was in the Sound and he was fixin to come to you for an alibi." She dropped her head and he said sharply, "You don't believe that?"

She did not answer. He went on: "I guess he's screwed two hundred since then. I seen him just the other day in his gallery, putting the make on some rich bitch was in there. He gave her a pocketbook. What was it he said? 'Show it to your friends, and come back to see me.'" His voice rose. "Why do you go on protectin him?"

"I—"

"All right. You got people left up there. You won't talk against him because you don't want them embarrassed. That and you're scared of him."

"Just go *on.*"

"You ought to know a lot more about men than you did three years ago," Danny said.

"I know that you're all bastards and I wouldn't screw another one of you except for money." Her voice was thick.

"That's a bad way for anybody to come to feel. You ought to hate him just for makin you feel like that."

217

"He ain't the only one."

"Well, he's the only one you can git even with. All I want from you is a statement. Just say you were mixed up on your dates. That it wasn't the sixth he was with you on, that it was the seventh. I don't want another blessed thing from you but that."

"And wind up in court and send my mother to her grave."

"Where do you think she'll go if you go to prison for accessory to murder?"

Now Mona raised her head.

"Sooner or later it's bound to come out. You'd do well to clear yourself now. Because I'm a cop and I'm after him. It's like taking out insurance."

She was looking at him once more, painted brows drawn from arches to flat level lines as she frowned. "We'll either git him for this," Danny went on, "or he'll do it again and— Either way, you'll be in a mess unless you make a statement now."

She hesitated, licking her lips. Finally, she said warily, "You son of a bitch. You really *are* a cop, aren't you?"

Danny fumbled in his coat. "There's my badge and gun," he said.

The only commercial air connection in that part of the state was a short-line feeder service flying out of the Coast Guard air station on the mainland. It took Danny Rush nearly as long to make a connection to take him there as it had to fly from New Orleans to Charlotte. It was after three in the afternoon of the fifth day when he saw below, through cloudy skies, the great checkered domes of the station's water tanks. Then he watched the runway come up, relaxing as the wheels met it smoothly and the plane taxied to a landing. He was the only passenger disembarking. In the tiny airline office he retrieved his suitcase, used the rest room, and hurried to his parked car on the special lot. Relieved to find it still there, he wondered who would bother to steal it and chided himself; he had to break the habit of always expecting the worst. He touched the document in duplicate in his coat pocket and smiled.

He wished the car would fly too. The need to show what he had accomplished to Paula, to see her face and savor her delight and admiration, to plan another move, to hurtle on with this momentum to success, pushed him like a great invisible hand.

Signed, he thought, sealed, and delivered. It had cost him money, though, over and above the typist's and notary's fees. She was a whore, and whores did nothing free, not even to save themselves. She had demanded two hundred dollars, and he had talked her down to a hundred, payable after she had signed the statement. It had taken him nearly all of one day to get it right and get it typed in the proper form. He knew the proper form because of his experience with Bubba Dixon, so maybe some good had come out of that after all. Anyhow, it was done, and it was ironclad. And he was broke, with only four dollars of the money left in his pocket. But that didn't matter now. Wallace Gordon, he thought, you don't know it, but the heat's on you. He wondered if Gordon, confronted with these documents, might not break down, confess. But no, that was a dream. Gordon was not the type. There was more work to do, a lot of it, to build a case; only the easy part of it was over, the hard part yet to come. But he could do it. He knew that now.

He drove swiftly across the spur of mainland, pushing the old car to its limits. He crossed a bridge and was on the Currituck Banks, the upper end of the Outer Banks. A light drizzle fell, but the road was good and, as if it had decided to make itself part of his luck, the old car ran smoothly, without clunk or hesitation. He sped past the Wright Brothers Memorial at Kitty Hawk and the adjoining municipality of Kill Devil Hills. Where that merged into Nags Head, a towering mountain of sand, a great dune more than a hundred feet in height, thrust its tan bulk against the sky, climbers like ants on its flank: Jockey Ridge.

Nags Head, like Shoal Island, was thickly settled, swarming with tourists; he left it, crossed more bridges, and then he was on Shoal itself. Passing the turnoff to the Old Village, he felt a trifle guilty about not stopping to tell Larry, Felix, and Hogan the news, but he would come back as soon as he had seen Paula. Driving down the beach front, he cursed the herds of people wandering blankly and without urgency across the road, delaying him. His chest felt stuffy with impatience, his heart was pounding; he begrudged every half minute that he had to pause. "Get your ass in gear," he growled to an old man who halted right in the middle of the pavement to raise high, triumphantly, a huge king mackerel as he called out to someone across the street. But finally he reached the cottages and pulled into the chuck-holed court. Then he said, "Aw, shit." Her car was gone.

He got out, knocked at the door. Maybe it was busted again and in the garage. He hammered hard, but no one answered. Danny mumbled more profanity in his disappointment and, very slowly, got back in his car. The edge taken off his anticipation, he drove at a more sedate pace back up the island to Old Shoal Village. Larry's car was parked beside Felix's truck. Well, they'd get a charge out of this, he thought, and his enthusiasm returned. He sprang up the rickety steps and entered the little house without knocking.

"Well gentlemen," he said, "mission accomplished. That girl sang like a—" He broke off.

There was something in this room, something invisible yet

tangible; he could almost smell it; it was stifling. Larry sat at the table with a tall glass of whiskey before him; Felix sat beside him dealing solitaire. In one corner Peter Hogan was packing a duffel bag. He straightened up and turned.

"Canary," Danny finished. Then, to Hogan: "Where you think you're going?"

"I'm leaving," Hogan said. He brushed hair out of his eyes.

"The hell you are. I just got a statement from that girl in New Orleans. This thing's breaking now and we'll need—"

"Danny," Larry said.

Slowly Danny faced around.

"They've found the killer," Larry said. "It was Harold Krause. He confessed."

For a moment he saw everything clearly and in an almost supernatural sharpness of outline: the grubby, rickety furniture, the unpainted walls, the littered trash and dirty glasses, the three men staring at him. He heard the rain on the roof in the silence. Then things blurred, swam in his vision. "They've— Bullshit," He said hoarsely.

"He left a suicide note," Larry said. "They published part of it in the paper. Day before yesterday they found him out by the sand pit. He'd stuck a rifle in his mouth and pulled the trigger."

"Why," Danny began in incomprehension and outrage, "It's not true, it's—"

"I saved the paper for you." Larry stood up, took it from the seat of another chair, and unfolded it. "Here's the part they published." He began to read: "'Everyone knows the crime I'm guilty of. It was whiskey that caused it. A murderer does not deserve to live. I don't want to live any longer. Three years of this kind of torture's enough. I hope now she will rest in peace.'"

He laid down the newspaper. "That's all they printed of it.

The rest was for his wife and kids."

"Lemme see that." Danny's legs would hardly support him as he seized the paper. He braced his hands on the table, reading. He swallowed hard, afraid for a moment that he would vomit. Then he straightened up, using all his willpower to grip and calm himself.

"That don't say specifically he killed Daisy Canfield."

"Who else was there for him to be a murderer of?" Felix asked.

"But he didn't do it! I know he didn't!" Danny touched his pocket.

"Anyhow, he thought he did," Larry said. "Of course, he was drunk. They found an empty fifth bottle in his car. Anyhow, it was enough for Bristow. He says the case is closed."

Danny dropped into a chair. "Like shit it is." He pulled out the affidavits. "You see these? Mona Shelbauer signed these down in New Orleans. She had come to hate his guts. She says she lied, she never was with Gordon that night. She's sworn to it."

They crowded close, reading. Larry was the first to finish and straighten up.

"You see?" Danny said. "We can still go ahead and collect the evidence. We can prove Bristow is a liar. We can reopen this case—"

"No!" Peter Hogan almost screamed the word, and his big hand grabbed at the affidavits. Purely by reflex, Danny knocked it aside, seized the papers, and jumped to his feet. Hogan backed away. "No, no, no," he said hoarsely. "You're not to do that, you can't do that!" He stood there, huge fists clenched, chest heaving as he panted. "Damn it, don't you see? I'm in the clear now. After all these years I'm in the clear. You stir it up again, all over again, and . . . and

. . ." His words trailed off. "I won't help you," he said. "I'm leaving. I'm pulling out. I won't help you crucify me for another three damned years."

Very carefully Danny folded the papers, returned them to his pocket. Hogan was terrified, defensive, raising his hands. Then he dropped them. "I appreciate . . . I appreciate everything you've done, Chief. I thank you for it. But . . . I came here looking for a miracle. Now it's happened and all this weight is off of me, and . . . and in God's name, if you have any mercy at all, you'll tear up those papers and flush them down the toilet, just forget Daisy Canfield."

"Forget," Danny said heavily. "Just forget her." Then he had to lash out. He took a quick step forward, cocked his fist, sent it slashing toward Hogan's face. Larry was almost as quick, deflecting the blow, pulling Danny's arm around. "Stop it," he said. "Stop it, Danny. He's right."

"No, God damn him!" Danny roared. "The son of a bitch with his marijuana and lettin that girl walk home alone and his fuckin coolness, I'll—" He struggled against Larry's grip, but Larry Besser despite his slenderness was strong. Danny would have had to hit him too.

Then it was gone as suddenly as it had come, the rage. "Okay, Larry," he said and let his arm drop. "It's okay now." He faced Hogan. "Sure," he said. "Get. Go ahead. We don't need you anyhow. But let me tell you something, Buster. Don't you ever come back inside the city limits of Harriot. Because if you do I'll find somethin to hang you on."

Hogan did not answer.

"Go ahead," Danny said. "Get out of here. It makes me sick to look at you. You're as much a murderer as any of them."

Hogan turned away. No one spoke as he pulled the draw-strings of the duffel bag tight. He took a cased guitar from the corner, slung it across his shoulder. He picked up the duffel bag, threw it across the other shoulder. He went to the door, paused there, looked back at them for a moment, and went out.

When the door closed behind him, Danny dropped into a chair. "Shit," he said. "Let him go. The three of us can—"

"Danny," Felix said. He had never risen from his chair. "It'd just be a waste of time now."

Chief Rush turned to him. "A waste—"

Felix raised his head, met his eyes. "You can't buck a dead man's statement," he said. "Besides, I'm runnin outa money. I got to find a job."

"Well," Danny said. "Well, this is very interestin. First you beg me to tackle this and after I've stuck my neck out and gone five hundred dollars on the hook, got the first hard evidence we've found, it's a waste of time." Then he shoved the chair around and looked at Larry. But he did not speak; he read his answer in the regret and shame and pity on Larry's face.

"I'll help you if you want," Larry said, "until school opens. But—"

"But you agree with Felix."

"Why send good time and money after bad?"

"Yeah," Danny said. "Yeah, that's one way to look at it, but Daisy Canfield's still dead and— Skip it." He reached for Larry's glass of whiskey and took a long drink. "Just skip it." He made sure the papers were in his pocket, got up, and went to the door. "Have either of y'all seen Paula today?"

"No," Larry said.

"I called her yesterday from New Orleans and she wasn't in. Well I'll go by her place. She's worth the two of you when it comes to this, anyhow. All the ideas have been hers."

"Danny," Larry said.

"Never mind," Danny said. "I'll see you later." He went out. The rain was falling harder now. On the highway he passed Hogan, standing in it, hitchhiking, thumb pointing north.

He drove back to Paula's cottage; the car was still not there. Without getting out, he spun around and headed for his trailer. It was, after all, home, a sanctuary where he could wash and shave and have a drink and deal with all these new developments. By the time Paula returned from supper, he'd have a plan. He got out and found the key and put it in the lock.

It did not fit. Danny frowned, rechecked it, tried again. Still it would not go in. He stood there in the rain, staring at it. Then he remembered the slip of paper which had been on his table for days, and he knew the lock had been changed.

He was surprised when he heard himself laughing, but all at once this seemed funny, downright comic. He was still chuckling when he got back in the car. He looked at his watch. Twenty minutes before the town hall closed down. Well, he was due a paycheck. He would pick it up and pay the rent. It would clean him out again, but that was an inconsequence. He would not think about it. Hell, for that matter, maybe he could move in with Paula.

When he entered the town hall, the clerk, Mrs. Hayes, called to him from behind her desk. "Hello, Chief Rush. Glad to see you back."

"Glad to be back," Danny answered automatically.

"Your wife's been calling. She'd like for you to call her right away."

Danny closed his eyes briefly, very tightly. "Yeah, I'll do that. Mrs. Hayes, I'd like to—"

"And Mayor Jordan said if you came in he'd like to see you

right away. He's in his office."

"Oh," Danny said. "Oh. All right."

Suddenly he felt numb, his legs stiff and wooden, as he walked toward the Mayor's office in the rear. When he entered, Jordan looked up, yellow light gleaming on his bald scalp. "Hello, Chief. Did you have a nice vacation? Would you mind closing the door? Sit down."

Danny caught a glimpse of his own reflection in the window behind the Mayor as he sat. His hair was mussed and wet, his coat sodden and wrinkled. He took out a pocket comb. "You wanted to see me?"

"Yes. Danny, I might as well get straight to the point. Bad news. I have to ask you for your resignation."

Chief Rush no longer felt any capacity for surprise or anger or even fear. "Why? Bristow finally—"

"Bristow has nothing to do with this," Jordan said. He leaned back in his chair. "Danny, we've been through this before, you know. I said these financial matters have to be kept straight. I warned you that you'd be in trouble if they weren't. Now Leroy Morton comes to me and says you're six weeks behind in your trailer rent and he has to lock you out."

"I'll pay him his trailer rent. Just give me my paycheck and I'll go right around and settle with him."

"Well, first, if you'll give me your resignation, effective immediately—"

"Listen, Mr. Jordan, let me explain what I've been doin. I—"

"Danny, please, I don't want to hear it. Anyhow, I think I know. Have you read the papers?"

"I've read 'em. But that's wrong. I've got proof—" He broke off, looking into Jordan's eyes. And all at once he knew there was no use in further talk." "Immediately?" he said. "Don't I git two weeks' notice?"

226

Jordan shook his head. "Well, then, two weeks' pay."

"Not when you're released for cause, Danny. It's in the city code. I'm sorry. There's nothing I can do."

"Well, of all the—" Now he did feel anger.

"I'm sorry," repeated Jordan. "You're entitled to a hearing before the Council, of course, if you want it."

Danny stared at him, jaw clamped. Then he took out his ballpoint pen, and Jordan handed him a sheet of letterhead. Danny pulled up close to Jordan's desk. "I hereby resign as Chief of Police of Harriot for personal reasons and with all good wishes effective as of this day. Daniel Wahab Rush."

Jordan read it. "Thank you," he said simply.

Danny shoved back his chair. "Now, if I can pick up my last check—"

"It'll be ready tomorrow. I'll arrange with Morton to come in and you can endorse it to him."

"You'll—"

"Well, Danny, there's town property impounded in that trailer. Nightstick, belt, flashlight. You understand."

"You mean I don't get no money?"

"We see that your rent is paid, and we take possession of the town property you're charged with and . . . I'm afraid there won't be anything much left over, but, of course, you get the residue."

"The residue," Danny said. "Yeah, I get the residue. Well, here's some residue for you." He fumbled in his coat and took out his badge and dropped it on Jordan's desk. Then, wordlessly, he left the building.

Uncertainly, on the sidewalk, he stood in the drizzle. Then he began to walk toward the white tower of the courthouse, gleaming in the rain.

In the foyer Bubba Dixon leaned against the wall, broom in

hand, match between his teeth. He grinned vacantly. "H-Hi, C-Chief."

Danny did not answer. The mild blank eyes followed him as he went up the stairs. In the big outer room of the Sheriff's office the secretary was taking her umbrella from a hat tree; Farnum, the chief deputy, was at a table filling out a form. Danny asked, "Bristow in?"

Farnum raised his head, eyes narrowing in a round face beneath a bristle of ginger hair. "Yeah, but—" Danny did not hear the rest; he was going directly to Bristow's office door, aware of Farnum rising from the table. Without knocking, he went in.

Bristow, in his shirt sleeves, lookéd up from behind his desk, pale eyes flaring in his gray narrow face. "Hello, Danny."

"Well, you did it. You got me fired, didn't you?" Danny was surprised at how controlled his own voice was.

Bristow leaned back. "It's okay, Bud, close the door." Farnum, just behind Danny, went out, and then they were alone.

Bristow said, "I heard that Jordan was goin to let you go. Money matters, I understood."

Danny looked down at him with contempt. "Money matters. You know damned well what kind of matters it was." He nodded. "Well, that's okay. I just come to tell you that I'm not the only one in trouble. Harold Krause didn't kill Daisy Canfield, no matter what you told the papers." Suddenly, on impulse, he took the affidavits from his pocket, selected the carbon, dropped it on Bristow's desk. "Read that and tell me now what you got to say. And you can't claim credit for it, because it says in there that it's me she's makin the statement to."

Bristow read it, thin mouth growing thinner. He put it

down, drummed his fingers on his desk. Then he picked it up again and passed it back to Danny. "All right," he said. "You stole a march on us. That is good detective work. We tried to crack her three years ago, before she left, but I guess she was still in love with him. If it's any consolation to you, the SBI had an agent about to catch a plane for another try when Krause shot himself."

Danny carefully stowed the paper. "Well, it don't matter. I'm going to—"

Bristow drew in a deep breath. "You're not going to do a damn thing." His voice turned rough. "You've done enough damage already."

"What?"

"Krause." Bristow stood up. "God damn it, I know Krause didn't do it. But he's dead now, and you killed him and—"

"I killed him?"

"You with your penny-ante game of cops and robbers with those beach bum friends of yours. You murdered Harold Krause just as sure as somebody murdered Daisy Canfield."

Danny stared.

"Of *course* he didn't do it; he was too drunk to drive that night, much less even pick her up and throw her off the bridge. But he was *afraid* he did. For a long time, he was afraid. Finally I persuaded him to give himself the benefit of the doubt. He stopped drinking, he made a whole new life for himself. But he was still hanging on by his fingernails. And then you brought this whole thing alive again and— It was all the push he needed. He went on a two-day bender, wrote the most despairing, mixed-up note I've ever read, convinced himself he was so rotten that he was bound to have murdered her, and while he was dead drunk shot himself. If you're not to blame for that, who is?"

Danny let out a long breath and shook his head as if

something buzzed around it. "Then if you know he didn't . . . Why did you close the case?"

"Because," Bristow said fiercely, savagely, "you forced me to. Krause's letter forced me to. No matter what I think, I can't repudiate a dead man's confession."

"You can now. With this affidavit, if— I need a badge. I want to be a deputy. I want to—"

"No," Bristow said. "We've got no openings. Besides—"

"Besides what?"

"The books balance now," Bristow said.

After a moment Danny said scathingly, "So that's the way you look at it."

"It's the way I've got to look at it. If you were in my position, you'd have to do the same." A flicker of pain crossed Bristow's face, he put one hand on his stomach. Sitting down, he said in a different voice, "It's all I can do. Look, Rush, Hogan was *with* her that night, and yet we couldn't pin it on him. All right, maybe we tried too hard, missed a boat somewhere else. The fact remains, regardless of Gordon's alibi, you can't establish any *physical connection* between him and Daisy Canfield that night. A whole battery of the best agents in the SBI have tried; I've tried; we've all failed. That"—he pointed at Danny's pocket—"means he lied, and *she* lied about that night, yes. But it still doesn't prove he killed Daisy Canfield or was even close enough to touch her." Bristow paused. "We hadn't forgotten him, that's why we kept so quiet, we didn't want to scare him, were hoping that—" He broke off.

Danny comprehended quickly. "That he'd rape or kill somebody else," he said bitterly.

"There would be no other way to get him," Bristow said. "Absolutely none."

"I'll see about that," Danny flared.

Bristow stood up again. "You get this straight, Rush. You'll see about nothing. You have no badge, no authority, and you're not going to have any. You forget Daisy Canfield, you hear? If I have one more word about you trying to stir up this case again, I'll—" He paused. "Skip it. You did a good job as far as you went. In a way I'm sorry things didn't work out for you. Maybe, if you stick around, when there's an opening, we might work out something."

Danny said nothing, only turned.

"Rush," Bristow said.

Danny paused, facing him once more.

"You've got to learn what can be done and what's purely hopeless. You've only got so much time and so many men, and you've got—" He gestured toward the map of the county on his wall, a great sprawling coastal wilderness. "You've still got to keep order in all of that. You've got to understand that—"

"When you can make the books balance, do it, and protect your ass," Danny said scathingly. "Christ," he added. "The way you operate, you'll be Sheriff forever." Then he spun on his heel and went out.

Chapter 14

Driving back toward Shoal Island, he was careful not to think. Indeed, he could not. This had all come so fast. He touched the papers in his pocket, was surprised that his courage was not broken; they existed; Gordon existed. Daisy had been murdered, and somehow he and Paula would get the necessary evidence, and when they found it, Bristow would be even more vulnerable. He would stay alive somehow, if he had to work part time on a fishing boat or at Dooly Gray's store, and when he had his case, he would make his arrest. Because he would get a badge and authority again somehow, even if he had to join the State Highway Patrol. He and Paula would not be beaten by Bristow or Jordan or any other little men.

Little men, he thought, that was it. Little men, so afraid. Afraid of their political connections, their reputations, their fortunes, and their jobs. So they picked only sure things in making their investments, and girls could die and be forgotten— "Shit," he said aloud and turned into the court of Paula's cottage, and then he jammed on brakes.

A car was parked before it, a long sleek Ford station wagon. Its tailgate was down, and as Danny watched, a tall scrawny man in sportshirt and slacks, followed by two children, carried a pair of suitcases up the steps and onto the porch. A plump, pleasant-looking woman with her hair in curlers held the screen door for them.

Danny sat behind the wheel for one frozen, confounded second. Then he cut off the switch, got out, ran across the court. The man had gone in the house; the woman saw him coming. Danny halted at the steps, rain falling into his face as he looked up.

"Where's Paula Murphy?" he blurted.

"Who?"

"The woman who lives here. Where's—"

"My name is Estok," she said. "My hubby's Wally Estok. The lady in the office just rented this to us. Who you looking for?"

"I— Paula Murphy." Danny whispered the words. Then reason returned. She got tired of this lousy place, he thought. She moved. Hell, she might be in the motel across the road. He sucked in breath. "Thank you, Miz Estok," he heard himself say and turned away.

Of course she would have left a message at the office.

It was only a larger cottage. He went to its back door and hammered. A stringy-haired little girl came.

"Yeah?" She wore a bikini that looked somehow even lewder on her breastless eight-year-old body than it would have on a woman more mature.

Danny said, "Your mama home? I got to talk to your mama."

"She's watchin television."

"God da— Look, young lady. You go git your mama, it's important."

He fumbled a cigarette from a pack as the little girl turned. "Mama? Maa-maa! A man's here to see you."

At least she wore no bikini. When she came, shuffling reluctantly, she had on a modest halter and a pair of baggy shorts. Her hair was up in plastic curlers. "Can I help you?" she asked.

"I'm— I'm Danny Rush, police chief in Harriot. I'm looking for Miss Paula Murphy. She was in Cottage Two."

"Oh, yeah, her. Well, she left yestiddy."

"Left," Danny said.

"Yeah, checked out."

"Oh," Danny said.

"The letter, Mama." The girl pulled at her mother's shorts. "Don't forget the letter."

"Oh, yeah," the woman said. "She left a letter for somebody. Lemme see." She turned back into the kitchen. After a moment, she said, "Whad you say your name was?"

"Rush," he whispered. "Danny Rush."

"Yeah. Then you're the one." She passed the envelope to him, opening the screen only slightly.

He looked at the firm straight-up-and-down solid writing on the envelope. "Danny Rush." It seemed a stranger's name.

"Thanks," he said. He held the envelope tightly and walked back to his car. He slid behind the wheel and managed to rip one end off with fingers that shook uncontrollably and draw out the single sheet of paper, with its typed single-spaced message.

Dear Danny,
I've done some cruel things in my life, but I suppose this

is the cruelest, but in the long run I hope it is kindness too.

The hell of it is, I didn't lie to you. I do love you, for you are indeed unique and in your own way wonderful. But there are kinds and degrees of love, and you want a kind and a degree that I am incapable of giving. Not your fault, a lack in me. There are many lacks in me and if you knew me better, you'd soon quit loving me anyhow. This is much simpler for us both. I am a different kind of person than you think. All you see in me is a mirror image of your own desires, and I could try to be that for a while, but I could never make it as an image in the long haul. I can only make it as myself.

And the case is closed. You'll by now know about Krause. I think it's best if all cases are closed simultaneously. I hope you had a pleasant trip to New Orleans, and as for the money, don't worry, we'll write that off with all the rest.

I hope you live a thousand years and always drink the rain.

Paula

Danny Rush did not know how long he sat motionless behind the wheel. He saw water sliding down the windshield in rippling streams. He read the letter once more and put it in his pocket with the affidavits. "This makes no sense," he said once. "This makes no fuckin sense at all."

His mind was like a toy he'd had as a child, a kind of telescope with one end full of broken bits of colored glass. You turned the thing around and around and the bits of glass whirled, shifted, blurred; but presently they fell into a pattern. He was waiting for his thoughts to do that.

Then it happened; the click came, and now his mind was working once again.

She could not mean what was in the letter, he was sure of that. There was no way she could mean it. It was beyond all reason that she could mean it. Women always thought twice when a man got serious; they tested him; they ran away to see if he cared enough to follow. They got cold feet. That had happened to her with him gone, but once he was back with her, he could reassure her.

But first he had to find her. Where would she have gone? Well, south, of course. He sat up straighter. Yes, and surely she would want to see the rest of the Outer Banks. Ocracoke and Portsmouth, which he had told her about but never shown her. She would have driven down to Ocracoke and got there last night. Today would have been too rough for her to go to Portsmouth, so either she would have waited or taken the ferry to Cedar Island on the mainland. Either way, he could trace her. She would travel slowly, sightseeing; he could catch up.

Suddenly, decisively, he turned the switch key and the car coughed into life. He whirled it out of the cottage court and onto the highway, pressing the accelerator, scattering pedestrians like quail. Once he glanced at the gas gauge, found the needle almost at empty. At the first service station, he pulled in. "Three dollars' worth," he told the attendant, waiting impatiently. When he had paid, he had a dollar left. Swiftly he drove on, through gathering dusk and slanting rain. The windshield wipers seemed to tick her name in terse syllables.

After a time he crossed the long high bridge and was on Hatteras. He did not slacken speed; it was dark now, but if he had no car trouble, he should make the last free ferry to Ocracoke all right. His heart quickened. She would still be there, waiting to go to Portsmouth; he knew it. He would spot her car outside some inn and— He constructed the scene in his imagination. Her surprise when she opened the door of her room, and the way he would take her in his arms. His need to have it happen was so intense that it seemed almost real; nearly, he could smell her perfume, feel the softness of her hair, her flesh.

Halfway down Hatteras the rain began to taper off. The storm was moving northwest; soon the skies would clear. Once, when he pulled over on a ramp to urinate, he could hear the boom of surf beyond the dunes. Before he got back in, he opened the trunk, unlatched his suitcase. It held half a bottle of bourbon. He took a long swallow, laid the bottle beneath the front seat, and drove on.

He was careful not to think about anything but her. If he thought about anything else, he would go crazy. When, in the dark, he passed the house where he had been born, he was especially careful not to think. If Wahab Rush could see what a mess his son had made of life—

Although he was hungry, he did not stop to eat, hoarding the final dollar. Twice more he drew on the bottle. He made the last ferry well before it pulled out.

The ride across the inlet took nearly three quarters of an hour. Standing at the bow, Danny let cold fresh wind batter his face and body. Overhead the clouds were breaking up; the moon showed through. The iron ferry bucked and pitched and smelled of diesel fumes. He went back to the car, had another drink. The whiskey fortified him, gave him hope and courage. He tried to hurry the ferry on, urge it with his body's weight thrown against the chained-up bow ramp. After an eternity, it swung against the bumpered pilings of the slip and neatly docked. Danny waited with impatience for the disembarkation signal, roared up the ramp and out on the narrow highway. With thirteen miles yet to drive, he turned south, pressing the accelerator pedal to the floor.

In full moonlight now, marsh and great humped dunes like sleeping elephants sped past, the ocean on his left, on his right the Sound. Except for an occasional ramp for sightseers and a tower built for visitors to look into the pasture which held the last remnants of dune ponies, there was no structure, nothing of civilization, until he reached the town.

Then, ahead, he saw it: the bulk of the Coast Guard station at Silver Lake, gleaming white, the big ferry to Cedar Island in its slip nearby, the spreading arch of ancient live oaks, the white thrust of the old lighthouse across the cove, vivid against the moonlit sky, a scattered spangle of lights that marked the farflung little houses of the village. His heart thudded almost painfully in his chest; for a second he was genuinely afraid of a coronary. There were only four or five motels or inns on the island; he could check them all.

He halted before the first one. Turning on the dome light, he squinted at himself in the mirror, saw a face he had never looked into before, one drawn and wild-eyed, bristling with a day's whiskers, its hair wind-tousled and on end—a wild man's face. His shirt was wrinkled, stained; he was coatless, sleeves rolled up. He rolled them down, put on his coat, heavy with the weight of the Magnum still in the inner pocket. He ran a comb through his hair. Then he got out and carefully surveyed the parking lot.

Her car was not in it. He entered the motel office, inquired if she had been there, received a negative answer, and drove on. But there were still three or four other possibilities.

He checked them all; and he found no sign of Paula. She had not been on Ocracoke. When he left the last one, it seemed to him as if he had been brutally scooped out with a rough instrument; he felt hollow and raw inside, bleeding. He sank behind the wheel and put his head down on his arms for several minutes, lights of fatigue exploding behind his closed lids. He cried a little and cursed bitterly and obscenely.

Of course he had no money to take a room; he had no money to take the ferry to the mainland either. He would have to drive back to Harriot tomorrow, get some somehow, if he had to wring that check out of Jordan with his hands, and trailer and Ruth and all be damned, go after her again. He would not let her get away.

He drove out of the parking lot and back along the highway. After a while he pulled over on a paved area, climbed a ramp that crossed the dunes. Then he was on the beach, which, here and at this time of night, was deserted. It stretched as far as he could see in both directions, its hard-packed sand glittering in the moonlight. The ocean boomed and roared and hissed as it hurled itself ashore, and the sea oats on the dunes rattled in the wind. With the bottle in his hand, Danny walked down the beach. Presently he sat down against a dune. He drank and watched the horizon. I would like to see a ghost ship, he thought.

None appeared. He sat there a long time. Sand fiddlers scurried away before him as he walked back to the car, swaying with whiskey and fatigue. He got in, drove back to the village. He did not go near the motels, but drove aimlessly around the back streets, which were narrow sandy lanes lined with little houses, sheltered by spreading live oaks, yaupon, and wind-tormented cedars. There were many little family graveyards: Dixons, Midgettes, Wahabs, Austins . . . The little houses slept. Some of them still had gutters running to their cisterns. *And always drink the rain* . . .

After a while he found himself on a road narrower even than the rest. On his right a small white board fence gleamed in the darkness beneath cedars, wind-bent, arching over the small graveyard it enclosed. He got out and went down the short path. At the fence he halted. There were four tombstones inside. He could not read them in the darkness, but he had seen them many times before, knew what they said: On one was engraved the name "Lt. Thomas Cunningham, R.N." Another bore the legend "Stanley R. Craig, A.B." Two were marked simply "Unknown." All said, "Body Found May 14, 1942." They were British sailors whose corpses had washed ashore here. This was called the British cemetery. There were artificial flowers on all the graves. The cemetery was neatly tended. It was quite a tourist attraction.

So far from home to die, thought Danny. "Unknown." And had, in their wildest dreams or deepest horrors, they imagined lying here? Dead and gone on an island they had never even heard of, and somewhere children, grown now, and women, with scarred hearts, knowing only that they were "Missing."

And that was what she did to you, he thought. Whatever you least expected, whatever plans you made, she always fucked you up and left you far from home in a place you never planned to be. But anyhow, he thought, they were through with loving. They had that much in their favor.

He got back in the car. He did not feel like driving on. He drained the rest of the whiskey in the bottle, hunched over on the front seat, and to his own fading surprise went to sleep.

Dawn awakened him. He sat up stiffly, head throbbing, rubbed a hand over a greasy, beardy face, smacked dry lips. His mouth felt burnt and fuzzy, dry. He would have to find a rest room somewhere to wash up in and use the toilet. He was surprised that he was not at all hungry.

After urinating in the cedars, he started the car. It was a fine, bright, calm day. He drove back toward the village. Silver Lake glimmered in the sun; the ferry had gone out on its first trip to the mainland across the Sound. The lighthouse was stainless white. Small boats rode at anchor around the cove. Fishermen brought early-morning catches from their gill nets in the Sound into the fish house at the water's edge. Well, thought Danny, he would have to spend part of the dollar on coffee, anyhow. He could use the bathroom in the restaurant of the inn over yonder at the highway intersection. He drove toward it, and as he edged into the parking lot, he put on brakes, hard.

Her car, the Mustang, was there.

Danny swung into an empty slot, jumped out, slammed the door behind him. He ran into the office of the inn. It was large, with a sofa, two chairs, a table full of newspapers, another littered with conch shells and sand dollars for sale. The young man behind the desk had not been there last night. Danny said hoarsely, "You got a Paula Murphy registered here?"

The boy stared at him, suspicion growing in his eyes. "I don't know," he said.

"Her car's out front. Check it. Hurry up, check it."

With agonizing slowness, the youth went to a card file. He thumbed through it front to back, then back to front. "We don't have any Paula Murphy registered."

"You *got* to—"

"Maybe she's just eating breakfast in the dining room," he said.

"Yeah. Yeah, maybe that." Danny hurried across the lobby, entered the dining room, which was also large, with many tables. He halted, panting; there were a lot of people, but Paula, he saw, was not one of them.

Heart thudding painfully, he took an empty table from which he could watch the lobby through glass doors. The waitress came and he ordered coffee.

He sipped it without tasting it, staring at the lobby, not even noticing that it scalded his mouth. Still she had not appeared and he ordered another cup. The waitress brought it, set it down.

And then, in yellow dress, she came, appearing from the stairwell, crossing the lobby, clutching the knitted fishnet handbag. She went to the table full of shells, picked up a splendid conch, turned it over and over, put it to her ear. As Danny crossed the lobby in three strides, she cocked her head.

"Paula," he said harshly and grabbed her arm and spun her around and she dropped the shell.

She stared into his face. "Oh, God," she said. "Danny, please, go back. Leave me alone."

"I can't, we got to talk. You can't run off."

"Oh, yes, I can."

"But why? You got to tell me why?"

She pulled her arm free. Her face was like a mask. "Danny, please, it will be better for both of us if you leave, right now. No more words are necessary."

He only stood there.

"All right," she said, hands twisting in the fishnet. "Danny, you want more than I can deliver."

"I just want to love you," he said hoarsely.

"That's what I mean. Danny, I tried to tell you gently . . . All right, I *do* love you. But I've loved many of my pupils, too; but they go on to other classes. Danny, why won't you understand? I am *not* what you think I am. I am not—what did I write?—the mirror image of your desires. I am something entirely different."

"I don't believe that," he said hoarsely.

She stared at him, and there was something like pain on her face. "Then I'll have to prove it to you," she said and turned away. She looked down at the shells. "Another man will be coming down those stairs in a few minutes. We spent the night together."

"Another—" He tried to grasp that. All he could think was that he knew now why her name had appeared on no register.

"It's Wallace Gordon," she said flatly.

"Wallace— Oh, now you're joking."

"Not in the least," Paula said.

"But he— don't you understand? How? He killed her. I got affidavits—"

"He's in the clear," she said. "But it doesn't make any difference, don't you see? He's not going to hurt me. I've given him everything he wants."

Danny backed off a pace. "I don't see how you could do it," he whispered. "He's a murderer."

"Only maybe." She toyed with the shells.

"How could you . . . do it with him?"

Paula turned. "Because I wanted to," she said. "From the first time I saw him, I wanted to, and while you were gone, I just let nature take its course. That's what I've been trying to make you see all this time, Danny. I do what I want to do. That's my life, the way I've made it." She paused. Her voice was gentler. "It doesn't mean anything, Danny. It's like trying a new cocktail because you've never tasted it. And if he's a murderer, it's just a different taste."

He could find no words for a full half minute.

"Is that what it was with me?" he managed finally.

"In a sense." Then still more gently, "Maybe a little more. Yes, it was a little more. Anyhow, it seemed the perfect time to end it; you were gone, the case was closed, it was all finished. . . . And I'll leave *him* here too today and go on to Florida and—"

Danny felt a chill down his spine, his skin actually begin to crawl. "Just like that."

"Go away, Danny, please. Go on back to Harriot, right

now."

When he did not move, she said, "All right." Before he could catch her, she turned away and ran swiftly back up the stairs.

Danny did not try to follow her. He did not know what he did next. When he was aware of himself again, he was sitting in his car across the road from the inn, under a big live oak, with his eyes fastened on the hotel's front door and on her car. His coat was laid across his lap, the weight of the Colt Magnum heavy in his crotch. When you looked directly at the sun, you saw a formless dazzling blur, white hot. Something similar within him had burnt up all thought, feeling, and emotion. He was only a white hot flame, it seemed to him. He waited, with no sense of time. It could have been an hour, two or three, before they came out. His watch told him that it had been forty minutes.

Closing the inn's door behind them, they stood in the graveled drive, Wallace Gordon with his arm around her. Danny thought he could hear the heat sizzling inside his skull. He thought his brain made a crackling sound. Rather warily the two of them looked around. Paula's yellow dress stood out vividly in the brightness of morning. Gordon towered over her, in sportshirt and slacks. They did not see Danny. As if relieved, Paula leaned against the man. They got into a big Oldsmobile parked beside her Mustang. Danny did not move as they drove away; on Ocracoke they could not go far.

Presently he started his engine and followed. He knew about where they were bound. He turned off the pavement along a narrow lane completely overarched with live oaks. An old man rocking on a porch looked curiously at his car.

Reaching another paved road, this one running along the cove, Danny edged the car out a little way. He saw the back end of the Oldsmobile as it turned into a parking lot a few hundred yards away, behind a small frame building that was a store. Danny waited for a few minutes, then he followed.

On Silver Lake's edge there was a wide paved lot. It ended at a clutter of small docks, where boats were tied up. On one of the docks was another store, Jack's, another small frame building over the water. Across the inlet the American flag above the Coast Guard station whipped in the wind; in the other direction the old lighthouse, brick, white-plastered, shone in the sun.

Instead of pulling into the lot where the Olds was parked with other cars, Danny put his car behind a small building which was the emergency generating plant of the electric co-op supplying the island's power. He had put on his coat now.

Paula and Wallace Gordon walked across the lot and out on a wooden pier, where a tall bulky man, face ruddy from the sun, waited in whites and a captain's hat. That, Danny knew, was the caretaker of Portsmouth Island. His wooden boat, a sort used by the Coast Guard years before, high gunneled and shallow draft, was tied beside the dock. He shook hands with Gordon, tipped his hat to Paula, climbed into the boat and helped the woman down. Gordon followed nimbly, and they sat together on the center thwart. The boatman started his powerful outboard and the craft swung away from the dock. Danny watched it plow across the inlet. With distance it diminished and finally, on the open sea, was only a white dot against the glaring blue.

Inside Danny Rush's mind the white dazzle made a sizzling noise. He turned away and began to walk around the inlet, the shoreline of which was littered with junk, trash fish, and flotsam. Presently, tied up at a rickety wharf, he saw what he wanted. He looked shrewdly in all directions; no one was watching. He cast off the painter looped around the piling, jumped lightly into the little skiff, started its outboard, and settled back into the stern. With ease he maneuvered clear of the docks and out into open water, headed for the sea. He passed the Coast Guard station, where a cutter rode beside the ferry newly in from Cedar Point and unloading. The cutter was not the *Wahab Rush*; she was on duty in the Gulf of Mexico.

Danny cleared the inlet's mouth and was in the open sea. He had not boated across this channel recently, but there were buoys, and besides, he could read the water, knowing exactly what, allowing for the wind, every degree of color, turbulence, and stillness indicated beneath the surface. Gulls shrieked and circled over him; the wind was fresh and forceful in his face. The boat met small waves head on and breasted them with a, to him, satisfying undulation.

His mind was still an opaque white flame. Only the necessary reflexes of seamanship penetrated it. Now, on the horizon, he saw a misty blot: Portsmouth. Once, nearly three hundred years before, it had been this coast's leading port. Tall-masted sailing ships had put in there for their cargoes to be lightered across the Sound to the mainland. Their ballast stones could still be seen along the shoreline. The town of Portsmouth then had been a brawling, lively, vigorous place. Then inlets had been formed and direct channels located to the mainland, and the ships passed it by, and it began to wither.

And yet, until only a few years ago, it had hung on. Completely isolated now, its people fished and salvaged and worked in a fish cannery that had provided it a temporary boom, and weathered the ferocious hurricanes that came beating up from the Caribbean every year. But the cannery had closed and somehow in latter days the storms had grown worse, and farther up the Banks and on the mainland there was prosperity; and one by one, family by family, the people had left their island. Finally only three had remained: two old women and a Negro named Henry Pigott. Their roots were too deep in the sand; like ghosts haunting the deserted village, they hung on, the black man, who had become a legend in his own time, the two white women, in a strange interlocking relationship, bound to one another by love: their fierce love of their island.

But age and sickness had done what hurricanes had failed to do; they were gone now, the last three. Wholly deserted, abandoned even by the Coast Guard, which had once had a station there, the town saw no humans any more save those willing to pay a stiff price for a boat ride across the Sound or who came in their own craft—those and the duck hunters who shot here every fall and winter. Soon, though, the National Seashore would take the island over, likely run a ferry, and there would be campgrounds and Coca-Cola stands.

The boat drove on past two small outlying spits of sand, once part of Portsmouth, now severed from it by the hurricanes. Ahead Danny could see the greenery of low thickly tangled brush, the gray roofs of houses, and, dominating all, the severe white lines and pointed steeple of the village church. The surfboat, returning to Silver Lake, passed him on the port side, and its navigator raised a hand in greeting. Danny did not reply.

He steered surely for the mouth of a blackwater creek where there was a flimsy dock, beached the skiff, leaped out, and tied it to a piling. He was sweating beneath the coat as he straightened up.

Although most of the island was overgrown with brush, the caretaker kept certain areas mowed. The landing was one of these, and from it lanes through the tangled thickets spidered out. Mosquitoes buzzed around Danny Rush as he strode up one such path. It brought him out behind two freshly painted houses, their yards also cut, though both had been uninhabited for years. The families still holding title to Portsmouth were of two sorts: the kind that still kept their homeplaces intact and those that let them go to ruin and be swallowed by the brush.

Danny halted in the back yard of the right-hand house, taking cover in a clump of fig trees. Now he fished inside the coat, and sun glinted on the heavy revolver as he brought it out. He was breathing hard. He spun the cylinder, catching the wink of brass cartridge rims; it was fully loaded.

Enough gun for the job; that was what they said of Magnums.

Almost every visitor came first to the Portsmouth Methodist Church. It was a clean-lined wooden structure always kept freshly painted white, its sharp pointed steeple dominating the deserted town, the grass around it newly mown.

With the gun in hand, Danny walked across the yard, went up the church steps. The door was fastened only by a hook in an eye; he flipped that loose and entered.

He passed through a vestibule into the little sanctuary. There he paused; it was wholly empty. The inside walls were of diagonal shiplap; the whole structure had been built by men who understood the power of the sea and of hurricanes and who had planned it with the solidity of a good sailing ship, designing it to withstand the same stresses. Light rayed in through frosted windows. There were gas lamps on each side. Rows of empty pews, polished to high sheen by generations of lean rumps and rough cloth, gleamed mutedly, hymnals still in their racks. Danny walked down the aisle.

At its end there was a table with a collection plate and a visitors' book; donations were solicited for the maintenance of the building, this ghost church, which now had no congregation of its own. Behind the altar rail there was a pulpit, a cabinet full of hymnals, and an old-fashioned pedal organ. Danny wondered if Peter Hogan had played that while he camped on Portsmouth Island.

He looked down at the collection plate before him. It held perhaps twenty-five cents in change and a twenty-dollar bill. The tattered visitors' book in front of it bore what he thought were two fresh signatures: "Joe Doaks" and "Jane Doaks." He touched them with a finger and the ink smudged. They must have laughed together at their little joke.

He turned, ran down the aisle, went outside, hooking the door behind him. Ahead, the brush was a solid wall, engulfing a decaying wooden house, its porch collapsed, vines and bushes curling through the dark, empty sockets of its windows. On either hand, right and left, the caretaker had cut roads through the scrub, exactly a jeep's width. Danny paused indecisively. Then he turned left.

He walked swiftly, gun in hand, along the jeep track. A thousand different kinds of plants, interlocked and stunted by ceaseless wind, made a wall on either flank, impenetrable and shoulder high. After a half mile, the lane ended in a big mown clearing, rectangular and larger than a football field. This was the air strip, and beyond it bulked the two wooden buildings of the abandoned Coast Guard station.

Danny approached them cautiously, like a hunter stalking game. The larger one, headquarters and boathouse, was locked. The water lapped at the shore at the foot of its short ramp.

The door of the smaller one, once mess hall and barracks, swung open on sagging hinges. Danny ran to it and peered inside. Two iron cots covered by rotting mattresses, more sodden ticks on the floor, a sink overgrown with scum, and the litter and debris of countless visitors everywhere—that was all.

He did not even take time to curse. He went back the way he had come, walking very swiftly, head up and eyes alert. He passed the church again, and once more he was walled in by scrub. In its depths houses rotted.

He crossed a rude wooden bridge over a small blackwater creek. He passed a family graveyard. He was going more slowly now; they had to be somewhere close by. He came to a wide clearing and shrank back. Three houses were ringed around its perimeter, these in not bad repair, and two with outbuildings. He peeped around the wall of scrub, holding his breath. Presently he loped into the clearing. One by one he looked into the houses. On the door of the last one was pinned a sign. "This is private property. Please do not destroy it." Across that someone had scrawled in pencil, "Shit," and all the windows were broken out.

Danny stood on its porch in a litter of broken glass. He fumbled for a cigarette, but he had no more. He held his breath. The wind rustled in the scrub with a sound as of some giant animal breathing.

Then he heard it: a tatter of laughter from somewhere farther along the trail: Paula.

Danny stepped down off the porch and walked along the trail, very slowly, the Colt pointed downward. He knew the terrain and knew that where the lane bent left ahead there was a family graveyard and beyond that another couple of houses in a clearing. Just before he reached the bend, he halted.

The laughter came again, more clearly now. He could barely hear it above that sizzling sound inside his skull; for a moment his vision blanked out. It was as if he had looked into the sun directly. They were in the little cemetery.

He went no farther down the lane. Somehow he managed to penetrate the brush. Bent low, he worked through it like a snake, sweat pouring off him, thorns raking at him, limbs whipping his face. He worked rapidly toward higher ground. He hoped they would not leave the graveyard before he got there. Presently he was in position, crawling on his belly through the scrub, with daylight visible beyond. Edging up to the border of the thicket, he saw them ahead and slightly below, not more than a hundred feet away. Gordon stood tolerantly with hands in hip pockets; Paula, yellow vivid against the green, bent over a little tombstone.

Danny worked quietly and silently to hook limbs behind each other to give himself a place to sit upright. Paula went to another tombstone, bent again, and pointed. Gordon looked bored and took out a cigarette. Danny gripped the butt of the Colt in his right hand and his right wrist in his left hand. With his arms extended fully and his elbows locked, he brought the gun down to bear, not on Gordon, but on the blot of yellow.

His vision partly obscured by that white dazzle outside of him as well as inside, he held his breath. The gun was rock steady, its front sight covering her. He sat like that for a long minute, lips curled back from his teeth. Paula straightened up. She turned to Gordon, seized his arm, still laughing, leaned against him, and rubbed her breasts against his biceps. Danny tracked her with the pistol, held steady for a second longer, and then said, "Shit."

The white dazzle faded out, the sizzling stopped inside his skull. Now he saw both of them in utter clarity, holding one another. Beside Gordon's big frame Paula looked like a doll.

That was it, he thought, his mind working clearly again. A doll, that was what she was. Not a child's, but one of those plastic dolls they sold in sex stores, complete with pussies, for use by masturbators. She masqueraded as a woman, but inside she was a plastic doll, for her womb was sterile, and she could accommodate the discharge of any lover without commitment, officer or murderer. She was an instrument, not a woman, for a woman took risk; by giving herself to a man she accepted consequences. There were no consequences for Paula. Sperm would not be absorbed by her plastic guts. If it ever were, she would have its fruit aborted. Nothing would ever flower in her, and she was not real at all. She was discardable. Even Ruth, who had at least borne Linda and Junior and accepted responsibility for them, was more woman than that thing down there refusing to give herself to anybody.

"Shit," he said again, and he raised the gun once more and pulled the trigger.

Its roar was thunderous in the hush; Paula screamed and whirled around, face a white blot above the yellow, as the slug powdered the top of a tombstone and whined off. Gordon spun around in the wrong direction, stared, whirled back in the right one, and Danny fired again, and dirt spewed between Gordon's feet. Gordon yelled something and seized Paula and they began to run. Danny fired again. A tombstone exploded into powder in their path, and they veered off. Paula screamed his name. *"Danny—"*

Then Gordon threw her down, hurled himself to the ground beside her. Danny laughed. He sent a bullet whirring close above their heads, another blew dirt in Gordon's face.

Danny rocked back on his buttocks, grinning, panting. Then he felt warm wetness running down his cheeks, though his grin stayed fixed. He looked down at the gun. One bullet left. He thought of Harold Krause. He sat there for fifteen seconds, looking straight down the gun barrel pointed at his head.

"Fuck it," he said then and turned the pistol and fired the

last slug into the earth between his feet. Despite the clawing brush, he stood up to his full height and began to walk. He shoved through the network of branches and vines by main strength and finally came out into the open. He walked along the jeep track until he reached the church. There he unlatched the door and entered.

He put the gun back in his pocket. He strode down the aisle through white-walled silence. It was odd, he thought, how light through church windows always looked different from any other light. He stopped before the table with the plate and book. He fumbled in his pockets, took out his last twenty cents, and dropped them in the plate. He unclipped his ballpoint and in the book, beneath "Jane Doaks" wrote in bold clear letters, "Daniel Wahab Rush." He went back and underlined the word "Wahab."

He latched the church door behind him, and walked unhurriedly down to the landing. He jacked the empty shells from the Colt, caught them, threw them far out into the water. He got in the boat, cast off, started the motor, and put out from shore, bound for Ocracoke. He steered well around Silver Lake and tied the boat up in a creek on the Sound side. Then he walked the two miles to his car.

When he crossed the causeway and was back on Harriot, Danny Rush took the fork that led to Finley Harbor. Gray was alone in the store. "Dooly," Danny said.

"Hello, Chief."

"You still want my Magnum?"

Gray's eyes lit. "You ain't jokin?"

"Not if you got a hundred dollars."

"Chief, I couldn't afford that. Eighty?"

"You go to hell, Dooly. It cost a hundred and sixty."

Gray hesitated. "Ninety."

"A deal," Danny said.

With the money in his pocket, he drove across the island. When he stopped the car before Ruth's trailer, Linda and Junior ran to him. "Daddy, Daddy, Daddy!" He scooped them up in his arms, blowing the gnats from their eyes.

Standing in the doorway, Ruth said, "Well, it's about time you come."

Danny put down the children. "Whyn't you git some spray for 'em?"

"I ain't even got money for groceries. Why you think I called and called? You're off somewheres having a high old time and—"

"Be quiet," Danny said. He dug into his pocket. "Here's eighty dollars; it's all I got, savin ten. I hope that will take care of you a little while." He drew in a breath. "I been fired. Until I find somethin else, there won't be no more. So don't git on me, you hear? I been locked out of my trailer and I'm off the force and I got to figure out what to do."

"How'd all that happen?"

"I don't know, it just happened."

"Well, I told you, I told you just as sure—"

Danny turned away, not even hearing. He went out of the trailer, and then he could go no farther and he dropped heavily on the trailer steps.

The children were pedaling their tricycles frantically back and forth. Bullbats and swifts swooped low over the clearing in the pines; the dying sun was an orange blur behind them to the west. Danny had never been so tired in his entire existence. Neither had he felt so free and sure of who he was. Or what, come hell or high water, he was going to accomplish somehow. He touched the papers in his coat pocket. His mind would not work right now, but tomorrow—

He almost jumped when a hand touched his shoulder. "I'm

sorry you got fired," Ruth said, most of the edge gone from her nasal voice.

"That's all right. I'll find somethin else."

There was silence while they watched Linda and Junior wheel around the yard in savage competition. "Well, if you need a place to stay tonight," Ruth said, "you're perfectly welcome here."

The sun blazed behind the pines; the children collided with each other.

"All right," Danny said at last.